SUSAN LYNN
SOLOMON

WRITING
IS
MURDER

An Emlyn Goode Mystery

Writing is Murder

Susan Lynn Solomon

For the real members of Writers Refuge
Lou Rara
Chera Thompson
George Morse
Eileen Werbitsky
Michael Marrone
Patricia Sweet

You teach me more each time we meet

Prologue

Watching the TV programs *Ghost Hunters*, *Haunted Collector*, and *Ghost Adventures* might give one the idea that western New York is the most haunted corner of the United States. It actually might be. In Buffalo's Central Train Terminal, passengers from a bygone era still wait for loved ones who never returned from World War II. The Iron Island Museum, once a funeral home, has a man wandering the halls in search of his ashes, never claimed by his family and abandoned in the basement. A soldier roams the Old Fort Niagara Castle, hoping to recover his severed head, dropped into a well by another soldier. In caves along the Erie Canal, tourists hear the voices of workmen who perished carving the tunnels that brought power to factories lining the shores. Then there's the Rapids Theater where a long-dead actress still performs, the Echo Club where a brutally slain woman still parties and Alexander Zelski, who ran a credit union and prohibition bar in the building, moans through the night. In addition, there's the Holiday Inn on Grand Island and dozens of other sites from Chautauqua County to Orleans County. Those who have sought spirits in these dark places say they've actually *seen* the ghosts.

None of these spirits have been known to harm the living, though. Not directly. But in a few instances, it's said that one crept into the body and mind of the living and caused him to kill. Such is the story of the Bennet House.

Local legend speaks of Wilson Blaine, an early laborer on the Erie Canal, who was haunted by the Tuscarora brave he shot to secure the land that now sits on Park Place in the old section of Niagara Falls. It's claimed that as the Tuscarora died, he cursed Blaine and all who would thereafter live on his land. Whether the result of the curse or of too much liquor, during a blizzard in 1827 Blaine slaughtered his wife and two children—shot them, cut off their heads, arms, and legs, then shot himself. That was the scene reported to the army at Fort Niagara when neighbors stopped by the stone house after the spring thaw. Through the years, lightning strikes burned rural structures built where Blaine once dwelled, and people moving along the canal to settle in the West died while seeking shelter on that land.

This is what the guide told my father and me during a Halloween ghost tour when I was twelve.

I mention this particular legend, because five years ago the ghost of the Tuscarora brave struck again. At least the attorney, Howard Kline, attempted this defense at Richard Bennet's trial for the murder of his wife in their home on Park Place. Here's how Kline presented the curse in court:

After being sworn in, police sergeant Dan Cummings testified he had been on duty in the Main Street precinct at 8:49 on the evening of February 7 and received a call from a hysterical woman who identified herself only as Shari. The woman said her husband had gotten drunk and was threatening her with a knife.

When the time came for cross-examination, Howard Kline rose at the defense table in the blond-wood paneled courtroom. "If you received that call at precisely 8:49," he began. "I believe that's what you just said, officer?"

"Yes, sir," Cummings replied. "8:49."

"Precisely?"

"Yes, sir. I marked the time in my log."

Dressed in the same black Perry Ellis suit and red and white power tie he'd worn each day of the trial, Kline stepped behind the defendant. With his hands on Bennet's shoulders, he said, "Apparently you didn't find the situation terribly serious… maybe a prank or something?"

"What do you mean? Of course I took it seriously," Dan Cummings replied.

"Did you?" Kline said. "Doesn't seem you did. After all, no one responded to the call until—" He leaned over the table, and pulled a page from a manila folder. "—11:15, or thereabout."

An aging cop near retirement, Sergeant Cummings sat up straight in the witness box. His lips went tight, and the lines deepened around his eyes that appeared as though they had seen too many similar cases. "It took that amount of time, because the line went dead before she gave me her full name, her address, or any other information. We were working on getting the location traced."

"Thank you, officer. Now tell me—"

"But I knew the situation was serious, all right," Cummings continued, "because I heard the defendant shouting and cursing in the background."

"Objection, your Honor!" Kline shouted.

"And the woman screamed just before the line went dead."

"Your Honor?" Kline said.

People in the gallery twisted in their seats, and whispered to each other.

Judge Aldernado rapped his gavel once. "I'll have order in here!" His gray hair in stark contrast to his black robe, he sat back in his chair with his lips pursed. "Your objection is overruled. You opened the door on this, Counselor."

Grumbling, Kline took his seat behind the defense table, whispered to Richard Bennet, then patted his arm. Bennet shrugged.

Detective Chief Harry Woodward testified next. After a few questions in which Dan Pettit, the prosecuting attorney, established that Chief Woodward was the first officer to enter the house, Pettit said, "I know you found a horrid scene, Detective, one you'd rather not recall—"

The judge raised his hand to stop Howard Kline as he began to object.

"—but please tell us what you saw in the Bennets' living room."

The head of the Niagara Falls detective squad appeared to be uncomfortable in the witness box. Perhaps it was the memory of that night of February 7, or maybe because, as a man six and a half feet tall, his knees looked to be nearly pressed against his chest. Twisting sideways in the chair, he rubbed his hand up his forehead and across his crew-cut gray hair.

"I saw the deceased on the floor between the living room and the dining room," Chief Woodward said. "She appeared to have been stabbed a number of times—the crime scene tech told me he counted sixteen wounds, several of them across her neck, almost severing her head. The ME has since confirmed this."

"Objection! Hearsay," Kline said.

"Sustained," Judge Aldernado replied. "Detective, please stick to what *you* personally know."

"Yes, your honor." Chief Woodward leaned forward, directly addressing Pettit. "I found the defendant asleep on the couch with an almost-empty bottle of scotch on the floor next to him. He held a bloody knife against his chest, as if he was cradling a baby—the DNA report…" He shifted in the witness box to look at the judge. "I've read the report and it's already been admitted into evidence…"

Glancing at the flag to his left—the New York State Coat of Arms on a blue field—the judge said, "Only what you *personally* know, Detective."

"I apologize, Judge… Uh, where was I?" Harry Woodward looked down at his notes. "Oh, yes. The curtains on the windows had been partly torn from the rods—one of them was completely off, and wrapped around the deceased's arm and waist." Again he consulted his notes. "I saw smudged blood in a trail from the banister at the staircase to the second floor, to the arch that separated the living room from the dining room. It looked like the deceased had crawled that far before she died."

"So, it appeared that Mrs. Bennet bled out from the initial stab wounds, but even then the defendant set on her, and—" Pettit made slashing motions. "—continued his vicious—"

"Your honor!" Attorney Kline rubbed his hand over his slicked-back black hair. He sounded put upon.

"Sustained. Spare us the theatrics, Mr. Pettit." To the jury, he said, "No evidence has been presented to support this."

Years younger than his opponent, in his creased brown suit, the prosecutor turned and smiled at the jury before asking, "Could an intruder have broken into the house?"

"We saw no signs of forcible entry. The front and back doors were locked. The windows also. We examined each of them. No indication they'd been forced. Took a locksmith to get us inside."

The prosecutor lifted a photo from the table. "May I approach the witness, your honor?" When Judge Aldernado nodded, Pettit handed the picture to Chief Woodward. "This photograph has been entered in evidence as Prosecution Exhibit 23-B. It's a picture taken that night by the crime scene photographer. Is that correct?"

The detective chief examined the photo showing a somewhat overweight short woman—Shari Bennet had been no more than four-foot-ten—with small eyes set close in a wide oval face. Her auburn hair had been shoulder-length until her killer apparently cut it off. The picture showed her hair in clumps on the floor.

"Yes. This is what it looked like the night of the murder." Chief Woodward handed the photograph back to Pettit.

After showing the crime scene picture to the jury, the prosecutor asked, "This wasn't the first time Richard Bennet had a knock-down-drag-out with his wife…" The attorney hesitated for a beat, as if waiting for an objection. When none came, he said, "Was it the first time, Chief?"

"No, it wasn't." Again Harry Woodward leaned forward, this time peering at the defendant. "When I examined our files in preparation for this trial, I found eight other complaints over the past three years."

Now the defense attorney had his turn to question the witness. "There are other complaints in your files, aren't there, Chief? Complaints from my client—the defendant." He turned, and looked down at Bennet. "Complaints that his wife… the, uh, deceased, had attacked *him*. Once with a tire iron, then with a kitchen knife—"

"Objection!" the prosecutor called out. "Counsel is testifying."

"Sustained," the judge said. "Do you have a *question* for this witness, Mr. Kline?"

The defense attorney cleared his throat. "Yes, Judge. Yes, I have questions. It's the house, isn't it Detective—the house and the land it's built on?"

"I don't know what you mean." Chief Woodward looked truly puzzled.

"Don't you, Detective? Don't you really?"

"Objection—"

"Look in your files all the way back to eighteen twenty—"

Dan Pettit jumped to his feet. "Objection, Judge!"

"Sustained."

Howard Kline refused to stop. "Time after time on the same parcel of land. It's the Tuscarora's Curse, isn't it, Chief Woodward?

Judge Aldernado pounded his gavel. "I said sustained, Mr. Kline!"

"You sweated my client for hours, and he didn't confess, did he?" White spittle covered the lawyer's thin lips. "Over and over, he told you he was having a drink in front of the TV, and that was the last he remembered, until—"

That's enough, Mr. Kline!" The judge's face had turned an angry red. "One more word and you're in contempt!"

The defense counsel caught his breath. He pulled a handkerchief from his pocket, and wiped perspiration from his forehead. "I apologize, your honor. I just wanted the jury to witness what happens when that damn Tuscarora's ghost takes over your mind. My client isn't guilty, you see. There's no *mens rea*—he had no criminal intent when—"

The judge also caught his breath. "Save that for your summation, counselor."

With a sly smile, Kline took his seat at the defense table.

***

The Tuscarora's Curse defense failed, and Richard Bennet was sentenced to life in the prison at Attica, New York. While ghost stories made good books, television, and films, Judge Aldernado instructed the jury its decision had to be based on the current facts, not ancient legends. I know the jury heeded the judge's instruction, because I sat on that panel.

The problem with the decision we made in the Bennet case was that the matter didn't end there.

Chapter One

A Writer's Life

This was a lonely profession I had chosen, or to be precise, a profession that had chosen me. Seated at the computer in an alcove in my living room, coffee or wine at one elbow and notes from my writer's journal on my lap, day-after-day and often late into the night I struggled to string words across the screen in a way they'd not been expressed before. Nouns, verbs (the speaking and the action kind), and adjectives. I moved them here and there while groaning and often yelling at my computer. Why wouldn't those damn words become the metaphor or the allegory I sought? This was the curse of having turned out two fairly successful books.

When I wasn't complaining, a clicking keyboard might have made the only sound in my house. Then, a few years ago, Elvira, a hefty albino pain-in-my-derriere, scratched her way past the French doors overlooking my patio and into my heart. After that, cat paws pattering across the tan carpet and the lacquered wood hall floor from my living room to the kitchen and frequent cat-snores from the overstuffed wingback chair next to my bookcases played in harmony with my typing. Entirely focused on my work, I allowed neither those sounds nor anything else to distract me.

Of course, there were the times that, while searching for something new to write, I couldn't help but be distracted by a police detective's body found in an alley, a man fried in a car behind the Bella Vita hair salon and a woman's body knifed in the ladies' room of Como's Restaurant. It annoyed Detective Roger Frey when I poked my nose into his cases. That didn't stop me. Those murders provided story plots which led to additional quiet days and nights at my computer.

Though there had been no murders in Niagara Falls to distract me since last Christmas Eve, new sounds now rattled my mornings. One of those sounds started about eight o'clock on a Saturday in late October. First I heard heavy footsteps descend the stairs from my bedroom, followed by a drawn-out yawn, and a baritone voice calling, "Coffee ready yet, Emlyn?"

Roger's voice tickled me from my toes to the top of my very red head. Several weeks after his estranged wife was institutionalized in the wake of the killings I now tried to write about, he had begun to spend several nights a week at my house. This man was a distraction I didn't at all mind.

"Coffee ready?" he repeated.

Lost in a paragraph that refused to do what I asked of it, I leaned back in my chair, and stretched my neck.

A thud on the carpet told me Elvira had jumped from the nest she'd made in my overstuffed chair. While my finicky feline barely tolerated most people, she'd become quite attached to Roger. I didn't blame her. These days I found myself also pulled in his direction.

When I reached again for the keyboard, a soft mew alerted me to the fact my writing that morning might have ended. As was so often the case, my cat was correct. Roger lifted the hair from the nape of my neck. He followed this with a gentle kiss. I don't know how it happened, but when I glanced at the computer screen, I saw *aaaah* typed on it.

Roger glanced at the screen, and laughed.

Elvira rubbed against my leg and mewed, as if to say, *What's wrong with you? Kiss the man back!* At least I thought that's what she meant.

In the two years this fur-ball had shared my house, I'd learned it was best to do what she demanded. This demand didn't require much prior thought. I swiveled in my chair and looked up into hazel eyes glittering with flecks of gold.

Roger gently stroked the creases around my eyes. "All red. You didn't get much sleep last night."

I gave him a weary smile. "The muse kept elbowing me."

With his size fourteen shoe, he nudged aside the books stacked near my feet. The Webster's Dictionary, Roget's Thesaurus and the Ciccarelli-White psychology text I'd been using for research toppled. His arm around my waist, he pulled me from the chair. "Give it a rest," he said. "Have some coffee with me."

I reached for my notes. "Can't. I've got to finish this chapter so I can take it to my writers' group this afternoon."

His eyes clouded when I mentioned this group. Roger didn't often display jealousy. Fact is, he seemed to show it only when I spoke of the people in Writer's Refuge (that's what those in my group had named it). More specifically, his jealousy might flare when I mentioned two of the guys in that group. But why shouldn't I have spoken of them? They were both wonderful writers… Okay, I admit to another thing. Just looking at those guys could make a girl's heart flutter a bit.

Roger's streak of green quickly faded. Darn it! Holding my hand, he led me to the kitchen. Once there, he pointed me to a chair at my round white dinette table. "Coffee first," he said. "I need some even if you don't. Plus I like your company." When he raised a mug, he gave a yawn so wide it showed the gap between his front teeth.

"If *I* didn't get any sleep last night," I said, "why are *you* yawning?"

He couldn't have been tired. When I climbed out of bed about two in the morning, his snores might metaphorically have cut through enough lumber to construct a house, so I knew his yawn came from boredom.

Roger thought of himself as a street cop. Chasing criminals to their lairs was his calling. At least that's what he'd been moaning about since Detective Chief Harry Woodward returned from his extended leave and told the City Council he wouldn't resume his position unless they appointed Roger as his Deputy Chief.

It didn't take long to confirm the reason he'd yawned. My guy poured more coffee into his white porcelain mug and dropped down on the chair next to me. His head in his hands, he glared at the headline on the first page of the *Niagara Gazette*.

"Another break-in on Independence Avenue," he grumbled.

"Probably just some kids looking for drugs," I said, hoping to cut this off before he drew the conversation in the direction he had every day for weeks. "If it were a major case, Harry would have you involved."

"Just kids? Right," he said. "It's the third time. And what am I doing about it?" He grabbed my hand and pushed my finger onto the headline. "Tell me what I'm doing, Emlyn."

When I started to answer, he cut me off with a groan.

"Nothing!" he said. "I'm pushing paper from one side of my desk to the other. That's what I'm doing."

Elvira looked up from her food bowl, and stared at him. Her expression seemed to say, *Oh, no. Here we go again.*

"Your job's important, Roger," I told him. "Harry needs you."

"He needs a cop, not a paper-pusher. I hear they're looking for cops in Rochester. Maybe I'll ride out there tomorrow and apply."

The cat let out a long *meeeow.*

I understood what Elvira wanted me to do. Pulling her onto my lap, I told her, "Sarah's book doesn't have a spell to make the man stop feeling sorry for himself."

I should mention I'm a direct descendent of Sarah Goode, who took the short drop from a Salem tree limb in 1692 after a few girls accused her of being a witch. Actually, my ancestor *was* a witch, and I've since learned that her... um, *peculiar proclivity* runs in my family's genes. The book I thought Elvira wanted me to consult? That was old Sarah's *Book of Shadows*—her diary of a sort—which had been passed down through my family's generations. In this book she wrote of her life and described certain herbs she might mix together to cause nature to do things the people of her day believed to be the work of the Devil. Nonsense, of course. But some people would still view my genetic heritage that way. This is why I had let only a few close friends know of my legacy. Roger knew, of course, as did my best friend Rebecca Nurse, who'd taken it upon herself to teach me old Sarah's arcane practices. Harry Woodward also knew—he had seen me work a spell or two when I figured out whose body had been left in Como's ladies room.

"I'm not feeling sorry for myself," Roger said.

"Oh?" I tapped his lip. "Then why are you sulking?"

Gripping his coffee mug, he pulled away. "Don't laugh at me."

I knew I shouldn't have, but the face he made—lips tightly pursed, brow wrinkled—was just so adorable.

I brushed his sideburn where his dark, curly hair had begun to gray and kissed his cheek. "Stop obsessing. I'm sure somebody will be killed sooner or later and Harry will let you help with the case."

I meant that as a joke. But when Roger's cell phone buzzed a moment later, I recalled something Rebecca had warned me of: someone with Sarah Goode's genes had to avoid spitting out such things, even if said in jest. Apparently a witch's idle thoughts could catch fire and spread.

After listening with his phone to his ear for what felt like five minutes, a grin lit his face.

"What?" I said.

He shook his head.

Something's altered his mood, I thought. *This could be a plot for another book.* I nibbled his ear. "Roger, tell me? Please."

He pocketed his phone and pushed back from the table. "I might be late tonight," he told me as he pulled his jacket from the hall closet and opened the front door.

My coffee mug in my hand, I followed him down the stoop and across the fifty or so yards of lawn to the driveway in front of his house. Roger owned the house next door to mine, and he would park in his own driveway even when he stayed with me. He'd told me he did that because, "an unmarried woman practically living with a man? Don't want to ruin your reputation."

Were it not such a sweet thought, I might have commented on the century in which he seemed to be living.

"What happened?" I asked again. "Was somebody killed?"

He glanced at me as he opened the door to his black Trailblazer. "I know what you're thinking, Emlyn." He raised his hand when I started to respond. "Don't say it. Yeah, I know you helped out a couple of times. But you can't get involved in this."

"But—"

"No *buts*. I've gotta go." Turning to me, he added. "I can only tell you this isn't the kind of case you poked your nose into before.

He climbed into his car and rolled down the window. "Enjoy working with your writers' group. Now be good, and let me do my job. I'll see you later."

My first thought caused my active writer's imagination to go haywire. My spine stiffened. *How dare he treat me like a brainless little woman?* Yes, I knew Roger would neither say nor think anything of the kind. So what? I was angry. Hadn't I helped solve crimes when he couldn't figure them out? My second thought loosened my spine and caused a flock of butterflies to flutter in my stomach. It had taken a long time for me to admit I loved this cop. Now that I had, the thought that he might be driving into a dangerous situation rattled me.

As he started to pull away, I called out, "Promise me you'll be careful."

He smiled, blew a kiss in my direction and backed onto River Road.

I continued to watch until he rounded the bend and was hidden by the trees lining both sides of the street. Walking across the lawn back to my house, it might have been the morning dew that caused my concern to get a bit doused. *I have to find out what's going on,* I thought.

Yes, I was in the middle of a new novel, but this wouldn't have been the first time I had worked on two stories—once I'd actually written four stories at the same time. I'm reasonably certain Webster's Dictionary had such an activity listed as a secondary definition of insanity, with a picture of me as an illustration.

My mind spinning, I tried to concoct a plan to squeeze information from Roger about what so suddenly yanked him from my house. It had to be something big if my nibbling on his ear hadn't worked. Focused on this, I nearly tripped over Elvira when I came through my door.

"Watch it, cat," I grumbled and pushed her aside.

She made a sound that might have been a groan and looked up at me with an expression that could have meant only one thing: *Oh, no. Not again. Don't you ever learn?*

Chapter Two

Staring Across Lake Erie

Just after lunch I gathered pages from my latest story, climbed into my new white Chevy Malibu (my former new car—a beautiful Subaru—had been murdered by Roger's ex-wife), and started the half-hour drive to Derby.

Weekend afternoon traffic was light along the I-190 and stayed light when I merged onto Route 5 and the Skyway that runs past the old grain silos. Beyond these, monohull boats, catamarans and even one trimaran, their sails lightly billowed, plied Lake Erie. When I glanced to the right, except for a maintenance crew, Buffalo's outer harbor seemed deserted. When Roger brought me there to see *Three Dog Night* a few weeks earlier, the place had been overflowing with concert-goers. His fists punching the air and his hips gyrating, it shocked me to see that this staid guy could really rock. Glancing again at the canopies that dotted the outer harbor, I wondered what else I didn't know about Roger.

A traffic light turned red and my brakes screeched as, lost in thought, I approached it at more than a few miles-per-hour over the speed limit. My car's engine idling, I stared at the rusted hulks of the steel mills in Lackawanna as if I might find written in the graffiti on the walls an instruction for getting a cop to tell me about his case. When the light at last switched to green, a panel truck abruptly cut in front of me. Again slamming my foot on the brake, I called the truck driver several words my mother would have scolded me for using.

Past Lackawanna, the lake turned as azure as the sky and I slowed a bit while driving past charming shops and restaurants on the outskirts of Hamburg (yes, we have one of those in western New York). This now-scenic drive on a sunlit afternoon stripped away all thoughts but those of meeting with my fellow writers. By the time I reached South Creek Road, I couldn't help but smile. A right, a left, and another right put me in front of Dana Smart's home. Through that summer and into early autumn, Dana had hosted the monthly meetings of our writers' group.

No sidewalks in this neighborhood, so I parked under an overhanging tree with my right-side tires on weed -strewn grass. With the manila folder containing my new chapters and those of the other group members under my arm, I approached the chain-link fence that protected Dana's yard. Barks and wagging tails greeted me at the gate.

"Hi, Lugzi," I said, reaching over the fence to scratch the head of the coal-black German shepherd. "Gonna let me in?"

He sniffed, then licked my hand. I wondered whether Elvira would have greeted Dana with as much enthusiasm. Maybe the difference between Lugzi's welcome and that which my cat would give explained why dogs weren't a witch's familiar. I mean, what witch would want her pet to welcome a stranger into her house?

Pushing that thought aside, I opened the gate, knelt and gave my attention to Ginger, a white Jack Russell mix. Sniffing the cuffs of my jeans, Ginger and Lugzi half-followed and half-led me up the steps of the deck and into Dana's house. The behavior of these dogs would have shocked Kathy Boone, a trainer of search and rescue dogs I had interviewed months earlier.

Once, Dana's house had been a summer cottage with a spectacular view across Lake Erie to Canada. In the years she and her husband had lived here, they'd turned the cottage into a comfortable year-round home. Reminiscent of my house which had also started as a summer cottage, on the first floor the kitchen flowed into a living space filled with books, bulletin boards and notes. As I had, Dana had set up her work space so that a twist of her neck toward the sliding glass doors provided the inspiration a writer needed: a view of life changing colors with the seasons. This season, yellow and brown leaves were scattered across her red-stained wood deck.

"I'm the first one here?" I asked as I dropped my folder on the edge of Dana's desk—a foolish question, since she stood slicing fruit at her kitchen counter and I saw no one else.

I handed her the box of cinnamon sticky-buns I'd brought as my contribution to the food the group would consume that afternoon.

What is it about the gathering of writers that jogs our stomachs?

"Anything I can do to help?" I leaned past Dana and snatched a slice of an apple.

Her curly, dark brown hair shook when she laughed. "Over there," she said. "Paper plates are in the cabinet next to the sink. You can put your buns on them."

The plates were in one of the lower cabinets. Petite, with an aquiline nose, Dana Smart was two or so inches shorter than my five-foot seven. As I began to pile the buns on the plate, Samantha Wold came through the door. Thin lips, straight shoulder-length hair the color of autumn wheat, she stood about as tall as my friend, Rebecca Nurse. Though she had been working on a young adult novel with a witchcraft twist, I wasn't convinced she believed in such things. Not that I would have shared my ancestor's proclivity with her, anyway—as I've said, the fewer people who knew of my genetic trait, the less I would suffer.

Samantha glanced at the sticky-buns, then at me. Clearly, she knew how these had gotten into Dana's otherwise healthful kitchen.

"Have one," I said. "It'll get your creative juices flowing."

She reached past the plate of buns and took an apple slice.

The deck door slid open. "Everyone here yet?" Mark Maitland asked.

In his early fifties, with a long, thin face and muscular build, he stood almost as tall as Roger. He was also one of the two guys in this group who started a conga drum beating in my heart. The other one—

"Am I late?" Ray Scannado called from the deck. Streaks of gray in his sideburns, mustache and beard, his writing, filled with dark metaphors, walked through a landscape of strange dreams. I suspected what I'd learned of my heritage drew me to him.

Chewing on a sticky-bun, then licking my fingers, I asked, "How's Mary?"

"She's well," Ray and Mark responded at the same time—they were both married to women named Mary.

The door again slid open. As Eli Nash stepped through, the two dogs scooted out. Apparently they thought there were now too many humans in their house.

Eli had a round face and a horseshoe of hair around his head. A retired high school principal, he now worked part-time at his sister's real estate agency. As he slid a sticky-bun onto a paper plate, he said, "Steve called me. He can't make it." Eli sneezed. "Sorry, I'm just getting over a cold."

"What about Daniel?" Dana asked.

"I saw him pull up just as I got out of my car," Eli answered.

"Let's get started, then," Samantha said.

I reached for a couple of the plates. "I'll give you a hand getting the snacks outside," I told Dana, and I popped another piece of a bun into my mouth.

***

Settled on the deck, snack tables at our elbows and pages of our works-in-progress on our laps, we passed the next hour critiquing each other's stories.

"I see where you're going with this, Emlyn," Mark said when my turn came to be critiqued. "You seem to have developed an underlying theme of guilt that spreads across several of your characters. Here, where you say, *Is guilt actually a spell—*"

Samantha flipped two pages of my manuscript. "I love your line about guilt as a spell that survives death. It's like you actually live with it."

In the slight chill of an early autumn day, my cheeks grew warm. The feeling of guilt that had led to the manner in which I clothed my plot felt all too real and had indeed survived my mother's death. I had been able to spread it across my story because I'd created a fictional heroine and assigned the pain to her.

Ray, a good friend, must have seen me crinkle the edge of the page I held. Moving the discussion in a different direction, he said, "The section that talks about the 1884 Van Rensselaer Pearson killing—I only see it mentioned once. If it's going to move your plot forward, you need to remind the reader about it a few times."

I took a deep breath, and scribbled a note.

Eli pointed to paragraphs in the middle of the third page of my new chapters. "You also might want to look at this—" His voice a bit raspy from the remnant of his cold, he read the paragraphs aloud. "See what I mean?"

"He's right," Dana said. "Those two paragraphs kind of wander."

"Maybe you could move this sentence up to here—" Mark pointed to the page on my lap to show what he meant.

"That'll work," I said, and wrote more notes. No matter how many stories I'd had published, I missed things. When a story got released, critics would have a field day pointing out the things I had missed. By the time those critics finished, my one desire would be to sit in a dark corner sucking my thumb, swearing I would never again set pen to paper—or, to be precise, fingers to keyboard. Working with these writer friends saved me from such a fate.

Daniel Bennet, the newest member of our group, had remained silent since we began our critiques. Not surprising. At five-foot-eight and a bit dumpier than a thirty-something guy should be, he seemed quite shy. I didn't believe shyness silenced him, though. The research in psychology I had been doing suggested that as the only unpublished member of our group, he was merely unsure of himself.

Critiques of my chapter finished, I put the copies on which the group members had written notes into my manila folder. Setting the folder aside on a snack table, I said, "Your turn, Daniel. You haven't shown us the new story you're working on. Can you at least tell us something about it?"

He stared out over the lake toward the Canadian town of Fort Erie and nearby Crystal Beach. Growing up in my corner of western New York, I had learned the history of this area and its haunted past. For thousands of years, the Iroquois had mined flint there for use as weapons and tools. After the British acquired the land from the French in 1764, they built a fort on the site. During the War of 1812, that fort had witnessed a bloody battle between the Americans and the British—more than 3,000 soldiers died in the fight. Not surprising that ghosts reputedly trod the fort's tainted ground. In 1888, an amusement park was erected at Crystal Beach and remained open for 100 years. Where the amusement park once stood, a condominium community was being constructed.

Following Daniel's gaze, I narrowed my eyes, attempting to find what at Fort Erie or Crystal Beach had captured his attention. Almost immediately I felt as though I'd been yanked from my seat and began to float over Crystal Beach. When I glanced down, though, I saw no new construction. Below me I saw a Ferris wheel, a carousel, stands peddling cotton candy and ice cream. Children in sandals, cotton shorts and t-shirts, their faces smudged, ate taffy and scrambled after their parents. I saw a young woman in a floral angel blouse and loose jeans sneak up to the roustabout operating the carousel. She touched his arm, kissed him. He reached into his back pocket, pulled out what looked like a legal document. He showed it to woman, then quickly shoved it back into his pocket. Deafened by the sound of the calliope, I couldn't hear what he said to her. It had to have been something nice, because she smiled and kissed him again. As I watched the woman and man, fog engulfed me. When it cleared, I had floated away from the carousel. Now I watched two adults. She had long red hair that fell almost to her waist and wore a tie-dyed shirt in psychedelic colors. His hair was dark and more conservatively short. Holding hands, they walked toward the Comet—the rollercoaster that seemed to twist and fly over the pier at the beach. I gasped. These were my parents. A child ran up and grabbed my father's shirttail... I now looked down at the amusement park when I was a child!

I shuddered. *No. This can't be happening!*

For months I had felt the past pulling at me, but this was the first time the past had wrapped me in its arms and refused to let go.

"You still with us, Emlyn?"

The Crystal Beach amusement park vanished at the sound of Mark's voice. I felt as though I dropped from a height back onto the deck chair.

I gulped back a frightened sob.

Samantha touched my hand and asked, "Are you okay?"

My heart racing, I twisted in the chair. I had to get my bearings. After a minute, my heartbeat slowed. I glanced around. At last recalling where I was, I smiled at Samantha. I smiled at the others. I scratched at what felt like a rash on my arm. "Sorry. I was just, uh… remembering something." I tried to fight back the flush I felt rise from my neck. "What was I saying?"

Eli looked sideways at me. His expression, reflective of years as a principal observing children, said he suspected something amiss. Of course, that might have been my imagination again gone haywire. "You… er, asked Daniel to tell us about the story he's working on."

"How about it, Daniel?" Dana sounded a bit impatient.

The newest member of Writers Refuge pulled at his stringy dark hair and turned his stare on me. "I… um, I'm thinking about… a ghost story. That is, I've started to write it."

"Okay," Ray said. "Halloween's Monday. It's a good time for a ghost story."

"Do you have some pages to read?" Mark asked.

Daniel picked at the shredded knee of his jeans. "Uh… maybe the next time we meet."

Dana gathered the pages on her lap. "This might be a good point to take a break. I'll put up another pot of coffee."

Samantha followed her into the house. Ray, Mark, and Eli settled at a corner of the deck, discussing the *Carnival of Parahorror*, staged two months earlier at Buffalo's Central Train Station. Daniel wandered to a corner of the yard, where he stood by the fence, watching an eagle circle in the cloudless sky. Still a bit shaky from my unexpected flight into the past, I also moved to the fence. I stopped about six feet from him.

For what felt like ten silent minutes, I stared across the lake, trying hard to understand what had happened to me. Why had it happened? I couldn't find an answer.

Maybe Rebecca will know. I'll phone her when I get home.

Having bounced against what felt like a brick wall that blocked the answer I sought, I turned my attention to Daniel. He looked at me with a puzzled expression. Could he have experienced what I had?

I moved to his side. In search of a way to broach the subject without giving away my heritage, I said, "The pages you brought to the group the last time we met were pretty good. Maybe I can... uh, help you work on *that* story?"

He looked down, and toed the dirt. "My grandfather worked over there... Ran the carousel at the park."

I felt as if the ground had turned to quicksand. The man I'd seen kissed by a woman at the carousel—could he have been Daniel's grandfather? "At... Crystal Beach?" I asked.

He nodded.

"T-then w-why not write about that?"

"Can't... I..."

"You what?"

"I've gotta write about a ghost."

I turned away from him. "Any ghost in particular?"

I heard him kick the dirt.

"There are plenty of haunted locations around here. Like, uh..." Fighting the scene I'd witnessed, I said. "Fort Erie."

"More than there," he said. "Last week, *Haunted Collector* went to the Echo Club."

I rested my hand on his shoulder, as much to steady myself as to reassure him. "Well, that could be a start."

"Uh-uh. Been done. They're all over the internet. Besides, I found…"

"What?"

Again he avoided my question. "It's like my grandfather… wants me to write this story."

My eyes narrowed, and I stared at him. "Your grandfather died last year." I remembered seeing Carlton Bennet's obituary in the *Niagara Gazette*.

"I'm not telling you his ghost came to me. It's something of his I found."

Again, I asked, "What?"

He pulled a sheet of paper from his side pocket, and held it out. "This is a copy of something my grandfather showed me before he died, but I know where the real thing is." Unfolding the page, he looked into my eyes. "I've got something I have check out before I get the real one. I'll tell you this much, though—" His voice dropped to whisper. "—if my grandfather was right, a lot of people are gonna be pissed. Get their hands on this page—" His eyes flicked around the yard, then he shook his head. "It'll be ashes."

His hand shaking, I caught only a glimpse of what was written on the page. I saw the name Hiram Bennet, and something to do with links and chains. I didn't see much more, because I twisted my neck when I caught a slight movement to my left. A shadow passed quickly along the ground, but when I looked, it seemed I had seen only fluttering leaves on the maple tree near the fence.

Daniel, who had been looking in that direction, seemed startled. He quickly refolded the page, stuffed it into his pocket, then brushed at the legs of his jeans. "Forget I showed you that," he said softly and walked back to the deck. Loud enough to be clearly heard, over his shoulder he said, "Um… maybe next time the group meets I'll, uh… have some pages to read."

After what happened later, I wished I had pressed Daniel. Maybe tried a small spell to make him show me more of what was written on the page he'd held. Better still, I wished I'd looked around to learn what had startled him. I didn't. My mind was still locked on what had happened when I looked across Lake Erie.

When I returned to the deck, I saw Samantha near the sliding door to Dana's house. She seemed to be engaged in a serious conversation with Mark. As I approached them, he looked at his watch, and said, "We should get back to the stories." He glanced at me. "Mary's parents are coming for dinner tonight."

From the corner of the deck where he sat talking with Ray, Eli said, "My time's also running short. Got a house to show this evening."

Dana came through the door holding the fresh pot of coffee. "You're showing another house?"

Eli gave her a nervous grin. "No end to the work. My sister's a slave driver."

"Let's get back to it, then," Ray said. He looked around. "Hey, Daniel, you ready?"

When I turned, I saw our newest member at the deck rail, again staring across the lake.

"Daniel?" Dana said.

At last, he turned to us and nodded. It took a few moments, though, until he joined us.

Chapter Three

Puzzles

At our critique session's end, Samantha quickly gathered her pages. Glancing at her watch, she said, "Almost five o'clock. Gotta dash. I've got a board meeting in an hour. Sorry. I'll see you all next time."

The dogs at her heels, she rushed from the deck.

"She's an officer in her father's company," Dana explained.

"I know," Mark said. "A vice-president or something."

I shook my head. "Whew. I'm so glad I work for myself. I couldn't take that kind of pressure."

Ray looked at me, and laughed. "Yeah. You just have to keep coming up with more dead people to write about. No pressure in that."

"None at all." I grinned at him. "Not as long as the guy I live with keeps getting murder cases to work on."

Dana stopped picking up the paper plates and coffee cups, and turned to me. "You and Roger are living together?"

"They are?" Eli said.

Oops. This was how gossip got started. Embarrassing as this might have been, at least it took my mind off the unintended flight I had taken to Crystal Beach. For the moment. My cheeks a little warm, I picked at my blouse. "Uh… Well… He stays at my house… Sometimes… When he hasn't been working late…"

My shoulders hunched, I glanced at Ray, silently begging him to again change the subject.

My friend with the dark dreams accommodated me. "Mark, Eli and I are planning a ghost hunt for Halloween night."

With a grateful smile, I said, "My father took me on a ghost tour of Niagara Falls when I was a girl. But hunting through a haunted house…" I rolled my eyes.

I've mentioned now and then that I'm a poor liar. When I try, my cheeks turn a little red and my arm itches as if I have a rash. These things didn't happen when I told Ray I'd never wandered through a haunted location. I didn't think my ancient relative appearing now and then in my backyard counted. After all, Sarah Goode showed up only when I would try to cast a spell, and then only after I had lit some incense sprinkled with the herbs she wrote of in her *Book of Shadows*. Roger refused to admit old Sarah *actually* showed up at such moments. He believed I had just gotten a bit high from sniffing the burning herbs.

"Never been in a haunted house?" Ray said. "What do you say, guys? Should we take her with us?"

Eli shrugged. Mark cocked a brow and closed an eye. Ray all but laughed. From these reactions, I couldn't decide if this was an invitation or a dare. A problem I'd had since fourth grade was that I couldn't ignore a dare. In fourth grade Freddy Silbert dared me to lock our teacher, Mrs. Meade, in a closet, then laughed at me until I finally did it. That stunt cost me a day of sitting outside the principal's office, a week of cleaning the blackboards and erasers in our classroom and a month of household chores—needless to say, my mother wasn't amused when she received a phone call from the principal. As a result, so many years later when it sounded as though Ray dared me to wander through haunted Niagara Falls locations, I responded, "What time should I be ready?"

Eli turned his back to us. Mark and Ray grinned at each other. I couldn't decide if my writer friends were engaging in a practical joke.

"About seven," Ray said. "I'll swing by for you."

Picking at the polish on my thumbnail, I said, "Um… what kind of costume should I… uh, wear?"

Eli snorted, then sneezed. Ray's and Mark's grins grew wider and they broke into laughter.

"What about you, Daniel? And you, Dana?" Mark asked. "You gonna come with us?"

"Count me in," Dana said, and looked at Daniel.

"Um… Uh…" He again pulled on his jeans. Since Samantha left, he'd also been checking his watch. Now his eyes flashed nervously around the yard. "I… have to leave. Call me later… I'll let you know." Grabbing his folder, he ran from the deck.

"What was that about?" Mark asked.

"I've got no idea," Dana said.

I shrugged. "He's been edgy all day."

Ray nodded. "I noticed that. I'll call him when I get home, see what's going on."

Ten minutes later, after helping Dana straighten up, Ray, Mark, Eli and I left. As I started the ride back to Niagara Falls, I thought about Daniel and wondered what had caused him such angst. *Probably had something to do with that piece of paper he showed me,* I thought.

Glad Ray would call him, I laid my concern aside and thought about the haunted house tour. An evening with these friends, focused on something other than our writing, would be fun. My musing about what might await us in haunted houses ended abruptly when cars behind me at the light on Route 5 blasted a wake-up call. The blare of horns made me jump. The tight seatbelt pressed on my chest. I had felt the same pressure on my chest when unseen hands carried me over the amusement park at Chrystal Beach.

Shaking again, I pulled to the side of the road, took my cell phone from my purse and punched in the seven numbers that would connect me to Rebecca. Her machine answered. *You've reached the Black Cat,* it said. *I'm either out of the shop or busy with a customer. Please leave a message for me.*

"Damn!" I muttered.

***

By the time I pulled into the driveway at my house, the sky had begun to darken. Nearly six o'clock, the russet and yellow leaves on the trees across the road had faded into the gray of evening. Next door, I saw an empty driveway. My stomach did a slow twist. Here was another distraction.

As much as my imagination might go blue at the thought of Ray and Mark, I loved Roger. Roger the cop. Out on the streets. Chasing people who might have guns and decide to shoot instead of talking to him. I pictured him walking up to a house to question a suspect in a murder case. In my mind, I heard a shot ring out just as he opened the door. I saw him grab his chest and tumble from the stoop. What if I had forgotten to take my cellphone when I left my house that morning? What if Harry Woodward had tried to call to let me know Roger had been shot? What if Harry had wanted to tell me Roger was... dead? Omigod! Two years ago, the wife of a detective had warned me of the constant dread which is the price of loving a cop... Damn my imagination! Why wouldn't it stay focused on a ghost tour?

"I've been through the end of a rotten marriage," I said to my Malibu's dashboard. "Why would I think of spending the rest of my life with a man who could get killed any day?"

No, I wasn't angry at Roger for what I imagined was his constantly placing himself in danger. There had been times I'd been far less careful than he. I shuddered at the recollection of a firebomb burning my leg and a baseball bat shattering my ribs. At least I'd known the trouble I faced. Sort of... All right, I'd had no idea what trouble I faced. Roger had known, of course, so right there was the issue. He had known the trouble I could get into then but I didn't know what trouble he might face now. This morning he'd refused to tell me. Damn him!

The therapist I'd seen after my marriage broke up would have said I was fighting to avoid the fear brought on by the strange flight I had taken to Crystal Beach. She would have said the anger I now felt at Roger was my way of avoiding having to deal with that other fear. Damn my imagination and damn my therapist for not letting me hide from the truth!

The folder with my story pages under my arm, I threw open my front door and stomped through it.

Down the hall, I saw Elvira's head pop up from her nest in my overstuffed wingback chair. Running her tongue across her mouth, she glared at me with her impossibly pink eyes. Her expression might have asked, *What are you grumbling about?*

"You don't want to know," I told her. In the living room, I tossed my jacket on the sofa and dropped down on the chair in front of my computer desk. "I wish *I* didn't know," I muttered as I pulled Sarah Goode's book from the top drawer.

The cat jumped from her chair. Parked next to my feet, she stared up at me.

"There's got to be something in here that'll tell me why that happened," I said while I carefully turned the brittle pages.

Elvira shook her head and mewed, as if to say, *Whatever you're gonna do, leave me out of it.* With that, she turned and began to strut back to her chair.

Halfway across the living room, she stopped and raised her head. Her ears taut, she listened for a moment, then scampered to the front door. In a minute the door opened.

With a laugh, a baritone voice imitating Desi Arnaz's Latin accent called out, "Lucy, I'm home."

How did that stupid cat always hear Roger coming before he opened the door?

"Good for you," I said under my breath.

I heard the hall closet open and close. "What are you up to?" Roger said as he rounded the corner from the hall. "How'd your writing session go?"

"Everything went just fine." I closed the calfskin cover of Sarah's book and tried on a phony smile.

He tilted his head, looked down at Elvira, then pointed at me with his thumb. "What's with her?"

Can a cat sigh and shrug its shoulders? It sure looked as though this one did.

With a snort, my hefty albino pain turned and sauntered off to the kitchen.

The way Roger watched the cat, I had the impression he was trying to decide if it would be safer to go with her. After a moment, he shook his head. When he came toward me, it was all I could do to hold back a laugh. The man tip-toed as if afraid heavy footsteps might set off a nuclear blast. When the bomb failed to detonate, he planted a loud, wet kiss on my forehead.

I pushed him away. "Don't be nice when I'm upset."

He took my face in his hands. This time his kiss was gentle and long. Not fair! I couldn't stay focused on my problem when the man could kiss that way. Like the remnant of snow under spring sunshine, my thoughts of Crystal Beach melted.

"Better now?" he whispered in my ear.

My cat must be psychic. I could come up with no other explanation for how she knew when the atmosphere in the house had cleared. Just as soon as I nodded and kissed Roger back, her head poked out from the kitchen door. Then she mewed, as if to say, *Thank the cat god that's over.*

Roger had known Elvira long enough to learn her language. Pecking one more kiss at my cheek, he looked at her from the corner of his eye and said, "You got that right."

I slapped at his hand. Obviously, he knew I would do that. Before the smack landed he'd danced three feet away from me, laughing.

"I hate you!" I called as he and the cat vanished into the kitchen.

His face appeared in the pass-through from my kitchen to the dining room. "Uh-huh," he said, "I love you, too."

He moved from the counter. I heard the refrigerator open, then his voice floated out. "That turkey casserole you made a few days ago, is there any left?"

I slid Sarah's book back into the desk drawer. "Give me a minute. I'll warm it up."

Chapter Four

Search for an Answer

Roger's stomach full, he at last told me about his day.

"Boring, boring," he said with a sigh. "But at least I wasn't stuck behind my desk."

Harry Woodward had done something he rarely did, Roger explained. The man had taken a day off.

"Your friend Rebecca's adoptive father came in from Cleveland and wanted to meet her new beau," Roger said with a grin so broad it wrinkled the skin around his hazel eyes. "He told me they planned to take her old man to dinner at the Ellicottville Brewing Company."

Now I knew why Rebecca hadn't answered when I'd phoned her.

"That doesn't explain why Harry called you in today," I said.

Roger rose from the dinette table, and took our dishes to the sink. While he washed them, he told me, "He needed me to cover for him."

I dried the dishes and put them in the cabinet next to the stove. "So what was the big secret?" Rebecca had already told me her dad came to meet Harry.

Staring at the backboard over the sink, Roger said, "Border Patrol planned a surveillance in town. They needed our squad as backup."

I rolled my eyes. "You couldn't tell me that?"

"C'mon, Emlyn. You know I couldn't. Not till it was over and the bad guys were rolled up."

I threw the dish towel on the floor and shoved him. "You were afraid I'd tell someone?" I growled

"Not on purpose. But something could've slipped in a conversation." He stooped to pick up the towel and tossed it onto the counter. Because he looked directly at me, he didn't see where the towel landed.

Elvira saw it, though. While Roger and I engaged in our small spat, she'd jumped onto the counter—the nosy animal wanted to get her two cents in (knowing my cat, she actually wanted to add ten cents to the argument). She didn't get the chance, because the towel landed on her head. She growled and jumped to the floor. Somehow, the towel remained over her face. Lacking hands, she twitched her body to shake it off. Then, with as much dignity as she could muster, head high, she strolled from the kitchen.

This scene put a brake on my annoyance before it had a chance to roll downhill to outright anger. I laughed so hard I couldn't get another word out. It wouldn't have mattered if I could. I knew Roger was right. I've mentioned at times that I keep a list of things I know are true, but just don't like—my "Kick-the-Damn-Bucket List." I had another entry for my list.

Settled now next to me on the sofa in my living room, my guy relented enough to tell me this much about his day: the people the Border Patrol had been after eluded them.

"A wagon and three guys in Border Patrol vests showed up at this house a couple of blocks off Pine Avenue," he said. "They surrounded the place, then Agent Partridge—it's his operation—jimmied the back door. Ten minutes later, he's back. He didn't find anyone in the house, he said. Guess the uninvited aliens he's looking for hadn't shown up yet."

Roger popped the cap off a beer bottle, took the television remote from the coffee table and turned on a college football game. "Oklahoma State's playing West Virginia." He turned to look at me. "This should be a good one."

I took the remote from him and lowered the volume. "So you got to lounge around in your office the rest of the day?"

Lifting his feet onto the table, Roger sighed. "Not even. The federal genius decided whoever he was looking for must've taken off when they heard us coming. He stayed to watch the place and sent the rest of us out scouring blocks all around looking for..." Roger shrugged. "Who the hell knows?"

I pursed my lips and stroked his cheek. "Aw, poor baby."

He smiled at me, then turned up the volume just as a voice on the TV shouted about a thirty-yard run that ended in a fumble.

"Can you beat that?" The sportscaster sounded out of breath. "Oklahoma had a chance to ice this game, and the tight end gave it away."

"Give credit where it's due," the sportscaster's colleague responded. "West Virginia's secondary is playing a heck of a game."

Roger leaned so far forward, I thought he might try to squeeze through the TV screen and wind up in the stands at the stadium. "This could be a major upset. Oklahoma State's a pick for the championship."

Three plays later, an interception ended any chance for a West Virginia win. The upset had eluded that team as easily as the people Agent Partridge chased had eluded him.

***

At eleven-fifteen Roger climbed to my bedroom. Left alone downstairs with my guy's day and the ball game no longer present to distract me, the memory of my flight across the lake to Crystal Beach crept back. It burned in my mind like a rampant forest fire. I hadn't told Roger about that strange incident. I've mentioned his belief that my trips to the past were drug-induced—the result of sniffing herbs burning on my altar. If I had told him what happened, he might have wondered aloud whether, instead of critiquing stories at my writers' group, we'd been sniffing glue. This would have led to an argument in which I didn't want to engage. After the breakup of my unfortunate marriage, I established a house rule: one argument a day is my limit.

So, with Roger snoring upstairs, I pulled Sarah Goode's book from my desk drawer and spent the next hour trying to decipher her handwriting as I searched for something, anything that would explain what had happened to me. The entry my ancient relative wrote on May 29, 1692 caught my attention and rattled my nerves.

> *I shudder on the straw in a corner of this cell where now I pass my days. To escape this place and the dread which is my sole companion, by the moon last night did I take flight. My one friend, Rebecca Nurse, had spoken of how this might be done. Years past had she been told of this spell by an Old One, who then warned of the spell's peril. The past, the Old One said, has powerful hands. Once a flight to it is undertaken, it might choose to not release its grasp. I feel those hands today. Shall I still feel this iron grip tomorrow?*

I turned page after page, praying Sarah had written of a remedy. I might have searched through her *Book of Shadows* until my eyesight failed, or at least for five or six more hours, if my phone hadn't rung just before midnight.

Stiff from sitting in one place for so long, swearing I would join a gym to get more exercise than constantly pounding my fingers on my keyboard, I shuffled my feet to the kitchen counter. To my ears, my voice reflected my weariness, when I said, "Hello?"

With no preamble, Rebecca said, "Okay, what trouble did you get into this time?"

"Huh? H-how…?"

"I couldn't fall asleep after me and Harry made… Uh, well, I couldn't settle down to sleep, so I started reading the cards."

I heard a strain in my friend's voice, which worried me more than a bit. This tone always boded trouble, and I didn't want any trouble now that my life had finally climbed to a calm plateau. My books were selling, I had at last settled in with my guy, and no one had tried to kill me in the past nine months. Everything had been fine until the *trip* I took today. Did that have something to do with what I heard in Rebecca's voice?

"I wanted to see what lay ahead for me and Harry," she said. "But the first card I turned over was the Queen of Cups. That's your card—"

"My—?"

"Uh-huh. It always shows up when I'm about to get involved with something you're doing."

I gulped and glanced over my shoulder at the étagère in which I kept my liquor.

"Then I turned over the Seven of Cups," my friend continued, "and you know what that means?"

Several times in the past, Rebecca had asked me if I knew the meaning of one tarot or another. She should have known by now I had no idea what they meant. I reminded her of that.

I heard her sigh. "It means your thoughts are about to get you all muddled again—probably in the next couple of days."

Now I knew why Rebecca sounded concerned. She feared I would find myself in the middle of some kind of chaos. When that had happened in the past, I'd dragged her into the morass with me.

"I, um…" I said.

"Do us both a favor. Stay in your house. Lock your doors. I don't need my kneecap broken again."

Roger's ex-wife had used a bat to break Rebecca's kneecap and shatter my ribs just after a woman whom everyone thought had been dead for years turned up dead again.

"I… uh, think it might be a little late for that," I said, and told her about what had happened at the meeting of my writers group.

I heard her swallow. Had she poured a glass of wine to settle her nerves? I sure needed one.

After swallowing again—harder this time—she said, "I told you not to try that time travel spell. Didn't I tell you that? You make me so mad sometimes, Emlyn!"

"What are you talking about?" I asked, although I knew quite well. She had referred to the spell I'd cast to carry me to a time before my birth, to learn the identity of someone who had been murdered back then. "Elvira and I got there and back all right," I said. "So what's wrong?"

She took another swallow. "This isn't the first time you felt like you were pulled into the past." She waited for me to answer. When I didn't, she pressed, "It isn't, is it?"

"Well…"

"Don't even think about holding back on me, Emlyn Goode. This is too important."

With a groan, I admitted it had happened before. "Though those times," I said, "I didn't actually get lifted out of my seat."

She let out a long sigh. "I've been afraid this would happen. The last time I came to your house, I thumbed through Sarah Goode's book. You were so anxious to try that spell she wrote about, you didn't read far enough. She wrote that once she'd tried that spell, she kept getting pulled back for weeks. She wrote it happened each time someone in Salem was about to be hanged."

"What?" I shouted.

"Your ancestor called being pulled back in time an omen. Now will you listen to me? Stay inside!"

I started to pant. "I will," I said, then thought for a second before adding, "Right after Monday."

I could almost see Rebecca shake her head and roll her eyes. "Why after Monday?"

"Well… You know Ray, Mark and Eli—from my writers' group? Monday is Halloween, and I promised I'd do a ghost hunt with them."

"Don't!" she said. "Stay. In. Your. House."

"I can't. It was…" I didn't want to tell her, but couldn't hold back the words "…a dare."

I knew I shouldn't have told her. As soon as I did, she moaned, "There's something very wrong with you!" and slammed down the phone.

My mother, God rest her soul, used to say the same thing about me.

My snoopy cat that had to hear everything going on in my house had been listening to my conversation with Rebecca. When it ended, she snapped her mouth closed and left the room.

Chapter Five

Almost a Quiet Time

Sunday, I spent a quiet day in my house. This had nothing to do with Rebecca's warning. It was just the habit Roger and I had gotten into since the start of the football season. A big late breakfast and the rest of the day we were parked on my sofa, watching teams beat each other up on the televised field. The prior night I had gone to bed, certain our day together would be lost. It might be football Sunday, but illegal aliens didn't stop sneaking across the border. Our reprieve came in a phone call from Harry. Border Patrol had called, he told Roger. The stakeout wouldn't pick up again until the next day.

Then Monday morning arrived. Halloween. When Roger came downstairs dressed in dark pants and a gray shirt—his stake-out outfit—I had a blueberry muffin and margarine ready for him.

From the doorway, he said, "A cat munching away next to my chair. My favorite girl and my breakfast on the table. I could get used to this,"

Need I say it? Clearly he wasn't a grammarian. While I poured coffee into white mugs (my kitchen and everything in it, including my dishes, were white), I couldn't help but correct him. "Your breakfast is on the table," I said. "I'm not."

"Huh?"

"I said…"

Elvira lifted her head from her bowl and looked at me with an expression that seemed to say, *This isn't an English class.*

I sighed, and told both the man and the beast, "Forget it."

Roger looked from the cat to me, trying to decide, I presumed, whether he had been insulted. After a moment, he shrugged and took a bite of his muffin. Then, sipping his coffee, he asked, "Who called so late the other night?"

When he hadn't said anything about it yesterday, I thought I'd gotten off the hook.

"Called?" I slipped onto a chair beside him and tipped a dollop of milk into my mug.

His mug to his lips, he glanced sideways at me. "I know I heard the kitchen phone ring around midnight."

"Um… er…" I hesitated this way because Roger's a police detective and he's quite good at his job. Once I told him who had called me at that hour, he would interrogate me until I told him everything Rebecca and I spoke about— including my unintended flight to the past and Rebecca's warning. I didn't want to tell him about her warning, because I'd then have to tell him about the planned ghost hunt, and that, because I'm incapable of ignoring a dare, I refused to stay in tonight. What would happen next? Because he cared about me and worried about the trouble I couldn't help but get into, my cop-buddy would probably drag me to the precinct, toss me into a cell and keep me there until the night had passed…

I've mentioned my overactive imagination? This was it at work.

Elvira twisted her neck and shot me a look that said something in the nature of, *Oh, give me a break!*

Roger put down his mug and turned in his seat so he could watch my face.

I didn't need the mirror hung in the hall to see myself flush until my face became the color of my very red hair. I saw it in his eyes. "It was Rebecca," I said at last.

"At that hour?" The interrogation had begun.

"Why not?"

"What was so important she couldn't wait until the morning to tell you?"

I felt as though I was again sixteen and trying avoid telling my mother I'd been out smoking cigarettes and drinking wine with Freddy Silbert beneath the bleachers at the Hyde Park little league field.

I took a breath. "She... had a great evening with Harry and her father. The two men got along famously, and she just had to tell me all about it."

My arm started to itch. I fought the need to scratch it. Well aware of the rash I would develop if I tried to lie, Roger would dig deeper.

When he narrowed his eyes, I nearly blurted, *That's my story, and I'm sticking with it!* Thank goodness I swallowed the words before they escaped from my mouth.

"You're sure that's what Rebecca wanted to tell you?" he asked.

This had gone too far. Certain in another minute I would confess to every crime committed since our nation had been founded including the assassination of Lincoln, I swallowed a mouthful of hot coffee.

Someone once said something about offense as the best defense. My throat scorched from the coffee, I let my anger flare. Shoving my mug aside, I stood up. My lips pinched, I hissed, "I'm not a criminal and I'm not your child. How dare you treat me like this?"

The nerve of the man. The unmitigated gall. He laughed! But then he took my hand, pulled me back onto my chair, and planted a kiss on my forehead. "I know," he said. "I was just practicing in case I ever get a chance to interrogate a prisoner again."

That didn't help. My anger having been released from its box, a forehead kiss would not tuck it back in.

A perceptive man, Roger must have seen the fire still flaring in my eyes. Before I had a chance to rise from the table and stomp from the kitchen, he wrapped his very strong arms around me.

"I'm sorry. Better now?"

My knees weak, the anger slid from my brain. Only memories of the times we had shared—yes, and the times this man had protected me from others *and* myself—remained.

Once again, Elvira raised her head from her white ceramic food bowl and looked up at us with an expression I took to mean, *I'm glad that's over. Maybe now I can eat in peace.*

After kissing me gently—a kiss I readily returned—Roger pulled his jacket from the hall closet. "Gotta run. Another boring day," he said as he opened my front door. "I'll be thinking of you while I sit in my car outside a house, drinking coffee and waiting for the Border Patrol's imaginary illegal aliens to show up."

I didn't hear from Roger the rest of that morning and afternoon. Not surprising. He rarely phoned while he was at work. I spent this quiet time at my computer, adjusting my story to account for the changes suggested by members of the writers' group. Lost in my work, I didn't come up for air until my stomach growled just before one o'clock. With a glance over my shoulder at my computer screen, as if I feared that when I turned my back, someone would sneak into my house and swipe my words, I moved quickly to the refrigerator. Watching my computer through the passage from my kitchen to the dining area, I stuffed some cold cuts between slices of bread. The sandwich sliding across my plate, I scampered back to my desk, where I gobbled the food while I typed. Focused on images of my characters running across my computer screen, I lost track of time until my phone rang. When I glanced at the toolbar at the lower right corner of the screen, I saw it was nearly five-thirty.

Elvira stopped snoring and looked up.

"Must be Rebecca," I said to the cat. "I'm sure she's checking to be certain I stayed locked in the house."

With a stretch and a yawn, I moved across the living room to the kitchen counter, and lifted the receiver. "I'm still here, Rebecca," I mumbled without first saying hello.

"Is this Emlyn?" said the somewhat muted male voice on the other end of the line. Clearly this wasn't Rebecca.

"Who are *you*?" I asked.

"This is Daniel," the voice replied.

My eyes narrowed. "Daniel…?"

When I hesitated, he said, "From… the writers' group?" He sounded less than sure of who he was.

"Oh." I took a breath. "Sorry. First time I heard you on a telephone. I didn't recognize your voice. What can I do for you, Daniel?"

"I… um… I need to talk to you. Can you… meet me?" His words came in a raspy whisper, and I had to listen carefully to make out what he said.

I glanced at the clock hanging on the soffit over my kitchen sink. "Now?"

"Please, Emlyn. What I've been searching for? I finally figured out where my uncle Richard must've hidden the original. Before I pull it out, I want to talk to someone about it."

I again glanced at the clock. "Ray's going to be coming by for me in about an hour. We're going on the ghost hunt, remember? Can we talk then?"

I heard him gulp. "I'm not going, Emlyn. Please. Meet me now. I don't know who else I can trust."

This was strange and growing more so by the minute. I'd only known Daniel a few months, and except for the facts that his grandfather once worked at Crystal Beach and that Daniel wanted to be a writer, I knew nothing about him. How could I be the only person he trusted?

Again in what was more a rasp than a whisper, he said, "Please, Emlyn."

I felt a metaphoric tap on my shoulder, and in my mind I heard my mother say, *If someone needs your help, you have to give it.*

"Yeah, Ma, I know," I said to my memory of her. To the guy on the phone, I said, "Where are you?"

It took a minute before he answered. I sensed he might be looking around to get his bearings. At last, he said, "I'll be outside the Tops supermarket. You know, the small one on Porter Road just off Pine?"

"Yes, I know it. I'll—"

"Emlyn," he broke in. "Please hurry! I think I'm in trouble."

Reacting to the panic I sensed in his voice, while I reached for my jacket in the hall closet, I said, "Stay where you are, Daniel. I can get there in fifteen minutes."

When I opened the front door, a cat-head poked over the arm of my overstuffed wingback chair. She shot a pink-eyed glare in my direction, and mewed, as if to say, *Didn't Rebecca tell you not to go out of the house today?*

I slammed the door on my furry conscience.

***

A nice thing about the small city in which I lived was that nearing six o'clock on a Monday afternoon, rush-hour traffic got spoken of by radio disc jockeys but was rarely seen on the roads. With only a single slow spot where Niagara Falls Boulevard passed the ramp to the I-190, I made it through the city and turned onto Porter Road in almost the promised amount of time.

I pulled into the lot next to the Mobil gas station and slowly circled in front of the Tops Market. I saw no sign of Daniel Bennet.

At no more than three miles-per-hour, I circled the lot, looking through the windows of parked cars. Daniel waited in none of them.

I drove past the McDonalds and peered inside in case he had gotten hungry while waiting for me. He apparently hadn't.

I looked at the digital clock on my Malibu's dashboard. 6:14. I grew more concerned by the minute. Daniel had called, begged me to meet him. I had rushed here, been no more than five minutes later than I promised. Where was he?

Maybe he figured out whatever troubled him, then went home, I thought, but decided that couldn't be. On the phone he had sounded more than troubled. The man had been panic-stricken. His raspy whisper suggested he feared a nearby and immediate danger. *I can't trust anyone but you, he said. His voice was almost trembling. That wouldn't have been the sound of a man who could solve his problem in twenty minutes.*

I took a deep breath. *Maybe he went into the market to wait for me.*

I pulled into a parking spot across from Tops, and went into the market. During the next twenty minutes or so, I wandered up and down the aisles thinking that any second I would see Daniel cowering against the shelves. Sometime near 6:45, still worried about him, I returned to my car, circled the parking lot one last time, then turned for home. Though I hadn't found Daniel in the market, I'd stopped briefly at the Prepared Meals section and picked up dinner for Roger.

When I reached River Road, my car's digital clock read 7:03. Several houses down from mine, I peered through the windshield to look for Roger's Trailblazer in his driveway. He usually returned around this time. I didn't see his car.

He's probably still backing up the Border Patrol.

I didn't worry about him on this kind of assignment. He wouldn't get hurt acting as a backup to a squad of federal agents. Actually, I felt sort of glad he hadn't come home yet. For a reason I couldn't identify, I still didn't want him to know of my plans for that evening until I returned home safe and sound.

Looking now at *my* driveway, I saw Ray's car. When I pulled in next to my writer friend, he rolled down his window, and said, "I almost gave up on you, Emlyn. Are you ready to drag a few ghosts from their lairs?"

"I will be in just a minute," I told him. I pulled my keys from my purse, slid from behind the wheel, and ran to my front door.

In the kitchen, I wrote a note to my guy:

> *I'm out with my writers' group* (I drew a happy face next to this line). *Not sure when I'll get home. There's a plate with meatloaf, scalloped potatoes, and green beans in the fridge. Heat it up in the microwave for three minutes.*

For a moment, I looked at what I had written. Then, perhaps out of guilt for my fib of omission, I added, *I love you.*

I placed a rather thick cookbook on the dinette table, leaned the note against it, then opened the hall closet. Earlier I had brought down my formal black satin mantle, and hung it in the there. When I took it from the closet, I felt a tickle of tears in my eyes. This cape had been my mother's. I couldn't recall why or when she'd bought it. I'd borrowed it from her years before when I had been invited to attend a local award dinner. Mom gone now, I refused to part with this reminder of her. Recalling how I had lost Mom caused a few tears to run down my cheek. Sniffing back the tears, I brushed my hand across the hood, tossed the mantle over my shoulders and hurried down the two steps of my front stoop and across my lawn to Ray's car. As I opened the passenger-side door, I glanced at the blood-red maple on my lawn, wondering if I would find it adorned with toilet paper when I returned. In the few seconds it took me to get into the car, I decided my house would be safe. The homes along River Road were spread a distance apart—most separated by stands of trees. As a result, few kids trick-or-treated in my neighborhood these days.

Ray shifted his car into gear and backed onto the street. "Okay," he said. "First we'll pick up Mark, then Samantha—Dana's driving up from her house."

"What about Eli?" I asked.

"He said he'd meet us where we're going."

I turned to Ray. Concern finding its way into my voice, I said, "And Daniel? Were you able to reach him?"

Ray shrugged. "I couldn't after we left Dana's house last Saturday. But he phoned me about two hours ago."

Thinking about the strange call I had received, my stomach turned a slow twist. "He called me, too, a little while ago. I hope he's okay."

I waited for Ray to say something about the call he'd gotten from Daniel. My friend only shrugged.

Because Daniel had also called him, I decided I must be overreacting—something, I admit, I'm prone to do. After all, how could I be the only one Daniel could trust if he had also called Ray? Pushing my concern to the back of my mind, I turned my attention to our plans for the evening. "So," I said, "just where is this haunted palace you're taking me to?"

Through his graying beard, Ray answered me with only a smile.

Chapter Six

Hunting a Ghost

Sitting next to Ray in the front passenger seat with Mark and Samantha in the back, for the second time in two hours I rode into downtown Niagara Falls.

Glancing to the left then the right, I asked, "Are we going to the Echo Club?"

Ray smiled.

We glided past the Hyde Park picnic area, so it couldn't be the Echo Club.

Now we drove under a sign set on concrete pillars and adorned with green and red iron grapes. This announced we had entered Little Italy. When we slowed for a red light on Pine Avenue, I glanced to the right at the ivory stucco walls and brown beams of a Mediterranean-style building. Set between a bakery and an Italian grocery —both of which had been there since my childhood—this building once housed the insurance agency where my ex had worked—the place where he met the blond bimbo who ended my marriage.

A block further on, we drove under another sign that marked the end of Little Italy.

"I know," Samantha said. She turned in her seat to look at Mark. "We're going to the Red Coach Inn."

"Keep guessing," he said.

Instead of turning onto Porter Road just before the Mobil station, we continued on Pine into an older section of the city.

"Are we going to the Rapids Theater?" I asked.

Neither guy answered.

I loosened my seatbelt so I could twist until I looked at both of them. "Okay. Enough of this. Tell me where we're going."

They both grinned.

"Tell me!" I shouted.

Patience had never been one of my virtues. My mother told me the day I was born, Dad barely got her to the hospital before I decided to pop out.

"Not yet," Mark said. "You'll see soon enough."

Samantha pulled back her straight, wheat-colored hair. "Why are you being mean?"

"They are, aren't they?"

She nodded.

"Grr."

She slapped my shoulder. "I don't need to hear you growl, Emlyn. We might hear enough of those in the house we're going to hunt through tonight."

"You know it's a house?" I said. "Did they tell *you* where we're going?"

Samantha's face turned a bit red. As if she were critiquing one of my chapters, she said, "You're always so exact. *House* is just a figure of speech."

In a few minutes, Ray made a right onto Park Place. A block off Fourth Street, this was, indeed, an old section of town, a section I hadn't wandered through since my teens. A few Tudor homes lined this street along with others which might have begun as cabins, then been expanded over the years. One house had a stone garage in the rear that appeared to have been constructed by an early settler in the 1820s. Nobody knew for certain, but when I was in school the kids believed that garage might have been the stone hut originally built by Wilson Blaine. Ray pulled to the curb in front of this house.

I gulped. "This is where Richard Bennet killed his wife." I had pushed this place from my mind and hadn't thought of it in five years.

The house had a dark red brick veneer. What had apparently been an open porch in front had been built up, with the posts now paneled in wood painted the color of the bricks. Instead of screens, this new sun porch had leaded windows. While most of the buildings on this block were clearly well-maintained, this one bore the effects of our harsh western New York winters. The house looked like it hadn't been touched by a painter or mason since Bennet was arrested. The brickwork had large chips, and there was peeling paint on the posts and panels. The small patch of front lawn, divided by a cracked walkway, looked as though it hadn't been weeded or mowed in a year. The *FOR SALE* sign on the lawn had been kicked over.

Ray climbed from his car. "This is our destination for tonight."

"The Bennet House!" A mixture of shock and fear made my voice quiver.

"Ooh. The Tuscarora Curse." Even in the dark car, I could see the shine of excitement in Samantha's eyes.

At that moment I recognized two things about Samantha Wold. First, unlike my earlier belief, she did seem to be thrilled by the paranormal. Second, she was far braver than I.

"Are you girls ready to hunt ghosts?" Mark said.

Samantha glared at him. "Who are you calling a girl?" She slung her purse over her shoulder and moved to the driveway.

I hung onto the handle of Ray's car door, not because I feared the curse—at least, that's what I told myself—but because I had sat on the jury that found Richard Bennet guilty of all but dismembering his wife in this house. I hadn't forgotten the gruesome murder scene photographs the prosecuting attorney had shown us.

Still frozen next to Ray's car, I called out, "How are we going to get inside? The house must be locked up. You don't plan to break in, do you?"

Ray laughed. "Not to worry, you big sissy. Eli's sister owns the real estate agency that's trying to sell this place."

Waiting in the driveway, Eli Nash must have heard what I said and what Ray answered. With a broad smile, he held up a key.

Knowing what had happened in this house, I truly didn't want to go any nearer. Still, as they used to say in old novels, I girded my loins and stepped onto the sidewalk. As I did, I asked, "Where's Dana? Aren't we going to wait for her?"

Obviously, God didn't intend to be gentle with me. No sooner had I spoken than Dana's Buick pulled to the curb behind us.

Still no Daniel. I didn't dare ask about him again. Maybe one of these writer friends was the person he didn't trust. He must have trusted Ray, though—Daniel had also called him. But the others? Of course, I'd known these people for years and could think of no reason why Daniel wouldn't trust any of them.

As Dana emerged from her car, her normally curly hair looked a bit frizzy. Staring at the house, she said, "Sorry I'm late. I… got tied up doing…" She glanced back at her car. "…something."

Ray stepped toward Samantha and me and took each of us by an arm. To Mark he said, "How about if we start in the garage? Maybe we'll find Wilson Blaine's ghost in there." With that, he pushed a button on his keyring and the trunk of his car popped open.

Mark reached in. From a black case, he took a couple of devices he called digital recorders. "Most times you can't hear a spirit trying to talk to you." He held up one of the devices. "These things are more sensitive than human ears."

He again reached into the black case, and held up another device. "This is an EMF meter."

"And that does?" Samantha asked.

Ray took the rectangular device from Mark's hand and turned it on. "People believe ghosts create electromagnetic fields when they try to manifest. See these colored lights?" He held the EMF meter in front of me. "If they flash from green to red, they'll tell us if any ghouls or goblins are around."

I had no need to wait until we were inside to see the image of a ghoul. Ray took a flashlight from his jacket pocket and held it under his chin. The way the beam lit his beard and mustache… I fought back a shudder.

Once more, Mark reached into the trunk.

"Come on," Eli called from the driveway. "Stop fooling around with that stuff. I'd like to get home before tomorrow."

"He's right." Ray looked at me and Samantha, and then at Dana. "The recorders and EMF meters will be enough for these amateurs."

As we started toward the stone garage, Ray gave each of us a flashlight.

"We'll need these," Eli explained as he opened to door at the side of the garage. "Since this place hasn't been sold or rented in the last five years, my sister told me the power's been turned off."

I could smell the mustiness in the garage as soon as Eli opened the door. Our flashlights scanning the floor and walls cast an eerie glow on cobwebs strung from the rafters and in the corners. Years of dust covered a wood work-bench on which rusted saws, screwdrivers and hammers were scattered. Dust also covered the concrete floor, except for one spot where the concrete seemed to have been swept, and a small pile of rubble had been pushed against the far wall. Footprints in the dust led to the rubble but went nowhere else.

"Ghost footprints." Mark traced them with the beam from his flashlight. "The TAPS team tried an experiment like this on one of their TV ghost hunts."

Ray knelt, and grabbed something from the floor.

"An axe?" Mark turned his flashlight on it. "That red on the blade—it's either rust or… blood. I wonder if this is what Blaine used to dismember his family." He lowered his eyes to the rubble.

We followed his glance with our flashlights. Near the wall, the concrete had been broken and a hole about a foot wide had been dug.

"Looks like someone's been busy in here," Samantha said.

Ray laid the axe on the floor. "Maybe someone was trying to dig a grave."

"I guess those footprints weren't made by a ghost, after all," Dana remarked.

Eli shook his head. "My sister won't be happy when I tell her about this vandalism."

I bent to examine the hole. "Not big enough for a grave. It's more like someone was trying to recover something hidden here. I wonder what it was."

As if to herself, Dana said, "I wonder if they found it."

"Found what?" I asked.

She shrugged. Looking at Mark, she said, "How would I know?"

"Maybe a spirit will tell us." Ray held out his digital recorder. "If someone's here, step forward and speak to us." He waited a full minute before saying, "Who's been digging in here?" Another minute passed, and then he said, "Tell us your name."

"See if you got anything." Dana sounded anxious.

When Ray played it back, we heard only a low static-filled hum. "Nothing," he said.

"And I'm getting nothing on this." Mark held his EMF detector out to show us. "It's the same point three base reading I got when we came in here."

Let's try the house," Dana said. "There's got to be ghosts wandering through there. Maybe Shari Bennet's ghost."

Samantha glanced at Eli. Her expression told me she was less than thrilled by the idea.

"Maybe Shari Bennet's ghost can tell us who really killed her," Ray said.

"You know very well who murdered Shari Bennet." I felt quite defensive about this. "On the jury, we went through every piece of evidence—"

Dana dropped her hands to her hips. "You only considered what his idiot lawyer showed you."

Ray glared at her. "Well, if the woman's ghost is still around, she might tell us who's right. Come on."

At that moment, I heard the wind howl up the driveway. As if the spirit of Shari Bennet didn't want us anywhere near her house, the door at the side of the garage slammed shut. Had I actually jumped as high as I thought I did, I would have cracked my head on one of the rafters.

Mark pointed at me, and let out a laugh so loud and long, I thought he might rupture his spleen.

Eli also laughed. "Are you ready for the house? From the way my sister described it, what's in there will spook you out even more, Emlyn."

"Thanks a whole heap, pal." I glanced at the door, considering a retreat back to Ray's car.

Dana took my arm. "You can do this."

As he twisted the doorknob, Eli glanced over his shoulder. "I can't... open... it. Feels like someone outside is holding it closed!"

I squealed.

"Just kidding," he said, and threw the door open.

As I went out, I hissed at him, "Ooh, Eli Nash. I'll get even with you if it takes forever. Maybe I'll kill you in my next book."

Single-file, we followed him to the narrow stoop at the back of the house. The glass on the storm door had been shattered. When I looked to my left, I saw that one of the windows had been broken and shards of glass were strewn across the lawn. It appeared as though somebody inside had crashed through it. While we waited, Eli took the key from his pocket. The hinges screeched when he pulled the door open. Hesitantly, one-by-one, we went in.

The back door opened on the kitchen, a room so dim that even the harvest moonlight through the broken window failed to penetrate the shadows.

"Okay," Ray said. "Let's form two teams. Emlyn and Dana, you come to the living room with me. Mark, you, Eli and Samantha go down to the basement." He pointed at a door dangling by one hinge to the left of the sink. "See if you can get any EVPs." Noticing a few blank expressions, he explained, "That's the ghost hunters' term for an electronic voice phenomenon. We use the digital records to capture those."

As we crossed into the living room, I lowered my flashlight to see if blood still stained the carpet. I saw none. Apparently the realty company had cleaned it up when they still hoped they could sell this house.

Most of the window curtains had been pulled off, and those still in place seemed to have provided a feast for moths. I saw a fireplace on the outside wall. The chimney on the house obviously rose from this. An urn sat on the mantel.

Could that hold someone's ashes? I wondered.

While the others walked around the dark room, their flashlights playing on the walls and floor, I moved to the mantel. A tarnished gold plaque on the maple-strained base of the urn said Carlton Bennet. The dates below the name were obviously those on which he had been born and died. *Interesting,* I thought. *Carlton was Daniel's grandfather.* With a backward glance at the urn, I returned to inspecting the room.

Sheets covered all of the furniture. When I played my light over the sheets, I'd have sworn I saw faces where they creased. While I stood peering at the ghostly visages, a breeze brushed my arm. It felt like something tried to get my attention. The breeze gained in intensity and it sounded as though it spoke my name. Startled, I jumped back.

"What's wrong?" Dana whispered.

I shivered. It took a moment to rationalize what had happened, and in that moment I decided a person with my vivid imagination had no business in what was reputed to be a haunted house.

"I just thought..." I shook my head.

Ray nodded, as if he, too, had heard the breeze speak. "I think a spirit is ready to communicate with us," he whispered, and held out his digital recorder. "Tell us your name."

"Why are you here?" Dana said.

Holding the recorder in front of me, Ray instructed, "Ask the spirit something."

"Uh... if you're Shari, do you know I was on your husband's jury?"

Dana touched Ray's shoulder. "See if we got anything."

We leaned close to the small speaker. I heard nothing but static. Ray, though, stood up straight. "Did you hear that?"

"Hear what?" I said.

"A voice. It said, '*Get out.*'"

We listened again. I still couldn't make out a discernable word.

"Why do you want us to leave?" Ray asked what he obviously believed to be a ghost. When we again listened, he nodded.

"What did it say?" Dana asked.

"I heard a different voice. A female, I think. This one said, *'Upstairs.'* We have to see who's up there."

At the bottom step, Dana held back. I moved in front of her.

The stairs creaked. Our flashlight beams criss-crossing on the walls, we climbed to the second floor. First me, then Dana, then Ray. As I reached the landing, I gasped. I heard a high pitched moan—I think that came from me.

Dana bumped into my back.

"What's the holdup?" Ray whispered.

I tried to answer, but words wouldn't come out. I could only point with a shaking hand. In the hall, doors to the three bedrooms and a bathroom were open. The attic was open and the drop-down stairs rested on the carpeted floor. At the base of the ladder, I saw Daniel Bennet sprawled in a small, dark-colored pool. I leveled my flashlight on him. His face was white, and his eyes were open so wide that just before he died, he might have seen a ghost.

I played the light down his body. All I knew of forensics was what I'd learned while doing research for a story. Still, from what seemed to be blood that started at his left ear and crossed his neck, it looked like his throat had been cut.

I moved my light to the nearest wall, and saw reddish-brown splatters. This had to be blood. Daniel's blood. No glow to the stains. This meant the blood had dried, so it must have hit the wall hours ago.

In that instant, a thought ran through my mind. *Could Daniel have been knifed by the Tuscarora brave? Could a ghost have done this?*

Chapter Seven

The Tuscarora's Curse

The living room of the Bennet House was as dark as the street outside. What might have been white paint on the walls appeared to be deep gray, except when one of us painted a section of it with the beam of a flashlight. Then the white walls looked a slightly lighter gray with almost-ivory places where framed pictures had clearly been taken down. On the wall near the banister bordering the stairs to the second floor, a hole had been punched in the plaster-board and a naked stud peeked through. Sheets that covered the furniture—a short couch, an armchair, two straight-backed chairs and a few tables—seemed yellowed by time and stained by what might have been bird droppings. Earlier, I hadn't noticed any of this.

Dana slouched on the couch between Ray and Mark. Samantha sat, stiff-back, on one of the chairs. I squirmed, trying to find a comfortable position on the other.

Eli rose from the armchair and traced the hole in the wall with his finger. "My sister is definitely not going to be happy about this," he mumbled. "She won't be at all happy."

"Please sit down, Mr. Nash," Roger said. As if he expected to be here for a while, he loosened his vest with NIAGARA FALLS POLICE printed in block letters across the front.

Eli seemed surprised to have been addressed so formally. Glancing sideways, he said, "Call me Eli, Roger. You know me."

Roger, indeed, knew Eli, just as he knew the other members of Writers Refuge. On more than one Saturday afternoon, we'd met at my house. As a deputy chief, Roger usually had Saturdays off, so he'd been in my house when my writer friends arrived. After graciously greeting them (and with what I took to be a somewhat jealous glance at Ray and Mark), he had gone next door to his own house to watch a ball game of some kind, I presumed, and left us to our criticism of each other's work. Today, though, Roger was all business.

"Please sit, Mr. Nash," he repeated.

Samantha looked at Dana, who looked at Ray. Mark shrugged. Eli dropped down in the armchair, and continued to peel the shadows aside with his flashlight.

Roger watched the beam dance along the walls for a few moments, then sighed. "Collins," he said to the uniformed officer standing beneath the arch that divided the living room and dining room. "Take that damn flashlight, would you?"

The young cop, also wearing a police vest, snatched the light from Eli's hand, and pocketed it.

"Now," Roger said, "what are you doing here?"

Though he addressed this question to all of us, he looked squarely at me.

"I, uh… that is, we, uh…" I phumphered.

Actually, *phumpher* is a perfectly good word. At least, it was when my mother would tell me to "stop phumphering, Emlyn, and tell me what you were doing!" You could look it up… On second thought, don't bother. I've checked my *Merriam-Webster's* and didn't find it.

"We… uh…" I tried again.

When the words still refused to leave my mouth, Ray said, "Mark, Eli and I took the ladies on a Halloween ghost hunt."

His hands on his hips, still staring at me, Roger said, "You thought that would be a good idea, did you?"

The sound of the cop-voice seemed to push Ray back into a corner of the couch.

"And why did you decide to... *ghost hunt* in this particular house?" Roger continued.

"I... um, wanted to see..." Ray stopped, and glanced around.

Mark said, "When we looked for a place to go this year, Ray and I found posts about the Tuscarora's Curse all over the internet."

Finding his voice, Ray added, "One site said no one had hunted in here before."

"The internet, huh?"

Mark nodded.

"The Tuscarora's Curse!" Samantha shivered. "What a perfect place to be on Halloween."

Roger turned his back to us. "Why didn't you mention to me you planned to come here tonight?"

I knew he directed the question to me. Still feeling a bit guilty for not telling him about my Halloween plans, I again phumphered a response.

"I see. Well, you and I will have a conversation about this later."

I wrapped my silk mantle around my chest. Feeling again like the sixteen-year-old my mother had caught smoking and drinking with Freddy Silbert—this time in the stand of trees across from our house—I almost said, "Yes, Ma." I saved myself from this embarrassing memory by gulping down my guilt. This enabled me to say quite clearly, "Oh, we'll have that conversation, will we?"

Officer Collins raised his hand to his mouth and snickered.

Samantha leaned over and gave me a fist-bump.

Obviously, Roger heard in my voice an echo from the doghouse he'd stumbled into. He cleared his throat and muttered, "Maybe we won't."

He shoved his hands into the pockets of his chinos. Once again a cop at work, he said, "Okay, let's go through this one more time. You got here about eight. Did you all get here at the same time?"

"I was already here waiting for everyone," Eli said. "I stopped at my sister's house to pick up the key—my sister's the realtor listing this place. Must've been an accident on the Hyde Park Boulevard. Traffic coming down to the falls was—"

"Yeah, I get it," Roger said. "What time did you get to your sister's house?"

"About six-thirty. My sister and I had coffee and talked for a bit about the trouble we're having selling the house."

"*We're* having?" Roger asked.

 Eli glanced out one of the living room windows. "I… uh, work part-time for her agency." After another question from Roger, Eli said, "She lives in Lewiston. A nice cottage on Cayuga Street. She's been fixing it up for years… Anyhow, I left there about seven-thirty, and got here just before the others."

"I'm sure she'll confirm the time you got to her, and the time you left?" Roger made it sound as though he'd never believe an alibi provided by a family member. "And the rest of you?" he asked.

We each looked toward Dana.

"I got here about ten minutes after the others. I drove up from Derby."

"Okay," Roger said. "Now, when you got here, what did you all do?"

I glanced at Ray. After I'd found Daniel's body, I truly couldn't remember anything else about that night. Ray glanced at Mark, as if he couldn't remember, either.

Samantha answered. "We went into the garage… I think. Isn't that what we did?"

Eli rubbed a hand over his scalp and nodded. "And someone had busted through the cement floor—" He pointed at the hole in the living room wall. "Just like someone vandalized that."

"Then we came in here." Mark pointed to the archway that led to the dining room then the kitchen. "Through the back door."

"I have a key to the door." Eli reached into his shirt pocket, took out the key, and showed it to Roger. "It wasn't us that broke in through the kitchen window."

"Then we split into two teams," Mark said. "Samantha, Eli, and I went into the basement. Thought we could get an EVP. Before we got too far into it—"

Eli finished the sentence. "We came running up, because we heard someone scream."

"I think that might've been me," Dana said. "At the top of the stairs, I saw Daniel…" Apparently, the recollection of finding his body caused her to whimper.

"What about him?" Roger asked. "He's part of your group. Wasn't he with you?"

I told Roger about the frightened phone call I'd received, and how Daniel had begged me to meet him, then wasn't at the Tops Market.

"I got the same kind of call from him," Mark said. "He had me looking for him up at the Boulevard Mall."

"Me, too," Dana said. "Except he asked me to pick him up near Shea's Theater in Buffalo. That's why I was a little late getting here."

Samantha nodded as if she had gotten a similar call. So did Eli and Ray.

Roger leaned forward, about to ask another question, but stopped when a man with straight gray hair and a grayer five o'clock shadow on his face came through the archway. The man had on a jacket with BORDER PATROL written across the chest.

"We've searched the area, Detective. Still no sign of our cross-border perps." The Border Patrol agent gave a quick glance at the hole in the wall, then looked again at Roger. "Don't think they're gonna show up tonight." Now his eyes circled the room, looking at me and each of my friends in turn. "Don't suppose any of you… picked up anything while you've been in here?"

"Like what, Partridge?" Roger asked.

"Don't know… uh, maybe something to tell me… who's using this house."

We all stared at him.

"No, huh?" The Border Patrol agent shrugged. "Well, then we're packing in, Detective Frey. Whatever you and Collins have going on in here is all yours."

With an annoyed expression, his eyes focused on me, Roger nodded. "Thanks, Partridge."

Now I knew why Roger and Collins had gotten here only minutes after I'd phoned him. He'd been helping to stake out this house.

As Agent Partridge headed to the back door, he said, "Yeah. Catch ya on the flip side."

A radio disc jockey once used this term when referring to the next day. When I was a child, my mother, whom I'd learned had been something of a hippie in her younger years, would say this when she tucked me into bed. The cop I now practically lived with seemed confused by the phrase. I decided I would explain it to him later— that is, if we were still speaking.

At last Roger removed his eyes from my face, and scanned those of the others in the room. "You can get out of here now," he said. "Leave your names and numbers with the officer." He pointed at Collins. "We'll want to talk to you again. Separately."

I pulled off my mantle, rose, and moved toward my detective boyfriend. "You don't have to gather their phone numbers. I have them, and you know everyone here."

He gave me stern look.

"Want me to give Officer Collins my number, too?"

Clearly in no mood for sarcasm, Roger grabbed my arm and steered me to Ray. "Take Emlyn home. Please." He handed me off, as if transferring a prisoner, and said, "Why is it bodies appear wherever you do?"

"Just lucky, I guess," I muttered, then turned on my heels and walked from the house. I slammed the back door and swore I would stay away from ghost hunting. Swore I'd stay away from the house in which Shari Bennet had been murdered. And I swore I'd stay away from the Tuscarora's Curse. Forever!

Here's the thing, though. As if the house had an opinion about my oath, I thought I heard it laugh just when I started down the driveway. Of course, that was probably my overactive imagination.

Standing at Ray's car, my hand on the door latch, I watched the others come down the driveway. Samantha next to Eli. Mark a few steps behind Dana. Finally Ray reached the street, looking back at the house while he walked. No one spoke. Like Ray, we all just stared at the house in which the body of a member of our group lay. We might have stood this way, each lost in our own private thoughts, for an hour, though in reality it could only have been ten minutes. Our vigil ended when the *wroo-wroo* of sirens announced the arrival of the Crime Scene Unit.

While we drove away from Park Place, Mark said so softly he might have been speaking to himself, "I can almost believe that place is cursed."

Ray nodded.

In the back seat, Samantha and I sat silently staring ahead. I don't know what thoughts played in her mind. Mine had gotten stuck on the phone call I'd received. Daniel had begged for my help, and I hadn't gotten to him in time.

Why hadn't I listened to Rebecca when she warned me to turn off my phone and remain snug at home? If I had, I wouldn't have gotten Daniel's call and wouldn't now be sitting in Ray's car with guilt buckled in the seat beside me. Just as bad, I wouldn't have seen a side of Roger—a cop focused solely on investigating a murder—I hadn't noticed before. The man now sharing my bed several nights a week had treated me as he would any other suspect! How could he? How… dare he? He knew better of me!

When I had driven to Dana's house just the other day, I passed the concert venue at Buffalo's Outer Harbor, and recalled the way Roger had pumped his hands, lost in the music of *Three Dog Night*. I'd wondered then what I didn't know about him. Now I knew.

Chapter Eight

No Time for Apologies

Seconds after Ray dropped me off, I stormed into my house. Grumbling, I threw my purse and hooded mantle on the living room coffee table and stood, staring through the French door at the naked trees that guarded the Niagara River.

A white head popped up from my wingback chair—I saw the head reflected in the window pane. My cat licked her lips and narrowed her eyes in what I recognized as annoyance.

I turned on her. "What's the matter, Elvira? I interrupted your nap again?"

She let out a short *meow*, which could only have meant, *Now what happened?*

I glared at the furry beast.

She must have read my face, because she stared back and again *meowed*. This time, she said, *You weren't supposed to go out of the house—didn't Rebecca tell you that?* At least, I thought that's what the cat said. Of course, I might have put those words in her mouth because they were on my mind.

I grumbled in response.

She shook her head, then her entire body. She jumped from her nest in the chair. With a sidelong accusing glance, she strolled past me and into the kitchen.

First Roger and now Elvira? This was too much. I followed her, ready to give that cat a good piece of my mind (well, at least the small piece I felt I still had). As soon as I rounded the door and entered the kitchen, my phone rang.

When I picked up the receiver, Rebecca said, "What happened?"

I felt my face flush. "What do you mean?"

"Something happened," she said. "The cards told me you went out tonight and something went wrong. What was it?"

Unlike my hefty white feline, at least my friend hadn't said she'd told me so.

"I… found someone I knew." I took a deep breath to fight back the painful recollection.

I didn't need to tell Rebecca the condition Daniel was in when I found him. I heard her sigh. "What is it with you and dead bodies? Okay, from the beginning, now."

In fifteen minutes or so, I told Rebecca all that had happened. I started with finding Daniel Bennet's body, then went back to the call I'd received from him, my search for him, the digging we'd found in the stone garage and the hole in the damn cursed house's living room wall. Then I told her of the way Roger had treated my writer friends—and me.

"He made me feel like a suspect," I said. "He thinks *I* killed that poor guy."

She *tsked*.

"He does!" I insisted, my anger overwhelming my shock at finding Daniel.

I could almost see Rebecca shaking her head. "Oh, Emlyn, Roger doesn't think anything of the sort."

"Don't laugh at me! You weren't there. You didn't hear the way—"

"Stop talking like that. The man's in love with you." It sounded as if she were shuffling her cards.

"I used to think so," I said. "Now I know he's just desperate to catch a killer—any killer—and he doesn't care if I'm it. You should've seen the way he's been sulking and carrying on these past months, complaining that he hasn't had a fat murder case to work on."

At the word fat, Elvira's head poked from the kitchen door, and she hissed at me.

"I wasn't referring to you," I snarled at my cat.

Rebecca sighed. "I can tell there's no use talking to you on the phone—even the tarot cards know there's no talking to you when you get like this." Before I could say anything further, she said, "I'll be there in an hour."

"You don't have to."

"I do," she said. "It sounds like you're gonna need a referee in your house tonight."

It was pointless to argue with her. Especially pointless because she had already hung up.

***

Rebecca came into my house just past midnight. As I turned to close my front door behind her, I heard a car door click shut. I leaned through the storm door, and peered toward Roger's driveway, thinking he had finally gotten home. I opened my mouth, ready to verbally tear into him.

Unless Roger had bought a new car and grown five inches in the past two hours, the guy pulling an overnight case from the back seat of a Buick wasn't him.

While I watched, Harry Woodward stood up to his full six and a half feet, stretched, then waved to me.

With a smile that didn't reach my eyes, I waved back. Leaving the front door open, I moved toward the living room where I found Rebecca on the sofa and Elvira stretched out next to her. Dressed as she usually was, in loose-fitting maroon pants with a yellow, red and green floral design and a knitted sweater vest, my friend's long, curly salt and pepper hair was tied back in a single tight braid.

I dropped my hand on the back of my overstuffed chair, needing the support to remain erect after this terrible night.

"You had to bring Harry with you?" I said.

She shrugged. "He refused to let me drive up here by myself at this hour."

At another time I would have rushed to Rebecca's side and given her a big hug, thrilled that my dearest friend had found the kind of relationship she had with Harry. Not tonight. Anger at Roger for treating me as he would a hardened criminal on his precinct's most wanted list had tossed a blanket over my kinder instincts. Of course, if at that moment I had been whisked to the past and landed in my psychologist's office, the shrink would have peeled off that blanket until I saw the grinning face of guilt beneath it. Then guilt would have told me it had come because I'd failed to help Daniel when he called. But that damn travel spell wouldn't whisk me to an earlier time when I needed it to. As a result, my anger persisting, I only thought to demand, "Did you tell Harry what happened tonight?"

"Of course she did," he said.

Because the man always wore rubber-soled shoes, I hadn't heard him come into the house or realized he stood behind me until I heard him speak.

I turned abruptly to face him. "Then you both know why I'm so…" I sputtered to a stop.

He laid his right hand on my shoulder. "Finding your friend dead, I'm not at all surprised."

Recalling Daniel, my eyes grew moist. I shook off Harry's hand.

"Come here." Rebecca reached out to indicate I should sit beside her.

Focusing on my anger at Roger let me fight back the painful memory. "I don't want to sit!"

Reacting to my tone, Elvira buried her head between the sofa's cushions.

Harry took both my shoulders and turned me to again face him. The man wore a long black overcoat and had buttoned his plaid flannel shirt all the way to his neck. His five o'clock shadow, now seven hours old, made his tight expression look warningly serious. "Emlyn, you need to calm down," he said.

Spittle on my lips, I told him, "I'm too mad to be calm." *Too upset about Daniel, also,* I thought, but I would deal with my feelings about him later.

How was it that fate chose this moment to show its face—or, in this instance, to open my storm door?

From the front stoop, Roger called, "Is it safe to come in?"

"No!" Rebecca said.

"I don't think so, Detective," Harry said and did the kind of neat about-face he would have demanded from his troops when he was a Marine colonel. In a few long strides, he reached Roger, and steered him from the stoop. "It'd be best if you and I go to your house and talk."

When the door closed behind the guys, my friend said, "Come over here by me."

"Don't want to."

"Emlyn!" Rebecca pointed to the floral sofa cushion next to her.

Behaving like the recalcitrant teenager I once had been, I moved to the front of the wingback chair and dropped down on it so hard it slid back against the bookcases.

"You're impossible when you get like this," Rebecca said. "Stick your lip back in and listen to me."

Elvira hesitantly raised her head, looked at my friend, and *meowed.* It was as if the cat said, *Her listen? You must be kidding.*

Rebecca pulled the pesky animal's head against her side. "Be quiet, Elvira. You'll make things worse." Now, she locked her eyes on mine. "Roger's a cop. He was just doing his job."

I leaned forward. "He wasn't. He—"

"Don't talk."

"No, he—"

She held up her hand. "You're talking."

"Grrrr."

"And don't growl. That'll clog your ears."

I slouched back.

She sighed. "You really *are* impossible."

The cat lifted her head and nodded.

My lips pinched, I closed my eyes. I stopped just short of holding my breath.

"You need to understand this," Rebecca began, then hesitated as though waiting to scold me again if I objected. When I didn't, she continued. "Roger knows you're not capable of killing anyone. But with other people— witnesses and possible suspects—in the room and another cop—"

"Irish was the other cop, and he knows Roger and I are a couple."

Rebecca and I had gotten to know Officer Collins, nicknamed Irish, when he saved us from a semi-crazed man with a pistol.

"Irish *does* know you," Rebecca agreed. "That's why Roger had to be even more careful."

"But he's also met the people in my writers group, so he has to know they also wouldn't kill anyone— especially a member of our group." Another thought struck me. "I'll bet he acted that way because he's jealous of how much I like two of the guys in the group."

"Come on, Emlyn. You know Roger better than that."

"Do I?" I said. "How well do I really know him?"

Rebecca *tsked* again, as if she couldn't believe I'd think such a thing. "For that matter," she said, "how well do you know the other members of your group? Are you sure not a single one of them is capable of murder?"

This stopped me. How well *did* I know them? I knew their writing, of course, and once in a while we'd gone out to dinner. Yet even on those social occasions, instead of leading to anything about our personal lives, the conversation would eventually circle around to the stories on which we worked.

So, I grudgingly thought, *maybe Roger wasn't so wrong to look at my writer friends as suspects in this crime.*

What I said earlier about fate arriving at an inopportune moment? Just as I calmed down enough to consider forgiving him for the way he had treated me, fate again walked in my front door.

"Emlyn, we need to talk," Harry said as he moved from the polished wood floor in the hall to my carpeted living room. His stern expression froze me. Seemed to freeze Rebecca and my cat, also.

When I finally found my voice, I stammered, "W-what's wrong?"

He moved slowly to my desk, rolled the chair over and sat facing me. "The dead man at that house tonight—"

"Daniel Bennet," I said.

Harry nodded. "You knew him?"

"Of course she knew him. He's a member of her writers' group."

"Please, Becca," Harry said. "I need Emlyn to answer me."

Her mouth fell open.

"I knew him," I said. "I… I found him." The memory of seeing Daniel laying in what must have been a pool of his blood caused my eyes to overflow.

Harry took a hanky from his jacket pocket and dabbed my eyes. "That's right. You knew him and you found him tonight. That's what you told Roger."

"What's going on, Harry?" Rebecca asked.

He shot her a warning look. To me, he said, "You also told Roger you'd spoken to the victim earlier. Is that correct?"

I nodded.

His voice softened, and he touched my hand. "Okay. You're doing fine. Now, did you have any contact with him between the time you talked to him on the phone and when you found him at the Bennet House?"

I shook my head. "N-no."

"The conversation you had with him—what was it about?"

"He begged me to meet him." I sniffed. "Begged me to…" I didn't need to time-travel back to my shrink so she could pull the blanket from guilt's face. It had curled up next to me.

Without turning to look at Rebecca, Harry told her, "Give Emlyn a tissue, please."

I blew my nose, then crushed the tissue in my hand. "He told me he was in trouble."

"But, you just said you didn't see him."

"I didn't. I drove into the Falls looking for him, but he wasn't… and… and I couldn't…"

Again, Harry patted my hand. "It's all right. You're doing fine. Now, while you were looking for Daniel Bennet, did anybody see you?"

"Uh-uh. No." I began to tremble. "Except…"

"Except?" he prodded.

"I stopped in the Tops Market and picked up dinner for Roger. I wasn't going to be here when he got home. But that's not where I usually shop, so no one knows me there."

Harry thought for a moment. "Do you have a receipt for the food you bought?"

I shook my head. "It didn't cost much, so I used cash and left the receipt on the counter."

"Did you get the cash from an ATM?"

Again I shook my head.

Harry rose, and rolled the chair back to my desk. With a sigh, he said, "You're making this harder for me. Okay, we'll check out what we can. Maybe there's a security camera by the registers. Meantime, you sit tight, and don't worry about anything."

Rebecca grabbed her oversized shoulder bag, dug into it for her wallet and pulled out a photograph. As she shoved it into Harry's hand, she said, "This is a picture of Emlyn and me. Show it to everyone at the store. Someone *has* to remember her being there."

He pocketed the photo. "You understand that even if a clerk recognizes you, Emlyn, even if you show up on a security camera, it doesn't mean much. You could have met Bennet at the house, killed him and still had time to stop in the market to establish an alibi."

I brushed the hair from my face. "Do you mean I… I'm really a suspect?" Shocked by the sound of it, my voice quivered.

"I'm afraid you're one of the suspects, so I'd advise you to get a lawyer." Harry looked at my friend. "Becca, I want you to remember everything said here tonight."

Her brows creased into a question.

"At no time did I warn Emlyn of her rights."

Her eyes lit with understanding. "So, nothing she said—"

"That's right. None of it can be used."

He turned to me. "Oh, and so you don't go thinking it's his idea, until you're cleared, I've ordered Roger to stay away from you. Can't have any indication of impropriety in this investigation. And one more thing. Don't go near this case. I know you'll want to, but we can't have you meddling. You can't afford to do anything that would call your innocence into question."

Chapter Nine

Accused

"Call my innocence into question?" I cried when the door closed behind Harry.

Had the Earth flipped on its axis? Two days earlier, I had been yanked from a perfectly good deckchair at Dana Smart's house, and propelled across Lake Erie to Crystal Beach. When I'd fallen back to earth, Daniel Bennet told me he knew where to find something that would make people unhappy. Unhappy enough to kill him? Obviously so, because today he'd called and told me he thought he knew where to find the original of the page he'd shown me, then I'd found *him*. Dead. Now, Roger, the man who yesterday swore he loved me, thought I could have killed Daniel. And here was the worst part: I couldn't straighten this out, because I had no idea what was going on!

If ever I reached a time to sit in a dark corner and suck my thumb, this was it.

As much as I wanted to do that, my friend with the long salt and pepper braid wouldn't let me.

"C'mon, Emlyn, snap out of it!" Rebecca demanded.

"Don't want to."

She groaned. "Great, I'm stuck here with a two-year-old. Want me to dig up some worms for you to eat?"

My lips curled and I choked at the thought.

"No? Then get a grip."

I groaned. "That's the problem. I *can't* get a grip. I can't wrap my mind around everything that's happened."

"Of course you can't," she said. "After the day you've had, you're exhausted."

"Not just today." I curled my legs up and rested my head in a corner of my wingback chair. "It started last Saturday at my writers' group."

Rebecca settled in the corner of the sofa nearest to my chair. From there, she leaned over and took my hand. "See? That's what I mean. You've gotta give your mind time to rest."

"I tried to get Daniel to tell us about a story he was writing—"

Still holding onto my hand, my friend began to hum.

Elvira twisted her neck and looked over at her.

Still humming, Rebecca glanced at the white fur-ball, and shook her head.

The cat seemed to nod, as if she understood the message Rebecca sent.

"—and I saw him stare over the lake," I continued. "When I turned to see what he looked at…" I yawned.

The humming swelled until it filled my living room.

"I felt like hands lifted me from my seat…" Again I yawned.

Elvira jumped onto the overstuffed chair and snuggled next to me.

Scratching the cat between her ears, I said, "I started to float…"

"Yes, float," Rebecca said.

"Crystal Beach…"

***

Wind musses my hair. Chilled, I pull the black mantle tight around me. My mother's hooded mantle. A blast of air yanks the hood from my head. The wind twists me. Like a plane with its rudder gone awry, I spiral downward. A dizzying spiral.

I open my eyes. Lift my head. Water below. Rippling. An ocean of water rippled by the wind.

A nearby shore. Just inland, cranes lift steel beams. Men in yellow hard hats guide them into place. I'm not spinning into an ocean. This is a lake. A large lake. Lake Erie. I know this, though I don't know why I know. The workmen guiding the cranes are constructing condos at Crystal Beach!

Another blast of wind. I have to steady myself, stop spiraling or I'll dive into the cold lake!

I grab the edges of my mantle, hold them out like wings. My spinning stops just above the waves.

I raise my chest, lower my right arm. Now I'm gliding on the wind toward the shore.

A speedboat rushes by below me. It casts up a wet mist. I raise my arm, shut my eyes, and dry them on my sleeve. When I look down, the speedboat has become a ferry, three decks, Canadiana written across its stern. This is how we rode to Crystal Beach when I was a child.

I follow in the Canadiana's wake. It docks near the rollercoaster tracks where the Comet soars over the edge of the lake. No condos under construction. This is Crystal Beach the way it once was. But, even this seems wrong. The sign for the rollercoaster calls it the Cyclone instead of the Comet. It hasn't been the Cyclone since a roller coaster tragedy years before my birth.

I glide over the shore. Below me is the amusement park, the Ferris wheel, the carousel the way I've only seen them in photographs. Strains of music from the dance hall waft through the air. A vocalist sings, "One, two, three o'clock, four o'clock rock…"

A woman in jeans, the cuffs rolled up past her ankles, jumps the line of people waiting to climb onto the carousel's platform and ride the carved wood horses. She brushes back her short brown hair. While I hover above, she crosses the platform to the center where a roustabout in a tight black tee-shirt manages the controls. The woman touches the arm of this rough looking man, kisses his cheek.

From the back pocket of his jeans, he takes a folded page. Two pages. Shows them to the woman.

Her smile grows. "You found it," she says.

He nods.

On the midway, a short man wearing a stained Yankees baseball cap stops near the carousel. He takes the chewed cigar from his mouth and calls out, "Ya don't own this park, Bennet. Not nearly. Not yet. Stop makin' out and get to work!"

Pushing the woman behind him, the roustabout leans forward and shouts back a few swear-words.

The cigar chewer stomps off.

The roustabout shoves the pages into his pocket. He kisses the woman, then points toward the waffle stand fifty yards away. "Later," he tells her.

He pulls a lever. The carousel slowly turns. The calliope sings. In its voice I hear Rebecca humming. The song swells, fills the air. It grows louder. The carousel turns faster. Faster. Spinning now. A blur. Inside the blare of the organ, horns, and drum is a metallic clank. Clank. Like metal smacking against metal. Something has gone terribly wrong with the carousel's motor.

My stomach twists with worry. People on the carousel have to get off or they'll be hurt. Maybe killed.

The man with the cigar stops on the midway, and points up at me.

"No!" I call down. "It wasn't me. I didn't break it!"

Men, women, stare up. Children hold their ears.

I shake my head.

There's a clatter. Crash. A bomb blast. A whoosh of flames. The carousel, the park, go up in smoke...

Startled, I jumped and nearly toppled from my chair.

"Sorry," Rebecca called from the kitchen. "I dropped a plate."

I opened my eyes. Daylight came in streaks through the mini-blinds on my French door.

Disoriented, I thought, *It's… just past midnight? Why's it light outside?*

On my lap, Elvira's head poked up. She gave me a pink-eyed glare, as if to say, *See? This is what it's like when you come crashing in here and rip me from a nap.*

Rebecca leaned over the kitchen counter. "I'm fixing us some coffee. It'll be ready in a minute."

At least, I think she said that. *Blah, blah, coffee, blah,* is what I heard.

I blinked, trying to clear both my sight and the haze from my mind. Licking my dry lips, I asked, "What time is it?"

She laughed. "Past nine."

"In the morning?" Again, I blinked to accustom my eyes to the light.

My friend came from the kitchen in her bathrobe and slippers. She carried two white mugs. One she put in my hand. The other she took with her to the sofa.

"Drink," she said. "I made it strong so it'll wake you up."

"What happened?"

She blew on her mug. "You fell asleep."

When I took a sip of the coffee, my eyes opened wide. "Good grief! You certainly did make this strong. What did you put in it?"

"Oh, a little of this and a little of that."

"Rebecca!" I held out the mug. "What's in the coffee?"

"Don't holler," she said. "It'll spoil the effect. I just added some marigold and gum mastic. With everything going on, I thought you'd need to think clearly."

I should mention my friend owns The Black Cat, an arcane shop in Ellicottville. In her shop she carries a variety of herbs and spices, many of which few people cook with anymore. Her shop also has shelves of books that explain how to brew those herbs and spices in order to achieve certain… uh, results. Of course, when women brewed them in old Sarah Goode's day, the result included a hasty witch trial, followed by a short drop on Gallows Hill. Fearing the brews Rebecca taught me to make might have a similar result in my day is the reason I'd let very few people know what my friend and I did with those herbs and spices. Yes, I knew I wouldn't have been tried and hanged as a witch, but if Grace Linden had learned what Rebecca and I were doing, she would have spread the word so quickly that half the people in Niagara Falls and the surrounding areas would be laughing behind my back.

As Rebecca's brew accomplished its task, the dream I'd awakened from swept back in. The short cigar-chewing man again accused me of destroying the amusement park. From the wings of this recollection, Roger and Harry all but pointed to me as Daniel Bennet's killer. All at once, engulfed by panic, I couldn't catch my breath.

Elvira stared up at me.

Rebecca's brown eyes narrowed with concern. "Are you okay?"

"D-d-doctor," I panted, and doubled over. "C-call a d-doctor!"

She jumped from the sofa and ran to the kitchen. A moment later she returned, but not with a phone. Standing next to my chair, she straightened me up and held a paper bag against my mouth and nose.

"Breathe into this," she instructed.

I glanced sideways at her, and pushed her hand away.

"Do it!" She placed one hand behind my head. With her other hand, she again covered my face with the bag.

I had only two choices: do as she ordered or stop breathing altogether.

"That's right. Slowly. Breathe in, breathe out."

It took five minutes or so for me to stop laboring to breathe. When I at last fell back in the large chair, Rebecca wiped the perspiration from my face.

"Better now?" she asked as she returned to the sofa.

I nodded, and took a few more breaths into the bag. "Sorry," I said. I felt my cheeks grow hot. "For a minute I thought I was going to die."

"You just had a panic attack. Wanna tell me what caused it?"

My cat twisted her neck to look up at me, and let out a long *meow*. It was as if she said, *Yeah, tell us what brought that on. Don't wanna be living with a corpse if it happens again.*

I didn't want to tell my friend—or my over-fed albino nerf ball. Not, at least, until I found a way to process the dream I'd had. I needed to process it, because something more hid within the dream. Something I couldn't quite—

"Well?" Rebecca said.

The cat nudged my arm with her head.

Clearly, at that moment those two nags had more strength than I. So I related my dream-flight to Crystal Beach, the pointing fingers and the explosion that woke me. I mentioned that something about the dream nagged at me. Something I had seen or heard. Something… Try as I might, I couldn't put my finger on it.

When I finished, my friend seemed lost in thought. Finally she murmured, "It's a sign."

"A sign of what?" I asked, hoping she would unravel the knot I struggled with.

Instead of answering, she rose, went to the kitchen and returned with her very large floral shoulder bag. Sitting again on the sofa, she reached into the bag and pulled out her well-used deck of tarot cards. One below the other, she laid cards in a line on the coffee table.

The first she turned over depicted a fist holding up a sword. She looked over at me, and said, "The Ace of Swords. This guides your decisions. But it requires you to think clearly. If you don't... There's danger if your thoughts go in the wrong direction."

When she turned over the second card, I saw a robed and turbaned man standing next to a kneeling woman. Six-pointed stars surrounded the man's head. "The Six of Pentacles," Rebecca said. "It means decisions you've made are upsetting your relationship..." She thought for a moment. "You didn't tell Roger you were going on that ghost hunt, did you?"

I shook my head.

"Thought so. That's what started this. If you'd told him, he would've told you not to go to that house. If you didn't go, you wouldn't've gotten into an argument with him. And, if you'd listened to me, you wouldn't have left your house at all and you wouldn't be suspected of killing your friend, Daniel."

When I started to protest, she held up a hand to stop me.

"See? This is why people pointed at you in your dream. You know you started this and you feel guilty about it."

My cat nodded.

I glared at the animal and shoved her from my chair. "So what do I do now?" I asked Rebecca.

She turned over another card. This one showed a man staring at pewter cups. "This is the Seven of Cups," she said. "It explains the end of your dream."

Elvia looked at her; so did I.

"The clanking metal you heard in your dream and the explosion at the end? You're overwhelmed. It's like dust flying up after an explosion is clouding your vision.

The Seven of Cups says you can't fix what's gone wrong by yourself. You need help."

My cat looked up at me from the floor. Her *meow* seemed to say, *I'm* always *here to help.*

Rebecca picked her up. Scratching the cat's neck, she said, "Not this time, Elvira. Emlyn needs professional advice."

My lower lip shot out. "I'm not going to a shrink!"

With a roll of her eyes and a deep sigh, my friend said, "That's not the help I mean."

"What then?"

"The kind of help Harry told you to get."

I looked at her with incomprehension.

"You need a lawyer."

Rebecca was right. By itself, the fact that I hadn't killed Daniel Bennet wouldn't free me from the quicksand that threatened to suck me under. I mean, Sarah Goode hadn't gotten legal help when she'd been accused of waltzing with Satan, and her story finished at the end of a rope. Another thing: I'd learned Rebecca's cards could peek into the overgrown forest in my mind. If they said I needed to contact a lawyer, perhaps they meant talking to one would begin to untie the knot in my dream.

I took a deep breath and sat back with my eyes closed. In my mind, I scrolled down a list of the attorneys I knew. This one handled slip-and-fall cases, this one did elder-law and this one specialized in commercial litigation. When I neared the end of my list, an idea struck me. I sighed with relief. Yes. In this circumstance, he would be perfect.

I jumped from my chair. "Get your jacket," I said to Rebecca.

Apparently startled by my sudden movement, she did a double-take. "Where are we going?"

"Didn't you just tell me I should talk to lawyer?"

As she stood, she said, "You're actually gonna to listen to me?"

For the first time since I'd found Daniel at the top of the Bennet House stairs, I laughed. "Don't I always?"

She looked at me through narrowed eyes.

Elvira shook her white head as if to say, *Uh-oh*.

Chapter Ten

Howard Kline

I had learned not to disparage the advice Rebecca gave when she read her tarot cards. In the past, those cards had told her to concoct a balm that saved my leg when I got severely burned by a firebomb during a reading of my first short story collection. Other times, her cards had warned of danger lurking at my mother's forty-second high school reunion and of a madwoman's attack that would hospitalize Rebecca and me. Her cards had told my friend to keep me from meddling when a body burned behind the Bella Vita hair salon during the summer solstice. To my regret, I hadn't heeded the tarot cards' advice those times. I wouldn't again allow my innate stubbornness to ignore the cards' advice. But in heeding the cards, I intended to do it my way.

I knew a lawyer who had shown an intimate knowledge of the Tuscarora's Curse. I didn't want to tell Rebecca the lawyer I had in mind, though. She had met this man, and to say that she had less than a stellar opinion of him would be an understatement. That's why I carried my cellphone to my bedroom where she couldn't hear me make the phone call.

After I made the appointment with the lawyer, I spent almost an hour dressing and fixing my hair and makeup. Having slept through the prior night with my head in the nook that formed one of the wings of my overstuffed chair, both of them were badly in need of repair. My friend, who normally wore no makeup and whose hair knew just one style, got ready to leave my house in fifteen minutes.

She spent the rest of the time shouting up to the bathroom on the second floor, "Come on, already! How long does it take you to change your clothes?"

"I can't go to a lawyer's office looking like a mess," I called back to her. "If I do, he'll never take me seriously."

I might have gotten ready more quickly if I hadn't smeared my eyeliner while I answered her.

Now, in my car on the Niagara Scenic Parkway, we headed for downtown Niagara Falls. If we stayed on this this road, we would have driven into the parking lot for visitors to the Niagara gorge. I enjoyed what our Tourist Board called one of the *Wonders of the Modern World*. Finding inspiration in the rush of water over the Bridal Veil Falls and the slow disappearance and reemergence of Maid of the Mist boats at the Horseshoe Falls, I often sat there with my writer's journal. But this wasn't my destination today. At the traffic circle about three-quarters of a mile short of the parking lot, I exited the parkway. I made a left turn, then a right onto Third Street—a block past the Seneca Niagara Casino—and found a parking spot next to a five-story building on the corner of Niagara Street. Before noon, few people were on the street.

When I unsnapped my seatbelt, Rebecca turned to me. "Please don't tell me you wanna see *him*."

The *him* she referred to was Howard Kline, Esquire. Rebecca had met Kline about a year earlier, when a rock icon of the 1980s had been murdered shortly after returning home to Niagara Falls. Kline had handled the woman's estate. Having seen him at work that time, Rebecca had formed the considered opinion that the man was too sleazy to be trusted. To be quite honest, I shared her opinion. Still, I needed to see him for a specific reason. Though he did not specialize in criminal law, I knew of one criminal case he had handled. Five years earlier he'd defended Richard Bennet when Bennet was tried for murdering his wife in the same house in which Daniel had been killed. That's what drew me to Kline's office.

"I don't like this idea," Rebecca said, as she followed me past a row of cement planters filled with chrysanthemums and calla lilies and into the building's dim lobby.

"This is a mistake," she muttered as the elevator lifted us to the third floor.

Holding tight to her arm in the elevator car's too-small enclosure, I told her, "Stop complaining. Your tarot cards said I need a lawyer. I'm just listening to them."

When (thank the Lord) the elevator door at last opened, she tried to hold me back. "The cards said you should find a *good* lawyer."

"They didn't say anything of the kind," I said and pushed past her, glad to be free from the cramped elevator car.

"Well, that's what they meant."

She tugged at my sleeve as we walked down the short hall lined with dimpled taupe paper. "Not *him*!"

"Hush," I said, stopping at a dark brown door bearing *KLINE & ASSOCIATES* in raised bronze letters. "I'm not going to hire him to defend me."

Rebecca's hands on her hips, she said, "Then why'd you drag me here?"

"*Shh*. We're here because I don't want to have *anyone* defend me in court."

"Huh?" Her eyes narrow, and her neck craned forward, she looked at me as if my mind had packed a suitcase and gone off for an extended vacation.

"This is the second time someone got killed in that house—and both of them were named Bennet." I shifted my purse from my right hand to my left and reached for the doorknob. "There has to be a connection."

She bumped me so hard with her hip that my hand slipped from the knob. "Didn't Harry tell you to stay out of this? I know he told you that. I heard him!"

I sighed. "*I* didn't accuse Harry of murdering a friend."

Tears gathered when I recalled Daniel's desperate phone call and then the sight of his body sprawled in the second floor hall of the Bennet House with his neck cut. I took a tissue from my purse and dabbed at my eyes. "Damn. My mascara must be running."

Her lips tight, Rebecca said, "Stop it. Right now! When are you gonna learn you can't fix everything?"

"But..." I sniffed. "I can, at least, make sure who-ever killed Daniel is caught."

"No!" She stamped her foot. "That's Harry's and Roger's job."

"They won't figure this one out, because they don't believe in curses and the Tuscarora's Curse is the key."

"What? How?"

I shook my head. "I don't know yet. That's why I've got to see Howard Kline. He made a big deal about the curse when—"

At that moment the door opened, and a short woman wearing stiletto heels and an ivory wool pantsuit that looked like a Dior knock-off leaned out. "If you intend to come in, then do it," she said in a harsh whisper. "Otherwise go someplace else to argue." With that, she turned on her spiked heels, and all but slammed the door on us.

"See? That's a sign," Rebecca said. She twisted toward the elevator.

I caught her arm and opened Kline's door.

We walked into a moderately large reception area lined in dark-stained oak and filled by a three-seat brown leather couch, two matching armchairs, and a polished mahogany table with copies of the *Law Journal* neatly stacked like a centerpiece. Unlike the time I'd been here before, the stark formality of this reception area was now softened by a vase with roses on a corner of the receptionist's desk, a potted geranium on the floor next to the desk and a hanging basket with morning glories draped down its side. The woman who had scolded us in the hall sat behind the desk. She had a heavily made-up oval face and black hair showing gray roots.

My eyes went wide and I bent toward the desk when I read the plaque with her name on it. *Mrs. Scannado*, a surname so rare, I knew of only one other person who had it.

Rebecca saw my reaction. She moved close to me, and whispered, "What now?"

She had her answer when I asked the receptionist, "Are you… related to Ray?"

Looking at her desktop computer instead of at me, Mrs. Scannado said, "Why do you ask?"

"Uh, well… You see there's a guy in my writers' group—"

She looked up at me. With a flicker of a smile, she said, "He's my son."

I felt a slight quiver in my stomach. Could this be the message the tarot cards had told Rebecca to give me? The cards had said I should speak to a lawyer. Had they known I'd choose this one? I'd followed the cards' advice and now I stared at a connection between two murders at the Bennet House and a connection between one of the murders and a member of my writers' group. I had no idea how those two connections might intertwine. Still, for the first time since I'd been yanked from my chair on Dana's deck, I felt as though I might climb off this Crystal Beach rollercoaster before it crashed and I got shoved into a cell next to Richard Bennet in Attica…

Okay, I know women aren't imprisoned in Attica. That's not the point.

So the cards had prodded me toward the first step in unraveling this puzzle within an enigma. The second step? Sarah Goode would know—using her herbs and spices, my ancient forbear seemed to anticipate everything. But without her book in hand, I could only try to guess what she might tell me.

"Is there... um, something I can do for you ladies?" Mrs. Scannado's voice threw a rope around my wandering mind and pulled it back to Kline's reception area. Why did the woman sound a bit nervous?

Rebecca shoved her sharp elbow in my ribs. "Stop staring at her."

My cheeks grew hot, and I suspected I flushed from my neck to my hair. "Sorry," I said in a hurry. "It's just that, er... You look so much like..." I touched my chin. "Except for the beard, of course... Sorry." I dropped my eyes, and examined a smudge on the toe of my shoe.

From my expression—or, more likely, my lack of one—Rebecca must have realized embarrassment had cost me the ability to think, much less to speak. Though he was the last person she would want to see, she said, "We're here to see Mr. Kline." With a glance at me, she added, "My friend has an appointment with him."

Mrs. Scannado's pencil-thin eyebrows furrowed into a perfect *V*. With what I thought to be a suspicious sideways glance in my direction, she lifted the phone and pushed the intercom button. "Ms. Goode is here to see you."

How does this woman know me? I wondered. I hadn't introduced myself, and I'd never met her before today.

I didn't get a chance to ask, because her voice went very soft—became almost a whisper—when she said, "Yes, sir. Eleven-thirty appointment... Called this morning..." Now Mrs. Scannado's cheeks grew a bit red. Glancing again at me, she said, "I can't. When she called, I told her you had the time."

No sooner had the receptionist hung up the phone than the door to the right of her desk opened.

The black Perry Ellis suit and red and white power tie seemed to be Howard Kline's uniform. He had worn this the other times I'd seen him—each day during the week and half of the Richard Bennet trial, and then here at his office, the day he had read Amanda Stone's Last Will and Testament to those of us who were her beneficiaries. With a smile that struck me more as a sneer, he stuck out his right hand and said, "Ah, Ms. Goode. How nice to see you again. You're well, I hope."

"Well as can be expected after finding Daniel Bennet." As I reached for his hand, he pulled it back far enough that I shook only his fingers.

"Yes. I heard about Bennet's… death."

My head tilted, I asked, "How?"

He looked at his fingers, then rubbed them together as though trying to wipe off any germs that might have passed from me to him. "Mrs. Scannado's son came in to consult me this morning. He had Dana Smart with him. Detectives showed up at their respective houses early this morning to interrogate them."

I nodded.

"I presume you've come to see me for the same reason?"

Rebecca pushed up next to me. "Emlyn only got into this because she tried to help her friend. She's innocent."

Howard Kline gave her what I can only describe as a smarmy grin. "Everyone always is."

He held the door open to let us pass into his inner sanctum. I expected to see a beehive filled with perhaps a dozen of Howard Kline's associates who busily searched for solutions to clients' problems. When we moved down the hall, I saw only a string of empty desks and deserted offices.

Rebecca also noticed this. Tapping Kline on his arm, she asked, "Where is everyone?"

His eyes straight ahead, he told us, "I'm working on a very confidential project. I gave most of my staff a leave so I can focus on it."

She stepped in front of him. "Then, how can you possibly take on Emlyn's case—or the case of Mrs. Scannado's son or Dana Smart?" She turned her face to me, and her eyes sent the silent message, *See? I told you coming to this bucket of sleaze was a bad idea.*

Kline stepped around her. While marching to his corner office, he said, "Don't worry your pretty little heads about things like that. I know how to take care of my clients."

As we passed the office just before his, I caught a glimpse of a woman seated at a long table. Her head down, it seemed as though her hand traced a line on a page in the book in front of her. Long wheat-colored hair covered her face. Something about her looked familiar. When I took a step toward the office in which she sat, Kline reached out and closed the door.

"This way, please," he said and ushered us into his office.

Chapter Eleven

Curse of the Tuscarora Brave

Almost the size of my living room, Kline's office filled the corner overlooking Third and Niagara Streets and manila file-folders filled much of the space in the office. Piles of files were on his desk, on the small, blond wood conference table, on one of the chairs and half the couch. While Rebecca and I waited, he moved a large handful of the folders from the conference table to the white radiator that formed the wide window sill. Blistering white paint on the radiator revealed rusted metal. I looked around. Worn almost down to the plasterboard, the walls also seemed in need of fresh paint. Among the grouping of framed photographs on the wall behind his desk—pictures of Kline shaking hands with a former mayor, with a local State Assemblyman who was under investigation for accepting a bribe and with Dan Petit, the City Prosecutor—were discolored rectangle ghosts of photos that had been removed. The look of this office seemed to be a stark contrast to the carefully-clad man who inhabited it.

Kline shoved another group of folders to the far end of the conference table. As he did, the top folder fell. I stepped from the doorway, and picked it up from the floor. When I handed the folder to the lawyer, I noticed the tab.

Kline frowned when his eyes flicked down to the folder. "Ahem, uh, yes," he said with a quick glance at me. "Make yourselves comfortable." He waved his hand toward the conference table and the surrounding unmatched wood chairs that looked anything but comfortable.

When we sat, he took a yellow legal pad from his desk and dropped it on the table. As he pulled out a chair, he asked, "Can I get you ladies anything? Coffee? Water?"

"Tea would be nice, if you have any," I said.

"I think I can rustle some up for you." He gave us another smarmy smile. Closing the door behind him, he left his office.

"What are you doing?" Rebecca whispered when I slid to the chair in front of the folders, and opened the one which had the tab that had caught my eye.

"Shh." I showed her the file.

"So? It's a contract."

"Look!" I pointed to the tab on the folder.

"Crystal Beach?"

I nodded.

"What's it mean?"

"I don't know."

Just as we began to scan through the contract, I heard Kline's voice in the hall. "You need to get this finished, but not here!" His voice harsh, it sounded as though it came from just outside his office. A muted voice replied. I couldn't tell whether a male or a female had answered him. Quickly I closed the file and placed it back on the pile of folders.

"Here's your tea, ladies," Kline said as he came through the door. He put a cup in front of each of us. Rebecca's cup had a small chip near the brim. "I didn't know how you take it, so…" Glancing at the pile of folders on the table, he hesitated. "I, uh… brought sugar and Sweet 'n Low, and, uh…" He moved the file I'd looked at to his desk. "…some cream."

Damn! He knows we looked at that file. A page stuck out. In my haste, I hadn't put it back exactly as I'd found it.

I held my breath, waiting for Kline to demand that we leave his office. To my surprise, he sat in the chair next to me, pulled a pen from his inside jacket pocket and picked up the yellow pad from the conference table.

"Now," he said, "tell me why the police think you killed that fellow."

Though he obviously knew I'd looked in his file, I didn't want to show any sign that I had come to his office for the sole purpose of snooping. As a result, like a character in one of my books, I had no choice but to play out the scene. While Kline made a show of taking copious notes, over the next forty minutes I told him what had happened. He stopped me just once.

When I began by relating how I had found Daniel, he told me, "If I'm to help you, Ms. Goode, start by telling me about the phone call that got you out of your house with no witnesses to confirm your story."

It startled me when he said that. *How could he know Daniel called me?* Then, I remembered he'd mentioned that Ray and Dana had been in to consult him. *They must have told him of the calls they received from Daniel, and he presumes that each of the writers' group members got a similar call.*

When I finished speaking of that horrid Halloween night, Kline flipped the pages to the front of his pad, then slowly turned the pages back, as if rereading an opus I had dictated. After a silent five minutes, he said, "I see the problem you have. From here on, if the police try to question you, tell them you have nothing to say without me present." He nodded, as if appreciating the wonderful advice he had given me. "Now," he continued, "if there's nothing else…"

He rose, ready to escort us from his office. I remained seated.

"Actually," I said, "there *is* something else."

His expression—that of a man admiring himself in a mirror—asked how, after his words of wisdom, I could possibly have anything further to say.

He made a show of lifting the top file from the stack on the table. "Yes, well…" he said, as if distracted by what he saw in the file. "You can see I'm rather busy today."

Rebecca nodded and began to rise.

I reached over, grabbed the hem of her jacket, and pulled her back down. "This won't take but minute. I'm a writer, you see—"

He nodded, "I'm aware of that. After you were here for the reading of Amanda Stone's Will, I read one of your books. Not bad. Although… the, uh, scenes in a courtroom didn't quite capture the finesse of our legal system. I would be glad to help you construct those kinds of scenes next time."

"Thank you." I made a mental note to seek the help of any lawyer but Kline. "That would be particularly helpful, because I'm thinking of doing a story about the Bennet trial."

"Oh?" He lifted a page from his file, and carefully examined it.

"You represented Richard Bennet at his trial for killing his wife, Shari, so I thought you might give me a bit of information about what went on behind the scenes."

Without turning his head, he lifted his eyes to look at me. "I don't think this is appropriate."

"You might recall I sat on the jury," I said. "I witnessed the trial from that angle, and—"

He closed the file and turned to me. "Ms. Goode, this is not something I can talk about."

I refused to give up. "You put on quite a defense— that he wasn't guilty because the Tuscarora's Curse made him do it."

Next to me, I heard Rebecca whisper, "A curse?"

Kline leaned toward me. "It's true. That's why he killed her. Preparing for the trial, we did extensive research into the curse. In the historical records—including the provost log from Fort Niagara—we found at least six instances of unexplained violence and deaths on that and the adjacent land. The Niagara Falls police records list another murder—this one in that stone garage—in 1926. The body had been buried under the cement floor."

"A curse made someone kill?" Rebecca said a bit louder.

"That's what Mr. Kline told us at the trial." To him, I said, "Did Bennet tell you he'd killed his wife, and if he killed her, why he did it?"

Kline pulled back from me, and his face stiffened. "What Richard told me is confidential. Attorney-client privilege."

"I asked," I said, "because when the judge sentenced him, Richard Bennet insisted he hadn't done it."

Kline cleared his throat. "Yes, well… uh, they all say that. Now if you'll excuse me, ladies. I *really* am quite busy—"

"So, for my story I need to know if claiming the curse made him kill his wife was Bennet's idea or yours."

He abruptly went to his desk, removed the file I had peeked in, then moved to his office door, and threw it open. In a harsh tone, he said, "I don't have time for this foolishness. In fact, Ms. Goode, I don't have time to take on your case—if there ever is one." He closed the door behind him, leaving Rebecca and me sitting in his office.

"In the books I've got in The Black Cat," she said as much to herself as to me, "I never came across a spell dark enough to make someone kill another person."

"I didn't think so," I said as I gathered my purse and my jacket.

It took a moment before Rebecca picked up her ten-gallon shoulder bag. Clearly she had something on her mind. She stared out the window for almost a minute, then asked, "Did you see the anger in Kline's eyes when he left his office?"

"And the way he bared his teeth? Yeah, I saw it." The look he'd given me had been more frightening than the idea of spending the rest of my life in prison. "Come on," I said. "We need to get out of here."

When I opened the door, I leaned through and peered down the hall.

"The coast clear?" Rebecca asked.

I nodded. When we came to the office in which I'd seen the woman examining documents the door was open. I peeked in. A vacant chair. No files on the table. Nothing in the room but an empty desk in an interior with no windows. Even the walls were bare. Had Kline closed his office door when he left us so he could hide the woman working there and her files before I had a chance to recognize her? Yes, a ridiculous idea. The woman must have been one of his lawyers, working on the big case he'd mentioned. Still, I couldn't purge from my mind the thought that the woman and those files had something to do with Daniel's death.

The angry meanness we had seen in Kline's eyes propelling us, Rebecca and I hurried on. I didn't know what lurked in her imagination. In mine, a fear ran rampant that he might cause us to disappear the way the woman in the now-empty office had.

Clutching each other's arms, my friend and I rushed through the door to the reception area. When we passed her desk, Mrs. Scannado halted us.

"This is for you," she said, and handed me a sheet of paper.

I glanced at it.

"It's your bill for today's meeting," she added with a stern look. "Do you want to schedule another appointment with Mr. Kline?"

Rebecca answered, "Not a chance!"

I rushed out the door to the hall, and made it halfway to the elevator before my friend caught up with me.

It felt like an hour until the elevator car responded. In that painfully long time, neither Rebecca nor I uttered a word. When the door at last whooshed shut sealing us in the small teal-blue car, she said, "Did you find out what you wanted to?"

Still troubled by what I'd seen in Kline's eyes, I just shook my head.

"Well, then that was a waste of time."

"I wanted Kline to tell me what in that house caused two people to be murdered."

"That's what I mean," Rebecca said. "A waste of time, because he didn't tell us." She shuddered. "Now the man knows you're nosing around."

I had to agree. I hadn't learned what I'd wanted to. All I had taken from my time with Howard Kline was a bill for $300 and the memory of the way he'd glared at me from his office door.

While I stood, struggling with concern about what the lawyer's expression might mean, I heard a clank from just above the elevator. The car jumped twice. Another clank and a grinding sound, then the car bounced once more, and stopped.

"Great," Rebecca muttered. "This is all we need."

She pushed a red button on the panel, and said into the small speaker. "Hello?" After a minute, she again pushed the button. "Is anyone there?"

This time, a static-filled male voice responded, "Yeah? What is it?"

"What is it?" she said to me. "The man's an idiot!" To the voice she said, "We're stuck in your elevator."

I heard what sounded like a metal wrench striking a pipe, and the voice said, "I can see that."

"Then get us out of here!" Rebecca shouted.

"I'm working on it," the voice grumbled. "It'll take me fifteen or twenty minutes."

During this exchange, I had pushed back into a corner of the elevator and begun to profusely perspire. Forcing my mind to focus on anything but the metal coffin in which I stood, I noticed chipped paint along the edges of the car's ceiling. I counted the cracks in the linoleum floor...

Have I ever mentioned I'm claustrophobic?

At last the elevator car moved. When the door opened, I ran from the building and didn't stop until I got to my Malibu. In my panicked state of mind, I concluded that coming to the offices of Howard Kline & Associates had been a bad idea.

Chapter Twelve

From Bad, to… OMG!

Before construction of the I-190 in 1955, River Road had been one of the main arteries between Niagara Falls and Buffalo. Though the I-190 with its 65 mile-per-hour speed limit became a quicker way to journey from here-to-there, many people still preferred the more scenic River Road route—not to mention the fact that they would save the dollar toll in each direction when the highway crossed Grand Island. As a result, vehicles on the street where I lived could sometimes move at the pace of an aged gastropod. This was the case as we returned from Kline's office.

"Stop complaining about the traffic," Rebecca told me. "We'll get to your house soon."

"Can't get there soon enough," I said.

Patience being far from my greatest strength, I stomped on the gas pedal and swerved to the left across the broken yellow line. I wanted to pass a van that, at a mere 20 miles-per-hour, seemed to be searching for a street to turn onto. Under my breath, I growled. River Road had no turn-offs for another three miles.

Her eyes wide, Rebecca shouted, "Look out! There's a car coming."

I hit the brake, and pulled back behind the van.

"Good Lord! Are you trying to get us killed?" she said. "From now on, I'm driving."

Grumbling and leaning forward over the steering wheel, I came around the curve in the road at an annoyingly slow pace. As the road straightened, I saw something which caused my heart to beat faster. A black SUV in my driveway. Roger's Trailblazer. Thoughts of Ray Scannado and Mark Maitland might have caused my stomach to flutter a bit, but Roger had staked a PROPERTY SOLD sign in the lawn of my heart. Gone was my anger at the way he'd interrogated me in front of my friends. The look Howard Kline had given me still rattling my emotions, I needed Roger to lean on.

Rebecca also noticed the SUV in my driveway. "Harry told us Roger had to stay away from you," she said. "What's he doing at your house?"

I didn't care why Roger had come to my house. Anxious to rush into his strong arms, I put my foot down on the gas. Defying the sound of an angry bass horn from a tractor-trailer on the northbound lane, I swerved in front of the van. As I did, my car skidded to stop on the edge of my lawn. The engine still running, I sprang from my car. On the balls of my feet so my three-inch heels wouldn't stick in the lawn, I raced to the SUV. As I drew near, I extended my arms, ready to receive the hug I badly needed. I stopped short when the driver's side door opened, and Harry Woodward climbed from behind the wheel.

Why is Harry driving Roger's car? I stared at him while he straightened up to his full height.

"I've been waiting for you," he said. His jaw set, he spoke through tight lips.

My stomach dove down several fathoms, and the hope I had when I saw the SUV scampered off like a rabbit fleeing a stewpot. *He's here to arrest me.*

My imagination taking a one-way flight to Devil's Island, I pictured myself in an ill-fitting striped suit with chains on my wrists and ankles…

Oh, the curse of a writer's imagination.

While I stood staring up at Harry, from the corner of my eye I noticed my car pull up next to the SUV. A moment later, Rebecca shoved the car key into my hand.

"You forgot this," she said. "Forgot your car, too." Then she looked up at Harry and caught her breath. "What's wrong?"

He took both my hands. "You need to come with me."

The dullness of his voice stunned me. It apparently also stunned my friend. "W-where are you taking Emlyn?"

With his thumb, he rubbed moisture from his eyes. I noticed that his gray eyes had red rings. "It's Roger," he said. "He's… been shot."

"He's n-not… not…" I gulped. I'm certain people in a perimeter of three miles heard me wail, "Noooooo!"

"I caught up with the EMT who brought Roger in," Harry told me. "The guy said he'd fallen into unconsciousness. Probably shock, but the wounds didn't seem life-threatening."

I don't remember much that happened after my knees turned to rubber. I recall being locked in an embrace between Harry and Rebecca. I remember her voice, gurgling with tears, asking, "What happened?" I think Harry answered her, but when his words moved from my ears to my brain they became jumbled. I only heard, "Alone… Door… Damn house… Shouldn't have…"

I don't know how I wound up buckled into the front passenger seat of the SUV with Rebecca gripping my shoulder from behind. I half-remember seeing a blue light that seemed to flash around us and hearing a siren's cry while Harry drove far faster than I ever dared. I had no idea where we were going.

In what felt like not more than minutes, we sped down Walnut Avenue and slammed to a stop on Tenth Street, just inside the parking lot next to a washed brick building with wide, tall windows. The Niagara Falls Memorial Medical Center.

Harry swung his door open and called to the young cop standing near the curb, "Look after Detective Frey's car, Collins."

I tried to exit the Trailblazer but got tangled in the seat belt. Seeing me struggle with the clasp, Rebecca leaned over the seat.

"Let me get that," she said, and shoved my hands aside. My panicked fighting to free myself from the car made it all but impossible for her to unlatch the belt.

Harry opened my door. "Sit still!" he ordered.

The command snapped by the former Marine colonel drew my instant obedience. In a moment, he freed me from the restraint and we three raced to the hospital's door. In the lobby, Harry rushed to the woman seated behind the information counter. Short, almost white hair, full round cheeks, and dressed in red and white, the volunteer behind the counter was Harriet Sovronsky.

"Is there any word yet?" Harry asked.

Panting, Rebecca and I caught up with him. On my toes, I leaned far over the counter. As I reached for Harriet's hand, I cried, "Tell me Roger's okay! Please, Harriet, tell me!"

I had known this woman since my childhood. When I lost my mom, she began to fill the hole in my life. Often we would have dinner together—an amazing cook, she tried to teach me her recipes. Just as often, I would turn to her for the kind of advice only a mother could give.

Now in the hospital, Harriet stroked my cheek and kissed my forehead. "Give me a minute to find out what I can." She ran her fingers across the keys on her computer. After a few clicks, she shook her head. "There's no information on him yet, Emlyn."

Tears of fear rushed to my eyes. I latched onto Harry's arm, and moaned, "He's not dead. He can't be... No! I won't let him be."

Harriet looked from me to Rebecca, then to Harry. "Chief, why not take Emlyn up to the waiting room?" She picked up the phone. "I'll see if I can get a doctor to come talk to you." Pushing my hair from face, she said, "Emlyn, dear, I'm sure your boyfriend will come through this just fine. Go, now. Go with the chief."

Harry holding me up on the left and Rebecca supporting me on the right, we crossed the gray faux marble floor, passed the glassed-in gift shop and the Tim Horton's coffee bar. At the elevator bank—if one can call two elevators a bank—we endlessly waited for a car to carry us upwards. When one at last arrived, we had to stand aside to allow a gurney and four passengers to be off-loaded.

All the while I stood muttering, "Come on, come on. You're not sight-seeing at the Falls. What's wrong with you people?"

I received several glares in return.

When we finally boarded, the elevator car stopped at every floor. When the car moved, it felt as though it did so at a speed of an inch-a-minute. Though I was certain it took more than an hour before we arrived at our floor, when I glanced at the clock on the waiting room wall, I saw only ten minutes had passed since we left Harriet at the information counter. A strange thing about my claustrophobia: worried for the life of the man I adored, it hadn't crippled me in the closed-in, crowded elevator car.

The only other time I'd been in this critical-care waiting room, it had been a grim place. Today, the atmosphere felt completely different. I saw leather armchairs, a flat screen TV hanging above a low cabinet, a light orange mini-blind to the right, to the left, a blond-wood table and chairs, and a rug in shades of green that stretched across the floor. Black and white floral prints lined one wall.

Feeling as though the temperature in the room reached 100 degrees, I pulled off my coat. Just as we settled around the table, the door opened, and a man of medium height and build walked in. Curly gray hair receding halfway up his scalp and his white lab coat unbuttoned, Dr. Charles Arnold, an old family friend, came toward us.

I wiped my tears on the sleeve of my rust-colored blouse, and rushed to him. "Tell me Roger's—" I broke into a sob.

He steered me back to the others at the table, then took a seat. Twisting his wedding ring, in the slow tempo with which he always addressed his patients, he said, "I've... spoken... with Doctor, uh... Carter. He, uh... operated on..."

Agonized by the pace at which he spoke, my heart crouched to leap from my chest, jump across the table and strangle the man. "Tell me!" I shouted.

Harry took my shoulders and pulled me down on my chair. "Doc," he said, "Did Roger make it?"

Dr. Arnold took a deep breath, and straightened the red bow tie clipped to his powder-blue shirt. As if afraid I might *actually* assault him, crisply, he said, "That's what I was telling you. Bullets caught him in the shoulder and leg. No vital organs damaged. They stemmed the bleeding in time. Your friend came through the operation in good shape."

At that moment *my* shape was far less than good. When the breath I had been holding escaped from my lungs, I deflated like a punctured balloon. My head banged on the table. Half conscious, I began to slump to the floor. Harry caught me and eased me back into my chair.

Rebecca looked at my face. "She cut her forehead."

Dr. Arnold lifted my chin, then my eyelids. I pushed his hand away.

"She'll be all right," the doctor said. "Wait here a minute while I get a bandage."

"Don't have to." Rebecca dipped into her shoulder bag and came out with one.

While she taped the bandage to my forehead, Harry asked, "When can we see Roger?"

"He's in recovery now," Dr. Arnold said. "Probably be there an hour or two." He turned my face, and examined my forehead. "You'll have a bit of a bruise, Emlyn, but it doesn't look like you did any real damage. Go home. Get some rest. Come back this evening."

I folded my arms across my chest. "Uh-uh. I'm not leaving."

Neither Rebecca nor Harry attempted to dissuade me.

The doctor shrugged and stood. As he left the waiting room, over his shoulder, he said, "I believe there's some coffee packets in that cabinet. You might want to make some—you'll be here awhile."

***

At the table, before me a Styrofoam cup filled with a dark liquid someone someplace had decided could be called coffee, my heart finally stopped racing. After two sips, my lips curled at the taste. No longer numb, I could at last ask what fear of losing the man I loved had prevented me from asking earlier.

Setting my cup aside, I said, "Harry, how did this…" I waved my hand around the room. "…happen?"

He swigged a gulp of steaming coffee. It must have burned his tongue, yet he didn't yelp in pain. Rubbing his hands together, he said, "I don't know all of it."

"What *do* you know?" Rebecca demanded.

He sighed and looked away, as if he didn't want to tell us.

"Harry, please." I said. "Whatever it is, I can handle it."

"It isn't you. It's me." He rose and began to pace. "It's my fault. I let him—" He stopped, loosened his necktie, then brushed his hands down the sides of his brown corduroy jacket. "Roger hated having to stay away from you. He wanted to check out the Bennet House, get a handle on what's going on there. Wanted to find anything that would show you had nothing to do with Daniel Bennet's murder. Once he did, he said, he'd be able to get back to you."

Those words opened the water taps in my eyes. How, even for a nanosecond, could I have doubted Roger's love?

Rebecca again reached into her shoulder bag. This time she pulled out a tissue and used it to dab my eyes. "I told you," she said.

I nodded.

His back to us, Harry said, "I should've ordered him not to go."

Rebecca pushed the tissue up my sleeve. "You know Roger. He wouldn't've listened.

"Then I should've told him to take a squad." Harry shook his head, and again sighed.

"Tell me what happened!" I shouted.

"He told the officers that got to him this much before he blacked out. He went around the back of the house to get in that way. Just when he opened the door, someone inside fired three shots. The guys told me two of the bullets hit him. I caught up with the EMTs that rolled him in here. They told me he'd been hit in the shoulder and thigh. Don't know anymore, that's when I came for you."

I gritted my teeth, already planning an evil spell I would heave at whoever did this. "Who shot him?" I hissed.

"Roger didn't know. The house was dark and the shots came from the doorway from the kitchen to the dining room. If I get my hands on the bastard—" Harry stopped, and turned to us. "I should've gone there with Roger."

Rebecca rushed to Harry's side, and rubbed his shoulder. "This isn't your fault. You couldn't have stopped him. Not Roger." She pointed at me. "He's as hard-headed as that one."

Her quip brought a flicker of a smile to Harry's lips. "They're made for each other," he said.

"Like you and me." Rebecca pulled on his tie, then, on her toes, kissed his cheek. "C'mon, Harry, you couldn't've known what would happen. You aren't clairvoyant. Tell him, Emlyn."

My voice as dull as Harry's had been earlier, I said, "It's not your fault. You couldn't—" I got no further.

Dr. Arnold poked his head through the door, and said, "Roger's out of recovery. Sooner than I thought. He's in a room. You can see him now."

We all rose.

The doctor held up his hand. "One at time, but only for a few minutes. He needs to rest." He looked directly at me, and repeated, "Only a few minutes. You understand me?"

As I said, Dr. Arnold had known me for years.

***

We came to a dim and rather bare semi-private room. It had curtains which could enclose patients during an examination, two closets, two hospital-green plastic chairs, two night tables, and fluorescent lights over the beds and in the ceiling. Roger occupied the bed by the window. An empty bed stood near the door.

Roger's eyes closed, he seemed to be asleep when I came in. I lifted a chair from where it stood against the wall, and placed it beside his bed. As soon as I sat, he blinked, and his eyes opened to narrow slits.

"Hi," he said, his voice hoarse.

"Hi yourself." I leaned over and pecked a kiss on his lips.

In the dim light, he looked pale. He took my hand with a weak grip. He groaned when he tried to shift his body toward me.

I eased him back and straightened the sheet. "Lie still. Hush." I put my finger on his lips.

With a slight shake of his head, he said, "I need to tell you…" He seemed to run out of breath.

"Tell me what?"

"I'm… sorry…"

"For getting hurt and scaring me nearly to death?" I squeezed his hand. "You should be sorry."

With a weak smile, he said, "No. For… embarrassing you in front of… your friends… at the Bennet House."

"We're past that," I told him. "You and I can get past anything."

I caught a glimpse of a white uniform standing just inside the door. About my height—which is to say neither tall nor short—she had auburn hair streaked with red and a stethoscope draped around her neck.

"You need to go now, Emlyn," she said.

I've mentioned at times that we who grew up in Niagara Falls for the most part know each other. I had gone to high school with this nurse. Janet Fargo. In school we called her North Dakota.

"I'll leave in a minute, Jan," I said.

With a smile, she came to Roger's bed and checked the IV drip running into his left arm. "You can see him again later. The doctor wants him to rest now."

I nodded, collected my purse, then leaned down and gave him a full kiss. Even in a hospital gown, his muscular chest left me a bit giddy. "Get well fast," I said as I left. "I need you—in a lot of ways."

From behind me, I heard Roger groan, then say, "And I need you to... stay out of this, Emlyn."

As I came into the hall, someone grabbed my arm. Startled, I spun around, and looked up into very gray eyes.

"You have to listen to him, Emlyn." Harry's whisper shook with concern.

I stepped back. "I can't. Someone shot Roger and is making it look like I killed Daniel Bennet."

"Don't be ridiculous," Rebecca said. "No one thinks you did it."

I chewed on my lip.

Again, Harry took my arm. "Either way, whoever's doing this is dangerous—"

"Very dangerous," Rebecca said.

"—and bad—"

"Very bad," Rebecca added.

"He shot a cop, dammit!"

I leaned to look into Roger's room. Janet Fargo, still smiling, leaned over him and adjusted the sheets on his bed. Turning back, I stared past Harry to the nurses' station.

He sighed. "Okay, I know you. You can't stop yourself from meddling. But if you're gonna do it, do it in your house. Sit and think about what you've seen and heard—you, know, like you've done before."

An orderly pushed a gurney holding a medical bag past us. In my worried state, something about his face and the way he carried himself seemed familiar. Narrowing my eyes and taking a deep breath, I wondered. *Have I seen this man anyplace near Howard Kline? He wasn't in Kline's office today, but was he there the day Kline read Amanda Stone's Will? Maybe I saw him in the gallery at Richard Bennet's trial...*

The orderly stopped outside Roger's room, took something from the bag, and peered in. The look in the man's eyes—

"Stop him!" I said at a volume not at all appropriate for a hospital. "He's gonna to try to kill Roger!"

Harry grabbed the orderly's wrist. Three nurses and a doctor raced down the hall. They formed a circle around the orderly. Janet Fargo rushed from Roger's room. "What's going on?" she demanded.

I pointed and sputtered, "H-he's—"

"What's that in your hand?" Harry said.

His eyes wide, the orderly showed us a vial of pills. "I-I was told to bring this to the patient in here." It sounded as though he spoke with a slight Canadian accent.

The doctor took the vial, and examined it. Calmly, he said, "You've made a mistake, young man. This is a sedative prescribed for Mr. Jordan." He pointed to the room across the hall, then turned to Harry. "You are?" he asked.

"Detective Chief Harry Woodward." He took his badge from his inside jacket pocket, and showed it. With a glance at me, he added, "I apologize for the disturbance."

"Still causing havoc, Emlyn?" Janet said.

One of the other nurses giggled. Her mouth open, Rebecca looked stunned.

I felt my face grow so warm, I thought in a moment the doctor would feed me Mr. Jordan's pills.

"Well, Detective Woodward," the doctor said. "Thank you for, um… catching this young man's error."

I stepped back, anger overriding my embarrassment. "He would've killed Roger if he gave him those pills."

Janet Fargo shook her head, as if she couldn't believe my dullness. "The orderly wouldn't have given Roger any pills. That's my job and I would've caught the mistake."

The doctor smiled at her. "You see, Detective? Everything in this hospital is checked and double-checked, so our patient was never in danger. Now, I believe visiting hours are over. You and your, er… friends are welcome to return when, uh… Yes." He led the orderly to Mr. Jordan.

His lips tight, Harry took my arm and pulled me to the elevator.

Chapter Thirteen

From OMG to... Damn!

Harry drove us home from Memorial Medical Center at a saner pace than the panicked drive we'd taken to get there. Plus it was silent. That is, until he pulled the SUV into my driveway. As soon as I pushed the button to unlock my door, I heard a second click, and was again locked in the back seat of the car. I pushed the button a second time, and a second time I heard a click that locked me in.

I leaned from the back seat to look at Harry. "What are you doing?"

His eyes straight ahead, he said, "Go inside, and stay there. It's my job to nab the guys behind this. Let me do my job."

"But—"

"No *buts*, Emlyn. I can't waste time worrying about what you're up to."

I opened my mouth to answer. Before I could, he twisted, reached over his seat, and took both my hands in a strong grip.

"And I can't be worrying that you're gonna drag Becca into another mess—I'm sure you remember how you both ended up in the hospital."

Next to Harry in the front seat, Rebecca rubbed her knee that had been broken when Roger's ex-wife smacked her with a baseball bat. Groaning, she said, "*I* remember."

What made me such an easy target for guilt bombs?

"Okay, okay," I said. "We'll stay inside."

"Becca, call me if Emlyn even thinks about breaking that promise."

She kissed his cheek. "I've got your number on speed dial."

Harry gave a sharp nod, then pushed the button to unlock the Trailblazer's doors. Rebecca and I slid out.

As he began to back out of my driveway, he rolled down the window, and said, "I've gotta get to the precinct and put the squad together. I know the way your brain works, Emlyn. If you think of something, don't do anything. *Phone* me."

Phone you? Right, I thought while we walked up the path to my front door. *When I figure out who shot Roger, I'll zap him with—*

My mind froze in mid-thought, my attention caught by the fluttering of the curtain over the kitchen window. Someone had gotten into my house! I reached out to Rebecca.

"What?" she said.

Holding my breath, I pointed to the window.

At that moment the curtain moved aside, and a white face stared out at us. Elvira was on the window ledge, sunning herself.

As if she had a map which showed the direction my thoughts had taken, Rebecca laughed. "How're you gonna concentrate on a spell if just a moving curtain stops you cold?"

I closed my eyes and released my breath.

Rebecca shook her head. "Harry's right. We need to stay tucked in till the killer's caught."

I know I've mentioned my propensity for bravery, which is to say I had none. I hoped the heroines I created would teach me this trait. Hadn't happened yet, but a girl could dream.

Still shuddering with embarrassment from my panicked *faux pas* at the hospital—I suspected my reaction to the orderly had its root in the threatening look Howard Kline had given us—I now felt overtaken by a fear the unseen fiend that had slit Daniel's throat and shot Roger would come hunting for me. Keys jingling in my shaking hand, I opened my front door. No braver than I, my best pal pushed past me. With a quick glance over my shoulder, I followed her into my house. The day reasonably warm, I left the door open so the sun could come through the glass on the storm door.

Obviously, also recalling Kline's look, Rebecca shouted. "Are you nuts? Close that before someone comes in after us!" She rushed from the kitchen, reached over my shoulder and slammed the door. "This time it might not be a mistake like with the pills."

What did I say about my friend's bravery? Still, it turned out to be good she did that. Just as the door closed, what sounded like a car in need of a new muffler, raced down River Road. Then, it sounded as though the car's brakes squealed in front of my house. Now, two things happened at once: Elvira shrieked and leaped from her perch on the kitchen window ledge, and the car's engine backfired. At least, I thought the *car* backfired. It couldn't have been the car, though, because the kitchen window shattered.

Rebecca and I dove to the wood floor in my hall. When we did, my purse slid along the floor to the living room. So did my friend's shoulder bag, its contents scattering on the carpet. My cat crawled from the kitchen. Elvira, lying so close to my face I could feel her panting breaths, glared at me with an expression that said, *Holy cat-gods! Who'd you start up with this time?*

Why couldn't I help but make an excuse to a cat? "Uh… no one," I whispered.

"She just *had* to talk to that sleazy lawyer," Rebecca muttered.

And why couldn't my dearest friend help but rat me out to a dumb beast?

As if the cat heard me think of her as dumb, she snorted, rolled over, and crawled to the living room.

Though we heard the car rumble off and the faulty muffler grow dim as it rounded the curve in the street, Rebecca and I remained on the floor with our arms covering our heads.

"Are they gone yet?" she whispered, as if a louder voice would bring more shots.

"Don't know," I said.

"What'll we do?"

"Pray a lot."

"I'm gonna call Harry." She patted the floor around her.

"What are you feeling for?"

"Where's my cellphone?"

"Maybe if you open your eyes—" I lifted my head, and pointed. "There it is."

Fearful the sound of the car driving away might have been a ruse and the gunman would be waiting on the lawn for us to become targets when we stood up, we crawled to the living room. Ignoring the other things which had spilled from her shoulder bag, Rebecca snatched her cellphone and ran to the sofa. Her knees pulled up, she covered her chest with one of the cushions—as if it would shield her from a bullet. I rushed to the French door and closed the mini-blinds, like that might keep a killer from smashing through the door. The sofa rattled when I jumped onto it.

"Hurry up, call Harry!" I whispered.

Elvira peeked out from the skirt of my overstuffed wingback chair and shot me a look that might have said, *What's wrong with you, whispering like that? Even if someone's still out there, he can't hear you talk. And closing the blinds and crawling around like a cat... Oh, come on!*

Rebecca understood the cat's expression. She looked at me and giggled nervously.

Elvira was right. If whoever shot at us wanted to come in and finish the job, he already would have. This had to mean the shots were only intended to warn me that I should stop snooping. This also meant whoever shot at us didn't know me very well.

***

When Rebecca told Harry someone shot at us, his voice on the phone was so loud that from halfway across the room I heard him shout, "Now you'll do like I said! Stay in the house. Don't move. Don't even breathe! I'll be there in ten minutes."

In what felt like far less than ten minutes, sirens screamed down the street. The *wraa wraaing* slowed to a dull drone in my driveway.

A tall woman, Rebecca had muscular legs that made up more than half her height. In other words, she was built for running. As soon as the siren's whining slowed, she jumped off the sofa and ran out my front door. Elvira, on the other hand… Well, good manners require me to call her hefty. By this, I mean her legs barely dropped below her belly. Yet as quickly as Rebecca dashed for the door, the cat ran at her heels.

Watching the cat, I thought, *Someday I'll learn how that overfed feline moves so fast.*

By the time I reached the door, I saw Rebecca in the driveway, her arms wrapped around Harry and her head buried against his chest. The cat had her front paws around his ankles. I must confess to a bout of envy. Roger wasn't there to fill *my* arms.

The Trailblazer, a patrol car, and a Crime Scene van in my driveway, with a second patrol car idling on the other side of River Road, I returned to the living room. After just a few minutes, the storm door opened and Harry walked in with Rebecca holding onto his arm. Elvira, her tail high, strutted in just behind them.

"Now you see why you can't mess around in murder cases?" Harry scolded. When I started to protest, he stopped me with a raised finger. "I don't care that you helped us solve a few killings. You can't keep doing it!"

"I—"

"No. Don't talk! For once in your life, just listen. This stops now. You understand me? Am I speaking a foreign language?"

I could only nod. I hadn't been scolded this way since eleventh grade when Mr. Franklin caught me pantomiming him while he taught our American History class. To make matters worse, I could have sworn I saw the cat stick out her tongue at me. That's what Janet Fargo North Dakota had done when Mr. Franklin had the assistant principal come in and yank me from the classroom. I knew I never liked that girl for a reason.

Finally able to get a word in, I said, "What about my kitchen window? I've got to get Freddy Silbert over here to replace it."

Much to my mother's chagrin, in high school Freddy Silbert and I had a symbiotic relationship. That is to say if one of us had been in trouble, the other sat beside her in the principal's office. After high school Freddy had trained as a glazier in his father's shop. Today he ran the business.

"Not a chance," Harry said. "*I'll* take care of getting the window fixed."

Because Harry had heard me tell stories of the antics in which Freddy and I had engaged, he must have suspected I would use my high school friend to do the snooping I'd been forbidden to undertake. This was precisely what I had in mind, dammit!

"But Freddy can do it faster and cheaper," I said in my most innocent voice.

Harry stared at me until I glanced away. Then he said, "All right. Since I've made myself crystal clear, I'm gonna go supervise the men doing a house-to-house to find out if anyone caught the plate number on the shooter's car. Crime Scene will look around the street for spent casings and in here for the bullets that broke your window. You and Becca are going to stay put. I'm leaving Collins parked outside to make sure there's not another attempt on you. He's got orders to cuff you and haul you in if you even open the door."

It took two crime scene techs only fifteen minutes to dig bullets out of my kitchen wall. When they were gone, Rebecca sat beside me on the sofa. I knew she noticed my clenched teeth, because she stroked my arm, and said, "Harry also bawled *me* out for going with you to Kline's office."

I slid away from her into a corner of the sofa. "How'd he know I didn't just go there to hire a lawyer in case I'm arrested for killing Daniel Bennet?"

She gulped.

"You told him why I went there, didn't you?"

She slid over until her shoulder touched mine. Tears in her voice, she said, "Don't be mad at me. Harry's tough when he questions someone. He spotted it in a second when I tried to lie to him about the reason you went to see Kline."

Elvira jumped from the overstuffed chair, scampered around the coffee table and sat at my feet. Looking up at me, she *meowed* in a way that said, *Are you just gonna sit there and wait for us to get murdered in our sleep?* At least, that's what I thought she said.

My cat had meowed words of wisdom. I hadn't time for an argument about how Harry learned what I'd done. I turned to Rebecca. "*I* certainly don't want to wait for the killer to come back."

She shouted, "No, no, no! Don't let the cat give you any ideas."

With a snort that had to mean, *What a wuss!* Elvira turned her back and strolled to my computer desk. After jumping onto the chair, she pawed at the desk drawer in which I kept Sarah Goode's *Book of Shadows*. Then she punched the drawer, and looked at us over her shoulder with an impatient expression that said, *Give me a hand here. I can't open this. I don't have thumbs.*

"No, Elvira," Rebecca said. "We were told not to do anything."

I rose from the sofa. "Harry just said to stay in the house and think. He didn't say I couldn't get old Sarah to help me do it."

I looked down at her, and saw my friend's lips and eyebrows in tight parallel lines.

"What did he say, huh? Come on, tell me his exact words."

She took a deep breath. "Well…"

"See? You know I'm right."

Still, she hesitated.

"Rebecca, because you ratted me out, Harry let me have it but good. You owe me."

She sighed. "If he finds out you're getting involved again, I'm gonna tell him you threw a spell that stripped away my will power."

"You mean your *won't* power, don't you?" I said, laughing.

With a moan, she answered, "Okay. Get the book."

Back on the sofa, the old calfskin volume open on my lap, I began to carefully turn the brittle pages. The writing had faded to a feint sepia over the past 320-something years. That, along with the odd way in which some words were spelled, made the text difficult to decipher, so when I tried to read a page, I had to use a magnifying glass to see and use my imagination to fill in some gaps. Fortunately, as I pointed out on occasions, I had a vivid imagination.

"Anything yet?" Rebecca asked after I'd been skimming down the pages for about a half hour.

"Uh-uh."

With a wisp of a smile, she rested her head against the sofa's cushions. She seemed pleased that I hadn't found a spell or even a random thought to serve as a starting point in figuring out why someone had to kill Daniel and then shoot Roger.

While I continued to read, the railroad clock on the wall next to my bookcases clicked off another fifteen minutes. Then, "Look at this," I said, and shifted the book to my friend's lap.

She yawned. "What?" She must have been falling asleep, because the word came out like a whine.

"Here." I pointed, and handed her the magnifying glass. "Read this."

Her lips moving, she silently read the section I pointed to. I didn't have to hear her. I had already read it twice. I fact, I could repeat it from memory.

17 February, in the year of our Lord, 1692.

What mischief Abigail Williams and Betty Parris make. As if possessed, at services this day last week their bodies twitched like they had been possessed, their eyes rolled back and their mouths hung low to their chests.

"What torments you, my children?" Reverend Parris asked.

"It is she," the reverend's eleven-year-old daughter replied, pointing first at the Parris's slave-girl, Tituba, then at Sarah Osborn. She then pinched her nine-year-old cousin, Abbie, who pointed to me, declaring, "It is she!"

Now do those in this Salem Town look at me askance and whisper after me, "There goes she, Satan's handmaiden."

Far have I fallen under a husband's debt, I who could once walk these lanes with my head high. What is written of me now in my shame—for I know I am written of—in the hand of the Right Reverend Parris? There is danger in what he has written, even, dare I say it aloud, death. I must learn what this minister's hand has put to paper. But how? Tonight will I make a simple of mugwort, so to dream what I must know.

"Well?" I said when Rebecca closed the book.

"Well, what?"

"Am I right? That's the answer, isn't it? We need to know what's in that file in Kline's office. The contract I saw will tell me who's doing this."

"Great. And how're you gonna accomplish this? Walk in there and say, 'Excuse me, Mr. Kline, but would you mind if I examine the file you tried to hide from me?'"

"Of course not. Sarah told us how to do it. We'll brew a simple of mugwort. Then I'll be able to see what the contract's about without him ever knowing."

Elvira had been sleeping while we read—I knew this because I heard her snoring. Now she lifted her head and nodded.

Rebecca swiped the book at the cat's large rear end. "If we get killed because you encouraged Emlyn, I'll never forgive you."

In response, Elvira glared at her.

Grumbling, my friend tossed Sarah's book onto the coffee table. "Go ahead. Work another clairvoyance spell. When I can't get you back into your body, I'll slap you into an asylum. Then I'll be able to go home where no one's looking to shoot me."

I stood up. My hands on my hips, I said, "If you're going to be this way, I'll do it myself!"

She didn't move from the sofa.

"I'm going to do it," I said.

She smiled. "Go right ahead."

"I've got mugwort. You gave me some, remember?"

"I did." She still didn't move.

I stood staring at her while the railroad clock clicked off a minute. At last, I blinked. "Uh, Rebecca, what's a *simple*?"

"You really intend to do this, don't you?"

I nodded. "I have to. Don't you see? Someone killed Daniel. Then he shot Roger. Finding out what this is about is the only way to keep him from killing a third time."

At that moment I truly believed I'd be able to stop the fiend with just the use of herbs and spices.

Chapter Fourteen

Simple It Isn't

"Okay," Rebecca said with a deep sigh. "Get the mugwort. I'll start boiling the water."

The door to the basement was next to the framed antique mirror across the hall from my kitchen. In the basement I stored my, uh… tools. Not hammers and nails and saws, though. My *tools* were the colored candles, a number of dried herbs and spices, my ceremonial knife and sundry other items I kept locked away for times such as this. Rebecca had made it clear that these things could be used only in connection with my ancient relative's, uh… recipes. To use them for any purpose other than this, she'd insisted, would make them mundane. Useless. I had heeded this instruction. She had also insisted I could use my tools *only* when she was around to make sure I didn't get into trouble… Well, obeying one of her two instructions made for a reasonable average, didn't it?

I dug the tool cabinet key from the utility drawer in my kitchen. My father had been a carpenter—have I mentioned this? Before he passed away he had made a living space of every room in the house but the basement. Dim and dank, with cinderblock walls and a single bare bulb strung from a rafter near the steps, those times I went down there recently I felt as though someone watched me. My big white fraidy-cat refused to go down to the basement—to me, a sign someone probably *was* watching.

Elvira, her back arched and her hair standing up, stood at the doorway as I ran down the steps and across the cement floor to the tool cabinet in the storage room. In the time it would have taken to snap my fingers once, I opened cabinet, had the jar with mugwort in my hand and ran back up the steps. Slamming the door as I came through, I slid on the polished wood floor in the hall.

Near the stove, holding the white teakettle, Rebecca all but doubled over from laughter when I skidded into the kitchen. "My brave friend," she remarked.

My lower lip protruding, I said, "Next time *I'll* boil the water while *you* go down there alone."

Still laughing, she said, "Sarah Goode was probably looking over your shoulder to make sure you only took what we need."

"Well… Sarah could have said something."

"Of course, it might've been the ghosts of some of the things you did when you were in high school."

I grumbled. "I never should have told you any of that." I shoved the jar into her hand. "Start brewing before I sic the ghosts of my past on you."

She looked at the jar for a moment, then at the teakettle. "Have you forgotten something?"

I blinked several times. "Like what?"

"A teacup."

I reached into the cabinet for one of my mugs. "Here."

Rebecca tilted her head. "You use this for coffee every day."

"Yeah. So?"

"Haven't I taught you anything?" She put the kettle and the mugwort jar on the counter. "We can only use a cup you put aside for use in spells."

I glanced over my shoulder at the basement door. "I, um… don't suppose you'd want to get one from the tool cabinet. You know, just to be sure it's the right cup?"

She shook her head. "Your house, your supplies. You get it."

From the way she grinned, I knew my friend liked torturing me.

I narrowed my eyes. "Could we send the cat to get it?"

Elvira arched her back and ran from the kitchen.

"Go." Rebecca pointed. She turned me around and gently pushed me toward the basement door. "And don't forget to also bring the bamboo strainer I gave you."

I hadn't noticed the creak when I opened the door earlier. *Gotta get Roger to oil the hinge,* I thought, then stopped with my foot raised above the first step. Roger lay in a hospital bed, shot because he wanted to find evidence of who really had killed Daniel. Now someone—it *had* to be the same person—had aimed his gun at Rebecca and me. If I were smart, I would do as Harry had insisted. I would forget about chasing killers and spend my time creating brave heroines for my stories.

Staring into the darkness, I told myself, *Come on, Emlyn, do this for Roger and Daniel.* This was sort of like in the movie *The Wizard of Oz*, when Dorothy, the lion and the tin man entered the haunted forest, muttering, *Lions and tigers and bears, oh, my.*

I turned on the light. Slowly, I descended to the basement. Again sensing a presence behind me, I glanced over my shoulder as I made my way to the storage room. I reached for the doorknob…

Flashing lights. Like July Fourth fireworks. Red. Yellow. Smoke swelling around the edges. It spreads. I'm in the middle, blinded. I feel myself tumbling. A breeze blows and the smoke clears. I'm not in my basement. I'm in the air, floating. Above me, clouds wafting in a pastel blue sky. I glance down. Below me, the Crystal Beach amusement park. There's the Comet, but again the sign calls it the Cyclone. Now I'm hovering over the carousel. Calliope music. My vision sharpens. I see the roustabout show a page to the woman. I hear her say, "Carl, you got it!"

This is the third time I've seen these people. What message does this vision send? The page. That's it. I need to see what's written on the page. Spreading my arms, I glide closer. I can see it—

On this Twelfth day of June in the year 1796, in that Loyalist Hiram Bennet has proved by deed and word written by General John Graves Simcoe, Governor of Upper Canada, that during the armed rebellion he be loyal to the Crown, so be it to he is granted these…

I've seen those words before. On the page Daniel showed me. What follows them?

A breeze ripples the page. I can't see the rest. I need to get closer… The breeze brings smoke that envelops me. A stiff wind now twists me. Again I'm tumbling…

"Ooow!" I hollered when my backside hit the cement floor.

I heard footsteps race down to the basement. In a moment, Rebecca stood over me. Reaching for my arm, she said, "What happened?"

I looked up at her. "I… don't know. I was going for the—" Recalling what I'd seen, I stopped. "It… happened again."

While helping me to my feet, she glanced around the basement, then bent and picked up a rake lying near me. "You tripped over this."

"That's why I didn't get a chance to read it all," I said.

Her long neck bent forward, she locked her eyes on me. "What couldn't you read, Emlyn?"

I shook my head to clear it. "I-I'm not sure. It was kind of clear, but—" Again I shook my head. "I don't know."

She brushed dust from my blouse, then looked at my palms. "You're all scraped. Come to the kitchen and I'll take care of that."

A bit woozy, I had to hold onto her arm while I hobbled up the stairs. When she had settled me on a dinette chair, I asked, "How long was I down there?" As if I had drunk more than a few glasses of wine, my words came out a bit slurred.

Is it possible for a cat to look concerned? If it is, I saw such an expression on Elvira's face when she sat at my feet. I sighed. There were times I believed that this cat more than merely tolerated me.

Rebecca glanced up at the clock on the soffit over the sink. "You were gone just a minute, maybe two at most."

Only a minute? I felt as though I had been over the amusement park at least an hour.

She pulled a chair next to mine and rubbed half of an onion on my palm.

At the first whiff, my lips curled. "I'm glad Roger's not here. With this as a perfume, he wouldn't come near me for weeks."

As if to prove me right, Elvira sniffed my hand and ran from the room.

"Hush," Rebecca said. "This is a healing root herbalists have used for centuries. It'll also keep you from getting hurt again."

I giggled, remembering that my Grandmother Goode used to rub garlic on an onion, then put it and her shoes in a box in her clothes closet. The garlic-rubbed onion, she told us, would protect her from getting sore feet. The first time Grandma said that, my mother had responded, "Of course it will, Mamma. With that smell on your shoes, no one will come close enough to step on your toes."

Rebecca hadn't yet finished healing me. After throwing the onion into the trashcan (a white trash can, of course), she tossed a few cloves into boiling water. As she carried the kettle to the table, she said, "Inhale this. It'll help you remember what you saw."

"Remember? Onion and now the smell of clove—I want to forget this!"

"Stop it!" She smacked my arm. "I'm trying to help you." When I'd breathed in the steam for a minute, she said, "Now tell me where you went this time."

"Crystal Beach. Again. And now I got close enough—" As if of their own accord, my eyes opened wide. "The file in Kline's office. It's connected somehow to what I've been seeing. Yeah. That has to be why my mind keeps dragging me to the past." I shoved Rebecca's hand aside. "I have to get into his office again and see what's in that file."

My friend must have hoped my trip in the basement would have pushed such an idea from my mind. Pulling on her long salt and pepper braid, she sounded a lot like Harry when she said, "Go back to that sleazy lawyer's office? Don't you ever learn?"

I jumped from my chair. "I *have* learned. I've learned that doing something is better than waiting around for something to be done to us. Now, help me!"

She slid her chair as far from me as she could. "You said you're gonna use clairvoyance to try and see what's in the file."

I looked out the window.

"You promised." Her eyes dropped to her cellphone on the dinette table. "If you try going out, I'll call Harry."

I sighed "Oh, all right."

"No fingers crossed?" She looked down at my feet. "No toes crossed?"

I closed my eyes and took a deep breath. "Yes, Ma, I'll be good."

"Okay. Start the kettle boiling again. Give me the key to your cabinet—*I'll* go for the cup and the strainer this time." When she opened the basement door, to herself, she muttered, "The last thing I need is for her to have another episode down there."

I glanced at the teakettle, considering how long it would take to boil water that way. Then I glanced at the microwave oven. "Much better," I said, and filled a glass measuring cup with water.

Just when Rebecca returned to the kitchen, the microwave beeped. She looked at it, then at me and shook her head.

"What?" I said. "Nothing in the books you've given me says I can't boil water this way."

With a grunt, she took the measuring cup from me. She put some of the mugwort into the bamboo strainer. Holding the strainer over the teacup, she poured the water through it. "Drink this. All of it."

"That's it? That's all there is to this brew?"

She rolled her eyes. "Why do you think it's called it a *simple*?"

The smell of the onion and clove had clogged my sinuses. The first sip of this mugwort tea clogged my throat. "Ugh!" I gasped, and tried to hand the cup to her.

"Uh-uh. If you're determined to try this, you've gotta drink the whole thing. Of course, we could open a bottle of wine and let the police figure things out."

I harrumphed. Staring at her, I held my nose and downed the liquid in three gulps. When I finished, I sputtered, "That's… awful."

With a grin, Rebecca said, "*Hmm.* I guess I could've sweetened the brew with some honey."

The *meeeow* from my living room sounded like laughter.

Growling, I said, "I hate you both!"

My rotten best friend took a quart container of orange juice from the refrigerator, and reached into a cabinet for a glass. I snatched the container from her hand.

Desperation playing havoc with good manners, I guzzled a third of the juice directly from the container.

"Feel better?" she asked.

I caught my breath, and nodded. "Okay, I drank that awful tea. What now?"

"Get comfortable." She took my arm, and we moved to the living room. When we got to the sofa, she turned me around. "Sit. Relax. Become one with the wind and the trees."

After my mind-flight to Crystal Beach and gagging on the mugwort tea, I felt weary enough that relaxing sounded like a brilliant idea. I settled on the sofa and covered myself with the gray afghan my grandmother had knitted almost a century before.

Rebecca sat in the far corner of the sofa, rested her head against the cushions, and closed her eyes. "Let your mind drift with the breeze," she crooned. "Float into the universe."

I took a deep breath and waited to drift. I heard the honking of Canada geese on their way to their annual vacation somewhere in Georgia. I heard a siren screech in the distance. I heard the thump of a bass on the radio in a car moving along River Road. I heard the railroad clock click off minutes. I didn't hear the breeze or see the universe unfold.

"Damn!" I muttered. "That terrible mugwort tea isn't working. I can't see inside Howard Kline's office. I can't see the file."

I shifted so I could lay with my head on the sofa's armrest. I lifted the edge of the afghan. As I pulled it up to my chest, something about it caught my attention. I examined two runes my grandmother had sown into this woolen cover. One was a diamond sitting on an inverted *V*. The other, far more complex, was a diamond with a large *X* over it. The first time I'd seen these runes, I had searched the internet to learn what they meant. One stood for possessions, the other stood for war.

Can land be a possession? I wondered. *Sure it can. And it can be fought over.*

I sat up, reacting to a flash of memory. Two memories, actually. The heading on the first page of the document I had seen in Kline's file—*CONTRACT FOR REAL ESTATE DEVELOPMENT.* Before Kline had returned to his office, I'd only had time to note the name of one party to the agreement: World Development Corp. This heading keyed a memory of the few words I'd been able to see on the paper Daniel had shown me while he and I stood looking across Lake Erie. It said that during the Revolution Hiram Bennet had been a British loyalist and had been granted something that had to do with chains and links.

I jumped from the sofa and rushed to my computer. Quickly, I logged on and began a search for chains and links.

"What are you doing," Rebecca called from the sofa. "You're supposed to be—"

I waved my hand. "*Shh.*"

She came to the desk, and stood looking over my shoulder. "You thought of something, didn't you?"

I nodded.

The first two pages of Google listings directed me to sites selling and installing chain link fences. No help at all. Halfway down the third page, I found a Wikipedia entry that provided ancient definitions of these terms. Chains and links had once been land measurements. A chain had equaled 22 yards. 100 links made up a chain.

Swiveling on my chair to look up at Rebecca, I pointed to my computer screen. "This is what everything has to be about."

She scratched the back of her head. "I don't see—"

"How can you not? It's land. Or, to be more exact, a war over some land."

"War? You mean, like with an army?"

I really needed to teach my friend about metaphors. "No," I said. "It's like somebody has a piece of land, and someone else is killing people to get it." I lifted the hair from my neck. Feeling rather proud of myself, I laughed. "I figured it out, and I didn't need any mugwort to do it."

Rebecca folded her arms across her chest. "Oh? And just how'd you figure it out?"

Still laughing, I said, "I remembered—"

"Uh-huh. And do you suppose, just maybe, drinking the mugwort tea you moaned and groaned about helped you remember?"

With a grumble, I said, "Doesn't matter how I did it." I printed the page, then stood, and held it out. "I've solved the puzzle!"

Excitement lit her face. "You know who killed your friend?"

I slumped back onto my desk chair. What I had found only showed me what someone *might* kill for. It didn't tell me someone actually killed Daniel over a piece of land. Plus, while I might have suspected Crystal Beach was the land which caused the killing, I had no proof. Worse, I had nothing to identify the killer.

With a sigh, I said, "I... don't."

"So, you're back at the beginning."

I couldn't tell whether Rebecca's tone held regret or relief. Stubbornness blocking the part of my brain which housed common sense, I said, "It's a start." Again I held up the page I had printed and headed for the kitchen. "Grab your shoulder bag," I said as I moved. "We've gotta show this to Harry."

She didn't budge.

I picked up my purse. At the front door, I called, "Are you waiting for the first winter snowfall? Come on!"

Gracefully, she sat on the sofa, crossed her legs, and smoothed he long maroon sweater. "You don't have enough evidence for Harry to do anything with."

I didn't, dammit! I needed more evidence, and I knew where it could be found. "Maybe I don't have enough yet. But once I get back into Howard Kline's office, I will." My car key in my hand, without waiting for her reaction I slammed the door behind me.

Chapter Fifteen

A Spy in the Closet

I ran down the front stoop then pulled up short, stopped by the sight of a white SUV with NIAGARA FALLS POLICE in black letters on its door. Parked in the street twenty yards from my house, it blocked my driveway. While I stood, clutching my keys and grumbling, the young cop climbed from the squad car with his arms out and his palms raised.

"Where you goin', Ms. Goode?" he called to me.

Hiding the keys behind my back, I moved sideways toward my Malibu. "I thought I would, um…"

He took off his black hat and walked toward me. "You know I can't let you go anywhere."

"Oh, come on, Collins. I just want to—"

He ran a hand though his red hair. "No can do. Chief Woodward will have my badge if I let you."

Just then, Rebecca rushed out of my house. "Stop her, Irish!" she shouted to the cop. "Emlyn wants to break into Howard Kline's office."

I heard her say this. Collins couldn't hear her, though, because a semi-trailer rumbling past blasted its horn at a Volkswagen trying to pass on the two-lane road. With his hand to his ear, the lanky young cop took five or six steps toward her.

I had my chance. I ran to my car. Before either Collins or Rebecca could react, I climbed in, locked the doors and started the engine. Stomping hard on the gas pedal, I backed up and spun the steering wheel. Leaving ruts in my wake, I swerved across the lawn and past the squad car.

As my wheels hit the pavement, I looked back and saw Collins run to the white SUV. He would need only a minute to make a U-turn and come after me. In another minute he would alert Harry about my escape, and minutes later, a dozen of Niagara Falls' finest would be looking for me. Needing to stay ahead of this pursuit, I sped down River Road. My brakes squealed as I approached the turn-off to Williams Road. The semi-trailer, which moments earlier had abetted my escape, was stopped at the light with the Volkswagen idling behind it. No time to waste at stop-lights, I cut through the Citgo station on the corner. When I neared the entrance to the LaSalle Expressway less than a minute later, I again stomped on the gas. Ignoring cars coming in the other direction, to the blare of horns I skidded into a left turn and crossed two lanes of oncoming traffic. As if the numbers on the white speed limit signs along the LaSalle were the merest of suggestions, my speedometer soon shouted I was doing eighty-five. Cutting around cars and vans that, lacking a death-wish, moved at a saner speed, I quickly approached the turn-off to the Niagara Scenic Parkway. On this older, narrower road, I slowed to only about seventy miles-per-hour. No more than ten minutes after leaving my driveway, I sped around the traffic circle. Two minutes later, I left my car in the casino lot where it wouldn't be easily seen by the police and dashed through the door to 345 Third Street.

In the dim lobby, I stopped and stared at the elevator. I heard grinding from deep inside the shaft.

"Uh-uh. No way am I going to climb into that again," I muttered and ran for the stairs.

On the third floor, out of breath, I leaned from the stairwell door and peered around. Seeing no one in the hall, on light feet I approached the offices of Howard Kline & Associates.

Years ago, I had read Ian Fleming's tales of James Bond's exploits. My imagination shifting into third gear, I now saw myself as *Jamie* Bond, international spy. Lost in this image of myself, I failed to recall that in each book Fleming's spy had been captured—and once or twice, tortured.

Just outside Kline's door, I held my breath, listening. I heard no voices from within, no sound of clicking from Mrs. Scannado's keyboard.

I glanced at my watch. 4:45 in the afternoon. *Could they have all gone home?*

Slowly and as quietly as I could, I turned the knob, and pushed the door a fraction of an inch.

Door not locked, someone must be here.

I cleared my throat, and waited for Mrs. Scannado to ask if there was something I wanted. I had my cover story prepared. I would tell her I'd left my pen in Kline's office—an old pen, a keepsake from my father. I didn't need the excuse. Nobody challenged me.

I slid inside, and moved quickly to the inner office door. My ear against it, I again listened for sounds of people at work. Hearing none, I carefully opened the door. Halfway through it, I heard voices from the hall behind me. Muted by distance at first, they soon became more pronounced.

"I don't know what I'll do when Mr. Kline closes the office," Mrs. Scannado said. I recognized her voice. She must have been returning from the bathroom.

I didn't wait to hear what the person with her responded. I rushed into the inner office, and closed the door.

As it had been that morning, the hall leading to Kline's corner office was empty. No one at the desks in the cubicles. The office doors were open, the rooms unoccupied. Except for the office nearest to Kline's. That door was closed. Apparently people were meeting in there. I could make out the voices of at least two men and one woman. Again holding my breath, I stood near the door, listening.

One of the males sounded angry. "I don't care how much is involved, I don't like how this is going. I only signed on for the construction job."

"Don't tell me, tell her." From the calmness of his voice, I had the impression this second male wanted to appease the first.

The woman said, "Does no good. She doesn't want to hear it." The woman sounded scared.

Who's the she *they're talking about?* If I could find that out, I might not need Kline's file. I leaned closer to the door.

"Well, someone better make her hear," the first voice said. "This project has already gotten way out of hand." He pronounced the word *pro*-ject. This first male had to be Canadian.

"I agree," the female said. "I didn't know this thing would end in a killing."

What's her name? Come on, say it!

I heard a buzzing sound that must have come from an intercom. A moment later, the second male said, "Thanks, Mrs. S. Yeah. We're just packing up to leave."

The door latch clicked. Jamie Bond Super Spy was about to be caught, tortured, her fingernails yanked off.

Damn! I just had my nails done.

Panicked, I scanned the hall for a place to hide. When I turned around, I saw the open door to the file room. Certain no one would look for me in there, I dashed for cover. Inside, I ducked down next to the vertical file furthest from the door. With my sweater-coat pulled up above my hair, I tried make myself as small as possible.

In the hall, the first male said, "Don't forget to close and lock the file room."

"Got it," the second said.

From between my fingers I saw legs in the doorway. "Hey, who left an old sweater in the back corner?"

I bit my knuckles to keep from screaming at him, *Old Sweater? I just bought this coat!*

He took a step toward where I cowered. I whimpered. Before he reached me, the woman said, "Forget the sweater. I wanna get out of here."

The man stepped back. The door closed. The light went out.

Catching my breath, I remained crouched for maybe five minutes. Might have been less—in my state of fear I couldn't tell. Then, believing the office must now be empty, I stood. Jamie Bond had outwitted the bad guys. Feeling my way down the aisle between the two rows of file cabinets, I reached the door. I could now complete my mission. The people I'd overheard hadn't spoken the arch enemy's name. All right, then. I would go into Kline's office, find the incriminating file. With the camera in my cellphone, I would snap a picture of each page. I would email the photos to Harry. When he saw them, he would pat me on the back. You've cracked another case, he would tell me. Never again would he doubt the skill of Jamie Bond, Super Spy.

I turned the doorknob, pushed the door. It didn't move. Lost in my imagination, I'd forgotten the guy had been told to lock the door. I was trapped in the narrow space between two banks of file cabinets. In total blackness. Until morning!

With my eyes open wide and my forehead so creased I thought no amount of face cream would ever remove the lines, I began to perspire. Feeling along the wall, I begged God to let me find the damn light switch. God couldn't answer this prayer. The only light switch was on the outside wall. My panic rising by the second, I paced from the door to the rear wall, than back again. Tears in my eyes, I dropped to the floor, then jumped to my feet, and rushed at the door. I threw myself against it, bounced off. I pounded on the door with both fists. Yes, I knew Kline's associates had left. Didn't matter. Claustrophobia had seized command of this spying operation.

"I'm locked in here. Let me out!" I shouted. "Please. Please!"

I beat the door harder. "Help me! Someone, please…"

I felt the walls coming closer together. Soon they would crush me. I'd be a human panini!

"Air… I need air," I gasped.

I sank to my knees, crying. For what felt like hours, maybe days, I continued to pound and cry and moan, my voice growing hoarse. "Help… Please…"

Then, at last, I heard voices from beyond the door.

"Good thing you caught me in the building's lobby, Detective. I was just leaving for home."

This sounded like Mrs. Scannado. Was her voice an illusion? While doing research for a story, I had read that could happen during a claustrophobic panic.

"Thank you for coming back up to check." This sounded like Harry.

"I don't see how she could have gotten into the office without anyone seeing her," Mrs. Scannado said.

"You don't know the half of what Emlyn can get up to when she puts her mind to it."

Even through the heavy door, Rebecca's voice sounded too real to be an illusion.

"I'm saved!" I rasped.

"Feel free to look around," Mrs. Scannado said.

Footsteps moved past the file room.

On my knees, I leaned against the door. Drawing strength from the thought I would be freed from this closet grave, I pounded, and shouted, "I'm in here. Get me out!"

I heard what sounded like a key inserted into a lock. A moment later the door opened.

I tumbled out.

Staring down at me sprawled on the carpet, Rebecca said, "You look a mess."

First an old sweater, now a mess? I would have told her she'd also have looked a mess if she'd been locked in a dungeon for a month. I didn't tell her, though, because I still gasped for air.

From behind her, Harry glared at me. "What the hell is wrong with you?"

Funny, that's what my mother used to say to me… No. I take it back. It wasn't funny.

As my breathing slowed, I saw spiked heels off to the side. I glanced up. Dyed black hair with gray roots, pencil-thin eyebrows. Wringing her hands, Mrs. Scannado said, "This crazy woman broke into our office. She's obviously a thief. Arrest her!"

A thief, huh? I opened my mouth, prepared to accuse Howard Kline & Associates of all manner of nefarious activities. I didn't get the words out, because Harry latched onto my arm and yanked me to my feet.

"Don't worry, ma'am, we know how to deal with this one." He turned me around and cuffed my hands behind my back. "Let's go, Bonnie," he said as he propelled me toward the office door. "Clyde's keeping a bench warm for you in your cell."

I gulped, knowing I would not have a fun ride home.

A sneering Mrs. Scannado led us to the Howard Kline & Associates office door. We waited while she locked it. Then, with Harry still clutching my arm as if I were a dangerous felon who might break free and take hostages, we followed her to the elevator. When she pushed the button, the grinding in the shaft began.

I tried to yank away from Harry, while I cried, "I'm not getting on that thing!"

Her thin eyebrows arched, Mrs. Scannado tilted her head in my direction "What's wrong with her?"

"You can't make me!" I'm sure my eyes looked as wild as those of a crazed killer. "Please, I can't be locked in."

"Claustrophobia," Rebecca said. "Maybe it would be better if we walk down."

Harry grinned at me. "No. We'll take the elevator."

I thought the criminal law didn't permit torture.

Just then the elevator door opened and Harry pushed me in. When the door closed, trembling, I leaned against his chest with such desperation, someone who didn't know me might have thought I wanted to pull off his clothes. This time the elevator showed mercy. Though it bounced and clattered, it didn't get stuck between floors. As we exited the building, I took in a lungful of cool air.

My nerves settled, I started to turn left toward the casino parking lot in which I'd left my car. Harry pulled me back, and led me to the white police SUV at the curb. Holding my head, he eased me into the back seat. When he closed the door, he tapped the roof and said, "Collins, you know what to do with her."

Chapter Sixteen

On Cruiser Control

The police cruiser turned left onto Niagara Street. When Collins slowed for the light at Rainbow Boulevard, with my shoulder I banged the grating that had me caged in the back seat.

"Okay," I said. "Harry made his point. You can take the handcuffs off me now."

When he leaned to look at me in the rearview mirror, I saw him grin.

I sighed. "Come on, Collins."

"Sorry, Ms. Goode, I can't. Chief Woodward said I gotta keep you cuffed."

"Aw, please, Irish," I said in my sweetest voice. "You can do this for me. I promise I won't try to escape."

"Like you didn't take off on me before?"

My hands pinioned behind my back made me extremely uncomfortable. Not quite claustrophobic, but close. "That was before," I said. "I didn't promise then." I grunted and leaned forward. "Pretty please."

He laughed at me.

At one time I had only to bat my eyes and guys would rush to do what I asked. I'd clearly lost my touch.

The light turned green. As the car slowly accelerated, the young cop said, "Ms. Nurse told me you'd probably try to flirt, and when that didn't work, you'd grumble. She said I should ignore you."

I groaned. *How absolutely* wonderful *to have a best friend who can't wait to have me locked away.*

Annoyance had stripped away the more rational thought that Rebecca actually desired to keep me—and her—from getting killed.

"Go on, then." I puffed out my chest. "Jail me." *I know Sarah's book will have a spell to break me out.*

What I just said about rational thoughts? In the center of my snit, it didn't dawn on me that, locked in a cell, I would have no way to get Sarah's book from my desk drawer. It also slipped my mind that if my ancient relative had known a prison-break spell, she would have escaped from her cell and not gotten hanged.

Fidgeting in the back seat of the police SUV, I watched Collins make a left turn onto Main Street.

"Uh, isn't the precinct that way?" I nodded to the right.

"Uh-huh."

"Then where are you taking me?"

"Where the chief told me to." Again he looked at me in the rearview mirror. Again he grinned.

Why does he think it's funny to not tell me where we're going?

My thoughts changed direction when I recalled that Mark and Ray had behaved the same way, refusing to tell me where we would hunt ghosts on Halloween. This started the calculator in my brain working.

Four of us in Ray's car, Samantha and I had no idea what haunted location we were on our way to search. Dana knew. Eli knew. They'd met us at the Bennet House. No sane person would deliberately lead others to his victim. Since I hadn't killed Daniel, it had to be... Samantha! No, wait. Maybe not. If someone wanted to make it appear as though he'd accidentally stumbled over Daniel's body, going on a ghost hunt at the Bennet House would be the perfect way to do it. Since only Samantha and I had no idea where we were going that night, Ray or Mark had to be the killer. Of course, Dana and Eli had also known where we'd be that night, and Eli had a key to the house... Whose idea had a night of hunting ghosts at the Bennet House been? From the way Ray and Mark grinned at each other when they spoke of this plan at our writers' group meeting, it had to be one of them. Of course, either Dana or Eli might have suggested the idea in passing, knowing the guys would pick up on it...

At this point, my calculation of who might have slit Daniel's throat got bogged down in a mire of *maybe—no, it couldn't be.* But at least I had narrowed the pool of possible killers to four. At last, a place to start. Leaning forward in the seat, I shouted, "Get me to Harry. Now!"

Collins didn't say a word. A few more turns, and he pulled into the lot next to Memorial Medical Center. He climbed from behind the wheel, then had to help me out—I had no idea it would be difficult to get out of a car with my hands cuffed behind me.

"Why are we here?" I asked.

Collins answered tersely, "Because the chief said we should be."

"Grrr."

"Won't help to growl at me, Ms. Goode. I've got my orders."

I rolled my eyes, and shifted my hands to the side. "You can at least take the handcuffs off me."

Without answering, he latched onto my arm, led me into the lobby, and pulled me directly to the information counter.

"Chief Woodward said we should meet him upstairs, ma'am," he said to Harriet Soveronsky. "Is Detective Frey doing better?"

She looked at my cuffed hands and *tsked* the way my mother would have. Mom would then have bawled me out for causing trouble. Harriet didn't. Shaking her head, she ran her fingers across her computer keyboard. "The detective's very much better, it seems." She pointed at the computer screen. "It says here that Nurse Fargo has been with him most of the day."

I narrowed my eyes. Through a tight jaw, jealousy spoke with my voice. "What's *she* doing with Roger?"

"Somebody had to make sure he stayed comfortable, Emlyn." Harriet sat back with a smile that filled her round face. "You weren't here to do it."

Chastised, I sighed. It seemed Harriet had inherited the East Coast guilt franchise from my mother.

Again Collins took my arm. As he pulled me past the gift shop, Grace Linden emerged. Stumpy, with short gray hair, she held a plastic supermarket bag. People said she had that bag filled with enough dirty laundry to mortify half of Niagara Falls and probably a good portion of north Buffalo. Collins turned me sideways so Gossip-Grace could see my cuffed hands.

Snickering, she said, "I knew they'd catch up with you someday, Emlyn. Do you need the name of a lawyer?"

Great! By tomorrow morning, most of my small city would know I had been arrested. It couldn't be a coincidence that Grace Linden came out of the hospital's gift shop at just this moment. Harry must have invited her to witness me perp-walked in handcuffs through the lobby. Plus Harriet seeing me this way, and chiding me for not being there for my guy... This was obviously my punishment for disobeying the chief detective's direct order.

My face burning from embarrassment, I struggled fruitlessly to keep Collins from pushing me into another elevator. When the door shut us in, I again felt claustrophobia rise along my brainstem. I closed my eyes and tried to hold my breath while I imagined I was hiking in Hyde Park. This didn't help. My panic rose more quickly than the elevator's slow climb to Roger's floor. At last freed from the elevator cage, I forced Collins to stop while I caught my breath. Then, without a word, he tugged on my arm to propel me forward. As we passed the nurses' station, I kept my eyes focused on a window at the far end of the floor so I wouldn't have to see the nurses turn to each other and giggle behind their hands. I did, though, hear one angel-in-white say, "I don't know what Detective Frey ever saw in her." Another answered, "Janet will be much healthier for him."

She'll be *healthier for him?* If we had passed a mirror, I'm sure I would have seen fire flare in my eyes.

When we entered the semi-private room, I saw a scene that looked posed like in a tableau: Roger sitting up in bed, his right arm in a sling; Rebecca perched on the second bed with her legs crossed; Harry by the window, his back turned, looking out; and Janet in a chair pulled up so close to my guy she might have been sitting on his lap. As I took a step toward them, the figures in the tableau came to life. Harry turned to me. Rebecca shook her head. Roger closed his eyes when Janet stroked his hand.

Idiot! I said to myself. *This happened because you weren't here to stake your claim to him.*

As we'd walked to this room moments earlier, I had been steaming. Now I became an erupting volcano. I broke free of Collins's grasp and rushed at Janet. "Get away from him, North Dakota," I shouted, "or I'll hit you with a spell that'll bounce you back to the middle ages!"

Of course, Janet had no idea of the craft I had been learning. Still, she jumped from her chair and bumped me with her hip as she double-timed it to the door. When I turned to spit more venom at her, she stuck out her tongue at me.

I glared at Harry. "She was in on it? What you did to me, she—"

He smiled.

"The other nurses, they also knew?"

Rebecca rose, came to my side and elbowed me. "That's what you get for breaking into offices after all of us told you to stay home."

Laughing, Collins pulled me back and unshackled my hands.

At last freed, I moved to Roger's bed. Leaning over him, I said, "And you, you rotten excuse for a boyfriend, you knew what they were doing to me?"

"Be gentle," he said. "I'm an injured man."

"Not as injured as you're going to be when I get done with you." I kissed him then, in a way a woman who's spent forty-something years learning knows how.

When I finally let him come up for air, he said, "Did you get it this time? Now will you let me and the chief chase the bad guys?"

"Slow down, Detective," Harry said. "You're not chasing anyone till your doctor says it's okay."

Roger shoved his sheet aside. "I only have flesh wounds." He groaned as he tried to swing his bandaged leg to the floor. "I'm perfectly capable of—"

My hands on his chest, I gently pushed him back against the pillow, then covered him with the sheet. "Stay there. I'd rather have my future husband alive than—"

"Husband?" Rebecca's expression grew so bright, her face might have served as a lighthouse beacon.

I felt the heat of a blush rise from my neck. Roger and I had never spoken of marriage… Well, actually he had and I'd made a joke of it. Ignoring Rebecca's smug smile, I rushed past my slip of the tongue before I tripped over it. "Harry's right. You're staying here and I'm staying with you."

"Stop right there!" Rebecca said. "Go back to the part about marrying him."

My friend had decided Roger and I should be a married couple the day she first met him and had tried everything she could—including a few herbal brews—to convince me of it.

"Yeah. Go back to the good part," Roger said, a lightness in his voice.

I kissed his forehead. "We'll deal with that when you're better." Mentally, I added, *if we ever do.* "Right now," I went on, "there's something I need to tell you."

Harry moved from his spot by the window. "I thought you'd learned your lesson. Does Collins have to handcuff you again?"

"You said you wanted me to think. That's what I did while Irish drove me here."

Looking down at the bed, Harry sighed. "Won't you give this man a little peace?"

"Did you figure out who did this to me?" Roger said.

I sat in the chair Janet had vacated. "I didn't get *that* far. But I think I've made a start."

Harry sat next to Rebecca on the bed nearest the door.

"Tell them about being pulled to Crystal Beach," she said.

I had no need to hide my flights through time from these men. They'd seen a few of my bumpy landings when I'd returned. But as I've already mentioned, they believed my out-of-body experiences had been the result of sniffing the incense I'd burned while casting the spells.

Harry rolled his eyes. "Did you get stoned in the back of a police car?"

Rebecca punched his shoulder. "No wise remarks. Just listen to her."

"Might as well." Roger glanced around his room. "What else is there to do in this place?"

With that less-than-heartfelt encouragement, I told them about the document Daniel had showed me.

"Chains and links, what's that supposed to mean?" Harry shook his head.

"They're old-fashioned land measurements," I explained, then told them what I'd seen at Crystal Beach and that I'd bet the same measurements were on the page the roustabout showed his girlfriend. "And that roustabout's last name was *Bennet*," I added.

To tie everything together, I told them about the document I had seen in Howard Kline's office—a contract to develop a piece of land. Then I related the piece of the conversation I'd heard just before I got locked in the file room.

"See," I said. "This has to mean Daniel was killed because he found a land grant."

Roger sat forward in his bed. "Presuming there is such a land grant that might make sense. This could be about someone not wanting that piece of paper to get out."

Always the skeptic, Harry remarked. "Even if this is all true—and I'm not saying it is—it doesn't tell us who wants the grant kept secret. You get that, don't you? I need a *who*."

I had an answer. A friend, one of those with whom I had slaved over words, must be the killer. "That's what I figured out while you had Collins drive me here."

I told them my logic about how Daniel's body came to be discovered.

"So, it has to be Mark or Ray that killed your friend?" Rebecca said when I finished.

"Or, maybe Dana or Eli," I said.

"I don't know." Harry's eyes turned up to the ceiling. "The autopsy confirmed Bennet's throat had been cut. A deep slash, with no hesitation marks, that cut his carotid artery—"

"From the blood splatters, I knew most of that when I examined the hall in the Bennet House where he was killed," Roger said.

"Would one of those four have the guts to slit a man's throat?" Harry asked. "I need evidence it's one of them, and Emlyn doesn't have any."

How could I help but love a guy who always leaped to my defense?

"Maybe so, Chief," Roger said. "But it'd sure be worth the time to interrogate to each of 'em again."

"Again?" Surprised, I turned to Harry. "You've already interrogated them?" I knew the police had talked to the group members to double-check their alibis for the night Daniel was killed, but an *interrogation*?

He stretched his shoulders and neck. "Not all of 'em. We saw Smart and Maitland about fifteen minutes before you got here."

Rebecca took his hand. "That wasn't an interrogation. They just poked their heads in for a minute to see how Roger's doing, so Harry talked to them."

A tingle of suspicion crawled up my spine. "How did they know Roger had been shot?"

"They didn't," Roger said. "They told us they were here to see someone named Gloria Hardwick that had a kidney transplant. They said she led a writers' group they used to belong to."

"Still, how did they know about you?"

Rebecca smiled. "When they were leaving, they heard two nurses talking about Roger and Janet Fargo."

Hearing that the nurses had really engaged in speculation about whether Janet could jump my claim to Roger's affection caused me to again grumble.

"What's with you?" Harry said.

Rebecca bumped against him. "She's jealous."

Roger laughed.

My cheeks burning, I said, "Well, maybe I am… A little." Quickly, I added, "But that doesn't change anything. It's still suspicious that they showed up just at this time. Harry, you have to talk to them, make them tell you whether they really came here to see Gloria Hardwick or if they wanted to find out if you knew who shot Roger and killed Daniel. And Eli, Ray and Samantha, too. It has to be one of those five behind this."

"Why not, Chief?" Roger said.

Harry thought for a moment. "Might as well. Got nothing else to go on."

Too soon there would be much more to go on.

Chapter Seventeen

Voodoo My Yard

Harry and Rebecca had left. I was still sitting next to Roger when, just past eight that evening, a doctor stopped at the room. From the way he filled the doorway, he seemed as tall as Roger but a good deal broader. As he came toward us, I noticed he had the weary eyes of someone who had been working for more than twelve hours. "I'm Dr. Carter, Mrs. Frey," he said. "I operated on your husband."

Roger glanced at me and grinned.

I took the doctor's outstretched hand. "I'm not, uh… Thank you for… Uh, thanks."

A moment later, Janet Fargo came in. While the doctor checked Roger's chart, she examined his bandaged arm. She then pulled down his sheet to check the bandage on his thigh. I watched while her hand slid up his leg.

"The bandage is on his other thigh!" I snarled

The doctor abruptly looked up from the chart. "Nurse?"

She tilted her head, and smiled at me. "Just checking to make sure there's been no injury to his muscle."

"I'm sure you were," I said through clenched teeth.

The doctor cleared his throat. "It looks like you're doing just fine, Detective Frey. I want to hold you overnight for observation. Then, all things being equal, I think you might go home tomorrow."

"That's great," Roger said. "No offense, Doc, but I can't wait to get out of here."

The doctor smiled. "Good. Then I'll stop in to see you tomorrow morning." To me, he said. "You must be exhausted, Mrs. Frey. Why not go home and get some rest?"

Janet smiled.

Glaring at her, I shook my head. "I'm staying here tonight."

With the sweetest voice, she said, "There's no need, Emlyn. I'll be here to look after Roger."

Clearly, there was every need. "*I'll* look after him, thank you. I'm sure you have other patients that need the muscle between their legs checked."

Dr. Carter looked from me to Janet, then at the empty bed. "I think it would be okay for you to stay, Mrs. Frey. What do you think, Detective?"

Roger answered with a grin so wide it showed the gap between his front teeth.

"Nurse," the doctor said, "let's give the detective some alone time with his wife."

Janet's eyes narrowed. "She's not his—"

"Nurse," Dr. Carter repeated with a stern tone. "Mrs. Frey is right. You have other patients to see to."

Muttering, she flipped her auburn hair as she left.

When we were alone, Roger took my hand and urged me next to him on the bed. "Mrs. Frey, huh? I kinda like the way that sounds."

It might have been the green dinosaur of jealousy breathing on my neck, but at that moment I also kind of liked the way it sounded.

***

I pulled into my driveway just past two the next afternoon. Rebecca, wrapped in a burgundy wool poncho, was waiting with a wheelchair. After I'd spoken with the doctor last evening, I had phoned and asked her to arrange for the chair. Need I say that Roger objected to this? He could manage just fine on crutches, he'd insisted. Obviously, I had ignored him.

While Rebecca helped me move him from my car to the chair, he complained, "Let me walk. You two girls will never get me up the steps to your house."

Rebecca rattled his chair. "Girls, huh?"

I would have liked to lug him up the steps, just to prove him wrong. I didn't need to.

Rebecca smiled at me. "Around the back?"

With that, we demonstrated the power of girls' brains. We rolled the wheelchair over the fallen leaves of the blood-red maple on my lawn, past the two steps leading up to my front door, then to the gate of my backyard. There were no steps up from the patio to my living room.

I pushed the chair, and Rebecca opened the gate. As she circled the corner to the back of my house, over her shoulder she said. "Don't you think it's time to take down your Halloween decoration?"

"What decoration?" I grunted as I pushed the wheelchair over a hump.

Roger grabbed the armrests of the chair, and stiffened. It must have hurt his shoulder and leg when the chair bounced.

"Sorry," I said.

Rebecca pointed. "I'm talking about that effigy on your beech tree."

I leaned over Roger's shoulder. The thing on my tree wore a red and green plaid flannel shirt and torn jeans. For a head, it had a burlap bag with painted eyes and a wicked smile. A carrot that might have represented a horn stuck up on either side of the head. The effigy's hands were yellow garden gloves. Below the eyes, it had red drips that might have been intended to represent bloody tears.

Staring at that thing, I said, "I didn't put up any Halloween decorations this year. Some neighborhood kids must have done this."

"What kids?" Roger twisted to look up at me. "We're on a road with scattered houses, and kids who live here are mostly grown."

He was right. So who would have put this thing in my yard? After what I'd been through the past few days, my stomach began to churn.

Rebecca took a step backwards. "That's a voodoo doll. Somebody's practicing obeah and is trying to curse you."

My jaw dropped.

"It has to be someone who knows you believe in these things," she added.

Roger looked from her to me. "A voodoo doll the size of a body? That's ridiculous! And the way that branch is bent, it's too heavy to be a scarecrow. Get me closer. I wanna see that thing."

I pushed the wheelchair along what appeared to be a double trail left in the fallen leaves until we were about five feet from the tree.

"This is close enough," Roger said, and leaned forward. He seemed to be looking at scars in the tree's bark. "There's something—"

Shuddering from more than an autumn chill, I said to Rebecca, "Help me get that thing down. I want it out of my yard."

"Stop!" Roger said.

"Huh?" Rebecca and I responded almost in unison.

"What's that thing stuffed with?"

"How would I know?" I said. "Probably straw or something."

He shook his head. "Hanging like that, straw would be sagging. It'd also be poking out at the wrists and between the buttons of that shirt."

"Maybe it's stuffed with feather pillows." Rebecca turned to me. "Take a look and see what's in that voodoo doll."

Latching onto Roger's obvious concern, I asked, "Why me?"

"You're the witch among us."

Roger stared at her. "I thought you were one."

"Nope," she said with a sigh. "I'd like to be, but the real craft runs in Emlyn's genes, not in mine. I'm not a descendent of the Rebecca Nurse that got hanged in Salem. I'm adopted. So Emlyn's the one who should examine that doll."

Hesitant to go near the life-sized doll, I groaned. Someone had to check it out, though.

As I took a step, Roger grabbed my hand. "Stay away from it!"

"Oh, come on," Rebecca said. "That doll's not gonna bite her."

"See the way the branch is bent? Unless I miss my guess, that thing's not a doll. If Emlyn touches it, she could mess up a crime scene." He leaned to the side and groaned as he tried to reach into his pants pocket. Pain in his eyes, he looked up at me. "Get me my damn phone."

Frozen by the thought of murder in my yard, it took me a moment to react. As I pulled the phone from his pocket, I stammered, "Y-you d-don't mean—" I pointed the phone at the thing dangling from my tree. "—that's a b-body?"

Instead of answering, he took the phone from my hand, and punched in some numbers. Seconds later, he said, "Chief, it's me... Yeah, I'm at Emlyn's. Listen, you've gotta get over here—and bring Crime Scene with you... Because it looks like we've got another murder is why." He listened for a minute, then said, "You got that right, Chief." Shaking his head, he handed me the phone.

"What did Harry get right?" I asked, as on wobbly legs, I began to push the wheelchair to the French door.

"He said I have a funny idea of what it means to get some rest."

Rebecca pulled the screen aside and pushed the door open. When I wheeled Roger into my house, my cat squiggled out from under the skirt of my wingback chair. She scampered over and sat, glaring at us. Her silent message seemed to be, *You were gone all night, and those crazy people could've hung* me*!*

"Don't give me that look, cat," I said. "Not after what Roger and I have been through." I glanced over my shoulder at what Roger thought was a body hanging from my beech tree.

Elvira narrowed her eyes and licked her lips.

"And don't look to Roger for sympathy. He had a worse day than I did."

Rebecca stooped, and picked up the cat. "Don't holler at this poor thing just because you're frightened. Look at her, she's trembling."

As the cat snuggled in my friend's arms, I would have sworn that feline version of Janet North Dakota stuck out her tongue at me.

I reached for my over-sized albino suck-up. "Oooh. If I get my hands on you... *I'll* hang you."

Tsking, Rebecca stepped back. "Pay no attention to that cranky old witch," she told Elvira. "Tell me what scared you."

In a story I would never use the phrase *whistling through a graveyard*. Too clichéd. Samantha had used it a few times in her story and I'd corrected her. Still, I could think of no other way to describe Rebecca's reaction to Elvira. Obviously frightened, she clung to something she could understand—my cat. My reaction? My home, my sanctuary, had been invaded by a body hanging from my beech tree. Anger was what *I* clung to. Long ago I had found anger to be a warm blanket that covered my abject fear. When my ex decided he wanted a blond bimbo instead of me, fearful of the life alone I faced, I had cried for a day. Then I had gotten angry, and that anger pulled me through.

I had sat down at my computer and begun to write a story in which he starred as the embodiment of evil. Now, anger again blanketing my fear, I found it downright annoying that Roger could remain calm.

Elvira responded to Rebecca with four staccato *meows*.

Holding the cat out, she said, "Did you see who it was?"

Again the cat *meowed*.

"Oh, you poor thing." She cradled the hefty animal like a mother would cradle her infant. "You must've been terrified."

Roger rolled his eyes. Because my guy refused to believe a grownup could converse with a cat, I presumed he intended to humor us when he said, "Okay, I'll bite. What did Elvira tell you?"

"She said someone came into Emlyn's yard last night—"

Elvira mewed.

"Yes, yes. I'll tell him," Rebecca responded. To Roger, she said, "It was a demon."

"Yeah, demon. Right." He shook his head.

Rebecca bumped his chair. As if Roger had pulled the blanket from her fear, tears filled her eyes. "D-don't b-be mean. Elvira's trying to help."

He had also pulled the blanket of anger from *my* fear, and I started to cry.

Fifteen minutes later, Rebecca and I were settled on my sofa. Roger, his wheelchair pushed close to me, held my trembling hand. Neither he, Rebecca nor I had said a word during that time. Our silence must have been the reason Harry knocking on my French door startled us.

As though she thought last night's demon had returned, my cat leaped from Rebecca's arms and dove for her hidey-hole under my overstuffed chair. If Roger hadn't been injured, I would have jumped onto his lap. From

Rebecca's wide-eyed expression, I thought she also wanted to leap onto his lap.

He sighed. "I'm surrounded by girls. Will one of you please let the chief in? Geez, do I have to do everything myself?" He let go of my hand and reached for the chair's wheels.

His groan defrosted my brain. "Coming, Harry," I called.

Chapter Eighteen

Starting to Stitch the Quilt Together

My house had what decorators call an open floor plan. This meant that standing in my kitchen, I could look out at my living room, the dining ell and the alcove in which I had set up my computer. No wall between these areas; where one stopped and the other started was marked by an étagère in which I kept the good china and crystal glasses I rarely used. Behind the cabinet's glass-paned doors, I had placed a few knick-knacks (including two china black cats wearing eyeglasses) my mother had left behind when she moved to Florida after Dad died. Mom now also gone, I thought of her each time I looked at those knick-knacks. In the cabinet below the glass door doors, I stored my wine and liquor—lots of wine, a bottle of scotch, one of vodka and the Courvoisier VSOP I sometimes used in recipes. I mention this because once inside my house, Harry looked at Rebecca, then at me and made a beeline to the étagère.

Standing behind Roger's wheelchair, I watched Harry open one of the doors, take two brandy snifters from the top shelf, then bend to the liquor cabinet, from which he pulled out the cognac. With a glance at me, he filled the glasses with more than two fingers of the amber liquid. Handing one to Rebecca and the other to me, he said. "Sit. We need to talk."

He took my arm and led me to my overstuffed chair. "Take a sip. It'll steady your nerves."

My hand shaking, the cognac nearly slopped from the glass as I raised it to my lips.

Rebecca was next to me, sitting in the corner of the sofa nearest to my bookcases. When I looked in her direction, I saw she held a nearly-empty glass.

Harry sat next to her. "Go easy on that stuff. I don't need you getting drunk."

When we were at last settled, he turned to me and sighed. "Can you tell me why, if there's a body anyplace in Niagara Falls, I'm gonna find you nearby?"

If I were less shaky, I might have laughed and said, *Just lucky, I guess.* In my present state, I responded with a nervous shrug.

"Chief," Roger said, "Emlyn had nothing to do with this." He waved toward the French door, beyond which a half-dozen white-clad crime scene techs searched through my yard.

"Probably not." Harry again looked at me. "There wasn't anything hanging from your tree when you got away from Collins yesterday?"

Rebecca answered—almost slurred, actually, "Uh-uh. No. Wasn't anything out there but fallen leaves."

"And you're sure of that, why?"

"Was standing at the French door when Emlyn—" She pointed vaguely to me, as if Harry didn't know who I was. "—ran out."

"And when *you* left the house?"

Clutching the brandy snifter to her chest, Rebecca said, "Wasn't anything on the tree then, either."

"No cars idling in the street?"

She held out her glass to Harry.

He took her glass and set it on the coffee table. "You've had enough for the moment. Now, about any cars?"

Looking longingly at the snifter, Rebecca shook her head. "Irish was out there. I went with him." She pointed to my front door.

"So you don't know how that—"

Harry got interrupted by a knock on the French door. A moment later, Officer Collins came in.

"Crime scene said to tell you they're finished in the yard, Chief."

"They find anything useful?"

The young cop pulled a notepad from his back pocket and flipped a few pages. "They said from what looks like footprints where it's a little muddy, maybe two people came through Ms. Goode's gate. Also, the leaves— the track looks like one of them shuffled his feet like he was weighed down, so they're thinking he probably carried the body."

"It *is* a body, then?" Roger said.

"Yes, sir. You were right about that."

"Any ID to tell us who he is?" Harry asked

"It isn't a he, sir. It's a woman."

My head snapped up. "A woman?" I pictured Dana or Samantha hanging from my tree.

"Yeah. Like that guy at the Bennet House, her throat's been slit." Collins looked down at his notepad, then added, "No ID on her, but she's an older woman. Round face. Straight black hair."

"Is that a description of anyone you know?" Harry asked me.

Dana had dark brown, curly hair. Samantha's was wheat-colored. The body couldn't be either of them. Relieved that at least another of my writer friends hadn't been murdered, I shook my head.

"Maybe if Emlyn looks at the body," Roger suggested.

Harry nodded. "Good thought. A body hung in her yard, it's gotta be someone she knows. Are you up to that?"

I gave him a far less-than-enthusiastic nod. After I slugged down the rest of my Courvoisier, I took a few staggering steps from the chair toward the front door.

Harry rolled his eyes. "Wrong direction." He took my arm and drew me to the French door. "Even if you recognize who the body is," he said, "can you see straight enough to know?"

I pulled away. Looking back at him as I moved to the door, I said, "'Course I can."

"Wait!" Roger said. "Let Harry open the—"

"Ow!"

"—door."

While I stood rubbing the side of my head, the damn man laughed at me. The mini blinds had rattled when I thudded against the closed door, and Elvira poked her head out from the skirt of the overstuffed wingback chair. I swear, that stupid animal also laughed at me.

Grumbling and still rubbing my head, I at last made it out to my patio, where I scraped my shin on the lounge chair.

Watching me stagger, Roger called to Harry, "Better get her back inside before she kills herself."

The psychologist I saw would have declared these accidents to be my thinly veiled attempt to avoid staring at the face of death. After finding Daniel, I would have corrected her. There was nothing *thinly* veiled about my psychological attempt. I mean, it was one thing to write about broken and dismembered bodies but altogether different to actually look at one. My high school friend, Laurie, was the funeral director who had tended to my mother. I had asked Laurie how she'd managed for so many years to prepare bodies for burial. She told me she focused on the comfort she brought to the families. This obviously made Laurie a good deal stronger than I.

Harry watched me rub my shin for a few seconds, then gave a sharp, decisive nod and brought me back inside. "Sit down, Emlyn, and don't take any more alcohol." As he started for the French door, he said, "There might be another way to do this."

"What way?" I asked, feeling relief at the thought I wouldn't have to look at another corpse.

He took his cellphone from the inside pocket of his corduroy sport jacket. "A picture of the face. See if you recognize her that way."

When I came into my house I couldn't sit. Anxious about the body in my yard, I went straight to the front door and stared out at the street. Five minutes later, I saw one of the crime scene buses pull out of my driveway. A minute after that, Harry came through the French door.

"Emlyn, come over here," he said. When I didn't move, he turned me around and settled me in my wingback chair. As if she were my comfort blanket, I lifted Elvira onto my lap.

"Are you ready?" Harry asked.

I closed my eyes and took a deep breath. "Show me the picture."

He must have seen me shiver. Instead of handing me his phone, he placed it on the coffee table. "Don't suppose I have to—that would only confirm who I already know she is."

Roger gave him a quizzical look.

"It's that Scannado woman from Howard Kline's office. I met her when we went looking for Emlyn."

Hearing who had been left in my yard cleared my head. "What?" I said. Of all the possibilities I had considered, Mrs. Scannado wasn't even an afterthought.

"Why'd someone want to kill *her*?" It sounded as though Rebecca's mind had also cleared. "Maybe she has nothing to do with your friend Daniel's murder."

Roger shook his head. "Emlyn starts snooping, someone shoots me then shoots up her house and now this body in her yard?"

"He's right," Harry said. "It's gotta be connected."

"But how?"

"That, Becca, is the million dollar question."

Elvira lifted her head from my lap and looked up at me. Her expression seemed to say, *Don't sit there like a dolt.* She smacked my hand with her paw, as if to add, *C'mon, snap out of it. There's a million bucks on the line. Answer him!*

"Stop it, cat!" I said. "I'm trying to think."

Roger managed to roll his wheelchair next to me. When he took my hand, he said, "You mean you haven't figured everything out? Mark your calendars, everyone. For the first time, Emlyn Goode doesn't have all the answers."

Oooh! There were times I truly didn't like that man. I raised my hand to smack him, then pulled back before I hurt his bandaged arm. I didn't like him at that moment, but I loved him.

He leaned to kiss my cheek, then rolled his chair back.

"You mean you really don't know?" Rebecca sounded disappointed.

I sighed. "I have part of it… I think. It has to be one of the writers in my group—"

"You've already told us that," Harry said.

"I know. But we can eliminate Ray Scannado. That was his mother's body in my yard."

"Okay," Roger said. "Let's go through this again. Why does it have to be one of the others in your group?"

"I thought you guys wanted me to stay out of this."

Harry clicked his tongue. "Yeah, like that's ever gonna happen."

Rebecca tapped my hand. "I've got the answer. It's one of them, because this all started when you took that flight during your last writers' group meeting."

"Flight?" Roger stared at me. "Just what is it you guys are smoking at those meetings?"

Glaring at Rebecca, I said, "*Flight* is just a metaphor. Right?"

Blushing a bit, she cleared her throat. "But... that's when it started, isn't it?"

I sighed. "Well, yes and no."

She kicked my ankle.

"Ouch!"

"You deserved that. I hate when you say yes and no. It can't be both!"

I rubbed my ankle, and looked at Harry. "Arrest your girlfriend, please. She just assaulted me."

He snickered. "Can't. She kicked you in self-defense."

"Yeah." Rebecca grinned at me. "Like with the laws in Florida, I stood my ground."

My furry white Benedict Arnold nodded.

"*Et tu,* fur-ball," I said. "Okay, I'll explain—" I closed my eyes. "Oh..."

"You remembered something?" Rebecca asked.

"It was such a small thing." I said.

"What small thing?"

"I... I didn't think it meant... But now..."

Clearly frustrated with me, Elvira growled.

"You make me so mad!" Rebecca pointed at Roger. "You kick her this time."

"Okay, okay," I said. "During the writers' group meeting, we were taking a break. Daniel and I were by the fence, looking over the lake to the construction where the Crystal Beach amusement park used to be."

Rebecca growled. "You told me that already."

"Yes. But, here's the thing. While Daniel was showing me that page with chains and links written on it, I got a funny feeling on the back on my neck. You know, like someone was standing behind me?"

"Who was there?" Harry asked.

I closed my eyes, trying to bring back that day. "I... don't know. When I turned, I didn't see anyone. But now I'm thinking someone must have been there and seen the page Daniel showed me—someone who didn't want that piece of paper found. Daniel's killer had to get that page."

Harry's eyes narrowed.

I looked directly at him. "It has to be. That's the only way any of this makes sense."

"If this invisible person killed your friend, why'd he shoot Roger, take potshots at you and then knife the Scannado woman?"

I shrugged. "I haven't figured that part out. Yet."

When I glanced at Roger, his eyes were wide open. "It makes total sense. Whoever killed Daniel Bennet didn't get that piece of paper. That's what he was looking for in the Bennet House when I walked in on him and he shot me."

I shuddered. "And now he's after me, because he thinks I have it."

"Then why kill Mrs. Scannado?" Harry said.

I moaned. "I don't know."

"And why dump her body in your yard?"

Roger answered. "Because if Emlyn has whatever that sheet of paper is, our killer thinks it'll look like *she* has the motive for killing Daniel Bennet and Mrs. Scannado."

A piece of this crazy quilt slid into place. "Having that paper would give me a motive for the murders," I said, "so I'd have to destroy it."

"Which is exactly what the killer wants."

Like an old married couple, Roger and I finished each other's sentences.

"But why'd they hang the body from your tree?" Rebecca said. "It would've looked like you had a motive if they just left it in your yard."

"Because someone knows Emlyn and knows she can't help but snoop into murders," Roger said. He thought for a moment, then looked at me. "It's like in *The Godfather* when they left a horse's head in a guy's bed. The killer's telling if you don't leave it alone now, you'll get hanged next. See? That's why I keep telling you to stay outta these things."

The way Harry's eyes blinked told me he was considering all this. At last, he said, "You know, in an upside-down kind of logic, that almost makes sense."

Roger smiled at me. "It does. All this time I've been spending with you, I'm starting to understand the convoluted way you think."

Harry held up his hand. "Assuming what Emlyn said is true, it doesn't bring us any closer to knowing who's behind this—" He stopped, and rubbed his forehead.

"What's bothering you, Chief?" Roger asked.

"It's the MO. In my experience, a killer sticks to doing it one way."

Roger's hazel eyes seemed to light up. "In this case, the Scannado woman and Bennet both had their throats cut—"

Harry took a deep breath. "And whoever went after you and Emlyn used a gun."

"Two killers?" I said. "Both after the piece of paper Daniel showed me?"

"Couldn't it be the same person?" Rebecca asked. "Maybe he got a gun, because… uh, doing it would be easier that way."

Roger shook his head. "Slitting Bennet's throat, then shooting me, then going back to using a knife on Mrs. Scannado?"

"Two MOs, two killers." Harry rubbed his jaw. "But maybe shooting you, Roger, was a mistake."

My guy touched his shoulder. "This sure doesn't feel like a mistake."

Signaling to Officer Collins, who stood by the French door, Harry told us, "But it could be. Might be one of the border guards thought you were his perp coming back to hide in that damn house. Pulled the trigger, and when he found out he shot a cop, was scared to admit it.

Collins, get me the number of the Border Patrol's office. Leave it on my desk—I'll call them when I get to the precinct."

When Irish left, I had another thought. I drew in a breath. "Don't laugh, but from the beginning I've thought the key to all this is Richard Bennet and the murder of his wife."

"So that's why you asked Kline if Bennet really killed her," Rebecca said.

"Uh-huh. And if you remember, he refused to tell me."

Harry turned to me. "Slow down, Emlyn. I gave evidence in that case. I was a hundred percent sure then that Bennet killed his wife, and nothing since has changed my mind."

"Yes, but—"

Roger reached for my hand. "She's been right before, Chief."

He sighed. "I know, dammit."

"So what're you gonna do?" I asked.

"Right now, I'm hungry. I'm thinking we ought to order in some dinner."

"And tomorrow?" I pressed.

Again Harry sighed. "Not that I think there's any chance you're right about Bennet killing his wife, but I think I'll take a ride out to Attica and have a conversation with him."

Chapter Nineteen

Anger on the Doorstep

Before we left the hospital, Dr. Carter had taught me how to change Roger's bandages and clean his wounds. For the next few weeks I would be my guy's nurse (take that, Janet North Dakota!). Of course, in Roger's mind, he would be my in-house bodyguard. The way he phrased it, he would be keeping an eye on my backside... *Hmm.* Harry and Rebecca? So we wouldn't all fall into Gossip-Grace's mouth (*falling into a gossip's mouth* is how my grandmother Goode would have phrased it) by appearing to have a *menage a quatre* in my little home, my prudish boyfriend insisted they stay next door at his house. This arrangement pleased the guys and Rebecca. While I kept an eye on Roger and he kept an eye on me, I wouldn't be able to chase after the killer.

Apparently, though, the Wicca God and Goddess had something else in mind.

Harry left after breakfast the next morning. Roger stretched out on my sofa with the TV remote in his hand, watching the ESPN analysis of this week's football lineup. Elvira, looking like a giant cotton ball, curled up near her food dish. Rebecca, dressed in her normal attire—loose fitting floral pants and a maroon sweater that fell nearly to her ankles—and I in my PJs and robe, settled in the kitchen and were now jabbering over our second cups of coffee. My cat, that somehow knew our peaceful morning was about to be disturbed, stood, arched her back and ran from the kitchen. Distracted, Rebecca and I didn't react until a minute later when someone pounded on my front door.

Rebecca jumped from her seat and backed up against the stove. I stumbled to the Formica counter to peer into the living room. I saw Roger raise the remote, click off the television. Reaching over, he pulled his service pistol from behind one of the sofa cushions. With his shoulder injured, this must have been painful, yet he didn't utter a sound. His lips pinched, he shook his head—a signal to be silent.

The pounding came again.

Roger's brow creased into a squint. I thought at any moment he would start firing at the door.

The pounding came a third time, now accompanied by a shouted, "I know you're in there, Emlyn. Open this damn door!"

Recognizing the voice, I released my breath. "It's Ray... Ray Scannado."

"You're sure?" Roger said.

"Yes, I'm sure." After years of critiquing at our Writers Refuge meetings and interim phone conversations with Ray about writing, I would have been able to pick out his voice from among all the others at a Buffalo Outer Harbor concert.

Roger nodded and lowered his pistol, but kept it tucked against his side.

I opened the door as Ray again began to strike it. His lips drawn back ready to shout, with his fist raised, he looked poised to attack me.

Startled, I shrank back. The wall-mirror rattled when I knocked it with my elbow.

From the corner of my eye, I saw Roger's pistol come up. "Don't move a muscle!" he snarled. "Don't even breathe."

Ray's fist dropped and he hissed, "You gonna kill me, too?"

I stammered, "K-kill you, Ray? W-what are you talking about?"

"A cop told me my mother was strung up like a Halloween decoration in your backyard. You gonna tell me you didn't kill her?"

"You're being ridiculous." With my brow creased, I reached for his hand.

He took a step back.

"Get outta my line of sight!" Roger shouted. I heard him groan—he must have leaned over so he could see past me.

Ray and I both froze.

I heard another groan from my living room. "Dammit, I can't see... Ow! Get in here, both of you!"

Glaring, Ray sidestepped past me. I stood for a moment, staring at the trees across River Road, trying to comprehend what had just happened. When I turned to follow, I caught a glimpse of Rebecca. She had her back against the stove and both hands covering her mouth.

I went to her and pulled on her arm to urge her from the kitchen.

In the living room, Roger was sitting up on the sofa with his pistol on his lap. Ray was in my wingback chair, clutching the armrests. His hair was a mess, his gray-streaked beard and mustache looked overgrown. From the redness in and around his eyes, it looked like he'd been crying. As Rebecca and I came in, the cat crawled on her stomach from under my desk. She looked at me with an expression that asked, *Is it safe to come out yet?*

"Yeah, it's okay now, Elvira." No surprise that Roger answered. In the time we'd been together, he'd learned to read my cat's expressions. Sometimes he actually understood her mewing.

Rebecca slid onto the sofa to the left of Roger. I moved a dining room chair to his right. When I sat, he asked, "Why'd you come pounding in here?"

Tears in his eyes, pointing at me, Ray said, "I want Emlyn to admit she killed my mother and tell me why she did it."

"I killed your—?"

Roger stopped me with a raised hand.

"See? She just admitted she did it." Ray leaped from his seat. Hands out, he took a step in my direction.

Roger lifted his pistol. "Hold it right there. That's right. Sit down." His lips pinched, his eyebrows in a straight line, he watched Ray return to the chair. "Now, suppose you tell me why you think Emlyn killed your mother."

Ray leaned forward. "It *had* to be Emlyn. My mother told me she'd caught her breaking into Howard Kline's office, looking to steal something from the file room. Mom said she had her arrested like any other thief."

Roger shook his head. "Nothing you said tells me why Emlyn would kill her."

Ray ran his hand through his hair. "Maybe it was revenge for getting her arrested." He rubbed his beard. "Or maybe she's gone crazy—have you thought of that? The way she's been acting the past year or more… And then her brain kind of went south during our meeting. So, yeah, she had a paranoid episode, and she killed Daniel—"

"I killed Daniel?"

"Yeah. Grace Linden told my mother she saw you being arrested—"

Ready to have a paranoid episode in which I would murder Gossip-Grace, I growled.

Ray glared at Roger. "Why'd you let her out? If you hadn't, my mother would still be—" his eyes again filling with tears, he let out a sob.

"What if I told you Emlyn couldn't have killed your mother because she was with me from the time she left Kline's office?"

I twisted in my seat. "Dammit! Don't ask him what if. *Tell* him it wasn't me."

Elvira lifted her head and seemed to glare at Roger. It was as if my cat intended to say, *Yeah, tell him that!*

At the same time, Rebecca said, "Yeah. Emlyn was in the hospital with you all last night." She turned to Ray. "You can ask that jealous nurse. She'll also tell you that."

Roger threw up his uninjured arm. "Will you all just knock it off? I'm trying to get to the bottom of this before someone else gets hurt." He took a deep breath. "Okay. We've established your mother was alive the last time Emlyn could've seen her—" He glanced at me, and shook his head, an obvious comment on my foolish stunt. "But if it had been Emlyn, what motive would she have had?"

Wiping his eyes on his jacket sleeve, Ray seemed to deflate. In a defeated tone, he murmured, "Oh, what's the point?"

"Even though Emlyn didn't kill your mother," Roger said, "the point is someone else might have had a real motive."

"And it could be the motive for killing Daniel," I added.

Roger glared at me.

"I've already told you I'm sure the two murders are connected somehow."

Roger's quiet questioning had its effect. Ray's rage melted. Now he sat back, his lips moving as if as he were making a silent calculation. At last, he said, "It could have been... I wonder..." He fell silent.

Half out of my chair, I wanted to demand that he tell us what thought he had stumbled over. Roger reached his left arm across his body and pushed me back.

It took a moment, but Ray answered without the need for prodding. "That paper. My mother thought Howard Kline might have had it—that's why she took a job in his office."

Roger's eyebrows turned down. "You're so sure the two murders are connected, Emlyn, but I don't see what a piece of paper—no matter how important it might have been to Mrs. Scannado—had to do with Daniel Bennet."

This time I jumped from my chair before Roger could stop me. "It does tie together. It really does! Mrs. Scannado took the job so she could search for that paper in Kline's files. That's what you just said, isn't it, Ray?"

He nodded. "Kline's receptionist is an old friend of my mother's. When she decided to take a leave of absence, Mom convinced her friend to recommend her to fill in."

"Okay," Rebecca said. "But what's that got to do with your friend Daniel?"

"Everything," I said. "The piece of paper Mrs. Scannado wanted to find is the same one Daniel showed me at the writers' group meeting—at least, another copy of the paper. It has to be. I'd bet the royalties from my next book on it. Plus, I'd bet it's the same piece of paper I saw in the hands of the roustabout when I—"

Rebecca's hand went to her mouth.

Elvira pawed at my leg. Staring at me, she gave a long *meeeeow*, as if to say, *Watch it! Tell this guy you can fly through time, he'll tell that crazy Grace Linden and you'll never live it down.*

I caught my breath. My saint with white fur had saved me from myself. I picked her up, sat, and snuggled my face against her neck.

Roger cleared his throat. "Let's stop ignoring what that piece of paper is. It's a land grant of some kind—and a worthless antique at best. The question is why it's worth killing over."

Like in Joyleg, I thought. I'd read that novel written by Ward and Davidson several months earlier—a man from the American Revolution shows up in modern times with land grants from George Washington and Catherine the Great... Another sliver of this puzzle slid into place. Why had it taken me this long to realize it? Shock and guilt had been my only excuse for being so dense. Shock at finding Daniel, guilt over taking too long to get to him, and oh, yes, being a suspect in his murder. Add to all that Roger getting shot, then finding Mrs. Scannado's body in my backyard... I came back to the present when Elvira growled and jumped from my lap. While figuratively kicking myself, I had apparently scratched her neck too hard.

Without apologizing to my cat, I said, "Maybe it isn't worthless. That grant was given to someone named Hiram Bennet in 1796—"

"How could you know that?" A tinge of Ray's anger and suspicion returned. "You'd only know it if you're the one who stole it!"

"Calm down!" Roger shouted. "Tell him how you know all that, Emlyn."

"Well... I, uh..." My eyes rolled up to the left. How could I tell Ray without admitting I'd seen it during one of my out-of-body flights to Crystal Beach?

This time Rebecca rode to my aid. "You told me you saw it when your friend Daniel showed you the grant. Remember, Emlyn?"

A flash of memory. Though it hadn't registered at the time, Hiram Bennet's name had been on the piece of paper Daniel showed me. Maybe that's why I saw it so clearly on the page the roustabout showed his girlfriend. Off the hook, so to speak, I had no need to mention my flights to Crystal Beach. Instead, I said, "The Bennet name on the land grant—it's probably been passed down through Daniel's family for generations. Do you know what that means?"

Elvira mewed as if to say, *Don't look at me. I'm a cat. How would I know about that kind of stuff?*

I had asked a rhetorical question. Having Googled the law about old land grants, I knew the answer. "It means that unless there's some record of one of the Bennets having sold the land, they own it."

This literally opened Roger's hazel eyes. At last he had a motive for the killings. "What land are you talking about?"

I had no need for an out-of-body flight to make a good guess about this. The construction of condominiums on the site had been written of in both the *Niagara Gazette* and the *Buffalo News*. "I'm talking about Crystal Beach," I said.

Ray groaned. "No Bennet owns that land. We do. It's my people's birthright."

"What?" I said, utterly confused. "The *Italians* own Crystal Beach?"

"I'm not Italian." Ray puffed out his chest. "I'm Iroquois, and that land has been my people's since our god, Hawenneyu, led us to it in the beginning of time."

Ray is Iroquois? I hadn't seen that coming. *All the years I've known him, the years we've worked together on my stories and his, I just presumed Scannado was an Italian name.* This thought recalled the question Rebecca had asked me after Daniel's murder: what did I really know about the writers in my group?

"Do you understand what you just gave me?" Roger said. "*You* have a motive for killing Daniel Bennet."

Ray collapsed into the wingback chair, as if stunned by being switched from the accuser to the accused. "I couldn't… How could you think I'd kill someone?"

"Bennet had the land grant, you wanted it. Grabbing for a valuable piece of territory sounds like an awful good reason to me."

"Hold on a second," I said. "Daniel's and Mrs. Scannado's murders have to be connected to that land grant. So, why would Ray kill his own mother?"

"Want to know why? I'll tell you." Roger's eyes narrowed. "When greed walks in the door, feelings for family fly out the window. I've seen that happen a dozen times."

I had seen Roger question a witness before, so I knew he didn't really think Ray killed his mother. He would've hoped the accusation would elicit more information. It did.

Ray again grasped the armrests of my overstuffed chair. "You're wrong. I didn't kill anyone. I didn't have to. Daniel told me he knew where the original land grant was hidden. He was going sign it over to me, so the land could go back to my people."

His lips tight, Roger asked. "Why would he want to do that?"

"When he called me last Monday, he said he'd found the grant along with a note from his grandfather. It said keeping the land for an amusement park was okay— millions of people enjoyed it. But now that the land would be used by just a few rich folk, it should be given back to the Iroquois who once lived there. Dan said to meet him at the Bennet House, and he'd give me the grant. Dammit, that's why we went there that night!"

Roger asked a few more questions. Then, as the railroad clock in the corner near my bookcases clicked close to noon, Ray insisted, "That's all I can tell you. I don't know anything else." He glanced at the pistol still on Roger's lap. "On my mother's soul, I swear I don't. Can I go now? I need to get to the funeral home and talk to Laurie. I've gotta make arrangements."

When Roger nodded, Ray left my house with the speed of a track star. Still a bit stunned, I went upstairs to my bathroom, got the gauze I'd brought home from the hospital and began to clean my guy's wounds. While I did, he turned on the television. He seemed content that he'd learned nothing from Ray to bring him closer to identifying the killer. Had he gleaned the slightest clue as to a name, he would have immediately called the precinct and gotten a team of detectives moving.

I had learned something, though. I had the answer to who had suggested where we should conduct our Halloween ghost hunt and why we should do it there. I'd been wrong in believing Daniel had been deliberately killed in the Bennet House so we'd find his body. Had I also been wrong about whether a member of my writers' group had killed him? I didn't think so. This killing spree had started after one of them saw the land grant when Daniel showed it to me. But which one? I didn't want to speak with Roger about this until I knew—or thought I knew.

Chapter Twenty

No End to the Madness

Roger again stretched out on my sofa. The TV remote raised in his left hand, he called out, "Do you guys know some kind of spell that'll make the Bills take the Seahawks on Monday night?"

I've mentioned that he believed magic is nothing more than slight-of-hand, and he certainly didn't believe the craft Rebecca was teaching me had any basis in reality. However, on the slightest chance that witchcraft could help his Buffalo Bills have a winning season, he would, as Samuel Coleridge wrote in 1817, willingly suspend his disbelief.

Rebecca laughed. "Can't do that. It'd start a war with the witches in Seattle."

While I enjoyed watching football with Roger and would cheer each successful play and moan about fumbles and interceptions as loudly as he did, I couldn't sit through the endless analyses leading up to the games. Since Rebecca shared my disdain of television sports talk shows, we sat in the kitchen drinking tea while she explained to me the healing properties of carnation oil. I had asked for this lesson, hoping to find a way to speed the healing of Roger's wounds. It hurt me to see my guy in pain. To see him bored and in pain hurt even more.

"You have to use *red* carnations," Rebecca instructed, "and they've gotta be fresh. You crush them and put them together with rosemary leaves. Then you'll need to get some sandalwood chips—"

"You brought sandalwood the time you came here to teach me about the solstice," I said.

She shuddered, remembering what had happened when she came to teach me the summer solstice ritual. "Don't wanna think about burning cars or any of the other trouble you keep getting into. Let's just focus on getting Roger healed. Where was I?"

"You told me I need sandalwood chips."

"Oh, yeah. You have to purify the oil of the leaves, then put the chips in a green jar."

"I have some green depression glass my great grandmother collected. Would that work?"

Another call from the living room interrupted us. "Emlyn, isn't there something in that old book of yours that'll at least give the Bills an edge?"

I sighed. "No, Roger. They didn't play football in the seventeenth century."

"Could you check the book anyway? I promise not to tell any witches in Seattle."

What I said about him being bored? I could only shake my head and hope the healing oil would work in less than the required seven days.

Ray Scannado had been gone about three hours when I heard the engine of a car in my driveway. A minute later, I heard a hard knock on my front door.

Rebecca abruptly sat up in her chair. "Oh, please, not again!"

Standing, I looked over the white kitchen counter to the living room. Roger had his pistol out, and aimed at my front door. There couldn't have been a threat coming our way, though. Elvira remained curled up under the coffee table.

I released my breath. "It's all right," I told Rebecca, as I went to open the door.

On my stoop stood Harry, all six-and-a-half feet of him. His gray eyes seemed darker than usual and his face looked drawn.

I pulled him inside, saying, "Good lord. Who ran you over?"

"I had a bit of excitement today."

"Come in here. Sit. You look like you're ready to fall on your face."

"Right about now I feel that way."

From behind me, I heard Roger grumble, "Shouldn't be doing this alone. I should be out there with you 'stead of lying here, useless."

Harry stepped past me. As he reached the living room, he must have seen Roger's pistol next to the remote on the coffee table. He glanced at the TV. "Thinking of shooting one of those sportscasters, Detective?"

Roger groaned as he leaned over and patted his pistol. "Point me in the direction of your excitement. I'll take it out for you."

Harry dropped onto the dining room chair next to the sofa. "I'm afraid it'd be rather late to help them." He ran a hand over his close-cropped gray hair.

Elvira's head popped up.

Roger slid up on the sofa's cushions. "Late?"

My friend Rebecca might be as prescient as my cat. As soon as she had heard Harry's voice, she lit the flame under the teakettle. Just when he sat, she came from the kitchen carrying a steaming mug. I had no idea what herbs she brewed—whenever I would ask, she'd just tap the side of her nose and smile. Whatever mixture she put in that mug clearly worked. When she handed it to Harry, he sniffed it once, took a sip, and the lines on his face immediately softened. After a second sip, he smiled at her with what could only have been adoration.

She kissed his forehead, then crossed the living room to my wingback chair. "Talk to me, Harry." Her voice had the tone of a wife urging her husband to share the burden of a difficult day. Had she been drinking her own brew?

He sighed, as if a weight had been lifted from his shoulders. He sipped again from his mug, then took a deep breath. "When I left here this morning, I drove to the precinct—"

"I thought you were headed to Attica for a talk with Richard Bennet," I said.

Roger, looking more alert than he'd been all day, answered. "Just can't show up at a prison. Gotta call ahead, make the proper arrangements."

"Besides," Harry said, "first I had to call Howard Kline. Find out does he still represent the guy."

"Even in prison," Roger explained, "Bennet has a right to have his lawyer there if he's gonna be questioned by the police."

Harry nodded. "He certainly had that right."

My head snapped around. In the years I'd been writing—and, yes, listening in on people's conversations wherever I went—I had learned to be aware of verbal nuances. As a result, I didn't miss this one. "He *had* that right? That's what you said? He doesn't have it any longer?"

My stomach sank. With all that had happened to the Bennets, I thought I knew the answer.

Harry nodded. "Yeah, that's what I said. When I called Kline, he told me Richard Bennet had been killed about month after he got sent to Attica. Shanked in the yard, is what Kline said. Even locked up, the man proved to be a bastard. The guard that investigated the killing reported Bennet had managed to offend the top guy in the White Brotherhood."

"Do you believe Kline?" Rebecca asked. Looking at Roger, she said, "Can anything that sleazy lawyer says be believed?"

Harry smiled at her. "I also know Kline, so I called the prison to check on it. He was right. Bennet got killed by some White Brotherhood wannabe."

Roger was very good at his job, attentive, intuitive. Where I had learned to notice inferences, he would be able to spot something omitted—and do it in an instant. As soon as Harry mentioned he'd confirmed Bennet's death, creases as deep as the Grand Canyon formed on my guy's forehead... Well, maybe not that deep, but they sure seemed close.

"Okay," he said, "It took you maybe a half hour to find this out, but you didn't get back here until just now. Something else happened, right?"

The lines returned to Harry face. "Two things. First, when I checked with Border Patrol about your shooting, I found out no surveillance had been ordered on the Bennet House. Seems that Partridge guy set the whole thing up without his bosses knowing."

"Did you find out why he did that?" I asked.

"No one at Border Patrol has any idea. When they found out about it from one of the guys that was on the operation, they went looking for Partridge."

Roger rubbed his wounded shoulder. "What did he tell them?"

"Nothing. They can't find him. No one's seen or heard from him in days." As if he thought this incredible, Harry shook his head.

"You said there were two things," I reminded him.

"Yeah. I said that. While I was on the phone with Kline, Collins came into my office."

Rebecca gasped. "Another murder?"

Harry nodded.

"And it's related?" Roger said. "Who is it this time?"

Harry's eyes shifted in my direction.

Without being told, I knew. Leaning forward, I grabbed my stomach, and moaned, "Oh, no. Please, God, no!"

Why is it that cats don't get credit for empathy and affection? When I moaned, Elvira scampered from under the coffee table, jumped onto my lap and snuggled against my chest.

"It's Ray Scannado," Harry said. "Couple of kids found him in some brambles off Whirlpool Street, not far from the Bennet House. I had Collins drive me to the scene. Weeds overgrown down into a ditch, good place to dump a body. Mightn't have been found for weeks if those kids cutting school hadn't gone down there to fool around. Crime Scene told me, from the way the victim's clothes were torn and pebbles they found in the abrasions on his face, it looks like he got dragged there. Cause of death, throat slashed. Like the other two. But this one looked like he'd been tortured first—Crime Scene said they saw what they thought were knife cuts on his arms and legs."

"I should've seen this coming," Roger muttered.

Harry's eyes narrowed into a question. "How so?"

"Scannado came here this morning." With that, Roger related in detail the excitement we'd had. When he finished, he reached across his body and took my hand. "I'm betting Emlyn's been right from the get-go. This is about that damn land grant. Anyone going near it—anyone that even knows about it—is getting taken out."

"Afraid so, Detective. And it's all tied into that damn house."

"The Tuscarora's Curse," Rebecca muttered.

"There's no such thing as a curse," Harry insisted. "Just people acting like…" Again he shook his head. "…animals."

Unwilling to give up the idea of an ancient curse, Rebecca said "But Roger got shot in that house."

"He got shot because there's something in that house our killer wants, and he won't let anyone go near the place till he finds it. In fact, Partridge being MIA, I'm thinking he concocted his operation so he could get into the house and search for it." Harry looked at Roger. "I'm also thinking it was Partridge that shot you, because you might've caught him tearing the place apart. Sure bet, he's also the one that shot up your house, Emlyn. I've got ballistics checking the slugs from your wall against what Border Patrol has on file for him."

Surprised by this idea, I said, "Then it's Partridge who killed everyone?"

"Can't be," Roger said. "It's him, he would've shot the others 'stead of cutting their throats. In fact, that would explain the different MOs."

Nodding, Harry added, "If Partridge is the cutter, we probably wouldn't have two MOs. Roger having worked with him, when he got to the house he could've gotten close enough for Partridge to also cut *him*."

I held my head to keep it from exploding. "So there *are* two killers on the loose?"

"Looks that way," Harry said. "Though at this point, Partridge would only be guilty of attempted murder."

I leaned back in my chair. "Whoever the killer is, I still think that roach, Howard Kline, is at the bottom of it."

While I had no idea what the others thought about that, I focused on whether I could find a *Roach Motel* big enough to snare a lawyer.

After a minute or two, Rebecca said, "There's one thing I don't understand."

"Just one thing?" Roger said.

She shot him a look. "If this is happening because of that piece of paper and the paper's in the Bennet House, why'd someone kill Mrs. Scannado?"

Harry brushed a hand down his cheek. "I'm thinking the perp scavenged the house the same way our guys did—yeah, and like Partridge was doing. If we didn't find anything, it's a sure bet neither Partridge nor the cutter did. So the killer's got to be figuring someone else has it. Mrs. Scannado working at Kline's office, the killer would've thought she got her hands on it for the Iroquois."

"Maybe he got it when he killed Mrs. Scannado," Rebecca said.

"No. Doesn't add. That damn paper's gotta still be out there, otherwise why kill her son?"

Searching for another piece of the puzzle, I asked, "Is it possible Ray knew where it is?"

"Dammit, what's wrong with me?" Roger groaned. "I *thought* Scannado held something back. If I'd been thinking straight, I would've stopped him before he ran off. Did that, he'd be alive and maybe telling us something that'd get us closer to who's doing this."

I squeezed his hand. "You did all you could."

"Damn straight," Harry said. "Condition you're in, you did right by making sure these ladies were safe and stayed that way."

"I've gotta do more than that. Lying here doing nothing's gonna drive me crazy." He glanced at his pistol on the coffee table. "Keep going like this, I might pick up that gun and shoot the damn television."

His voice stern, Harry said, "Your job right now is to get healed, Detective. I'll take care of running down clues—me and the squad will. I want *you* to make sure Emlyn and Becca stay put. This killer's not fooling around. If Scannado thought Emlyn could have that grant, it's a sure bet the same idea's crossed the killer's mind."

Another of my writer friends, a man I'd known and written with for years, dead. A man whom, if he weren't married and I didn't have Roger, I would have chased to the North Pole and beyond. And Ray's mother had been murdered, as had Daniel and his uncle, Richard Bennet. Whoever was doing this had killed four times—I had no doubt Richard Bennet had also been one of the killer's victims. The more I thought about it, the more certain I became that the killer had to be a remaining member of my writers' group. Mark Maitland, Dana Smart, Eli Nash, Samantha Wold. I should have been frightened he—or she—would come with a knife for me next. I should have been frightened and stunned by the bodies I had seen. What had I said about anger blanketing my fear? That anger was back.

Staring at Harry, I said, "*I* don't intend to do nothing!"

"Really?" He took handcuffs from his jacket pocket. "In that case, I'm arresting you for the murder of Daniel Bennet."

Elvira twisted her head to look at me. Her expression might have said, *I knew you'd get caught one day.*

"Hey, you know I didn't kill him!"

"Doesn't matter. I can hold you for forty-eight hours." He stood up. "Emlyn Goode, you have a right to remain silent. If you give up that right—"

I growled.

"Snarling at a police officer. That's gotta be at least a misdemeanor. What do you think, Detective?"

"Sounds about right."

Gnashing my teeth, I glared at Roger. "Some boy-friend."

Harry reached for my arm. "You have a right to an attorney—should I phone Howard Kline to represent you?"

I held up my hand. "Okay, okay. You've made your point. I'll stay in my house."

"That's better. Detective Frey, you'll call me if Emlyn breaks her word."

With a grin, Roger said, "You can count on that, Chief."

"While I'm a prisoner in my own house," I said to Harry, "what are you going to do to stop this insanity?"

"Well, since you're so sure all of this circles around Howard Kline, I think I'll have a chat with ADA Petit, see if I can get a search warrant for Kline & Associates. Becca, how about you walk me out to my car?"

As he opened my front door for Rebecca, Harry turned back to look at me. His brow cocked, he seemed to be wondering what trouble I might cause without leaving home.

Chapter Twenty-One

Consulting Sarah

I stood at the storm door, watching Rebecca and Harry walk down the path to my driveway. I could tell they were deep in conversation, because he, eight inches taller than Rebecca's five-foot-ten, leaned down as they spoke. When they got to his Buick Regal, he put something in her hand.

They're plotting a means of keeping me locked in my house, I thought—a reasonable supposition, since my friend must have believed I would run off searching for answers as soon as Harry left. When I did, she would have been certain I'd again drag her into danger. Rebecca knew me too well.

Harry stood at the driver's door, watching while Rebecca walked back to my house with what he'd given her clutched in her fist.

"No lingering kiss goodbye?" I said when she squeezed past me.

She responded with a grin and continued to the living room.

I remained at the door until Harry backed his car from my driveway and disappeared around the curve in River Road. Then I opened the hall closet and took out my red wool poncho. At the entry to the living room, I said to Roger, "Rebecca will get you anything you want. I'll be back before your bandages need changing again."

"Where do you think you're going?" he asked.

"No judge is going to give Harry a subpoena to search Kline's office. I'm not with the police—I don't need one."

I expected Roger would object in his strongest voice. He didn't. Quietly, he said, "Rebecca, would you get me my cell phone, please?"

"Going to call Harry, have him come back and arrest me?" Snickering, I reached for my purse. I'd be gone long before Harry could get back to my house. Even if he got here just after I left, with four routes I could take to the city of Niagara Falls, he'd never find me.

"Nope. Gonna call Janet Fargo. Have her come over and look after me."

I dropped my free hand on my hip. "Oh? When you were at the hospital she gave you her number?" I knew she hadn't. I'd pulled everything of Roger's together when we left Memorial.

Rebecca's grin widened. Opening her hand, she showed me a page torn from a notebook. "Harry gave me her number. He said I should give it to Roger when you tried to go out."

Damn! I'd been outsmarted by a detective chief who also knew me too well. Harry Woodward had correctly calculated that my jealous streak would lock me down better than any ball and chain.

I dropped into my overstuffed chair.

"Stick your lip back in," Rebecca said. "Sulking isn't becoming for a grown woman."

I stuck out my tongue at her.

She rolled her eyes. "Roger, you really wanna marry this infant? There are laws about adult men fooling around with children."

He opened his mouth.

"Don't say it!" I snarled. "Don't even think it, or I'll—"

"Yeah, yeah. I know." He laughed. "You know a spell that'll turn me into something unmentionable."

"Grrr." What use was being a witch if I couldn't frighten anyone?

Elvira poked her nose out from under the coffee table. She glared at me, as if to say, *Get over yourself. There's work to do!*

"What work?" I told the cat. "I'm stuck in here."

"Thanks a whole heap," Roger said. "I didn't realize spending time with me is being stuck."

Oops. Right there was a problem with my snits. Words got out of my mouth before they were proofread by my brain.

My face grew so warm my forehead must have become as red as my hair. Looking at the bare branches of the beech tree beyond the French door, looking at clouds sailing across the late afternoon sky, looking at anything but Roger's face, I *phumphered*, "I… uh… That's not… I didn't mean…"

When I at last looked at him, I saw his wide, toothsome grin. *God, what's wrong with me? I can't tell anymore when I'm being played with. Probably a side-effect of that out-of-body spell I can't control.* I vowed I would find a spell that could remedy the problem, after which I'd never again attempt a flight to the past.

Roger cleared his throat. "I've got an idea—that is, if you really feel like you've gotta do something."

"Yeah, I have one, too," I said. "I can get in my car, drive to Howard Kline's office and beat him silly until I find out what he knows."

His hand near his ear, Roger mimed talking into a phone. "Hello, Janet?"

I grumbled.

"Actually," he said. "I've thought of something you can do right here. How about if you look in that old book of yours, see if you get any ideas?"

Elvira's head popped up. Rebecca did a double-take. I glared at him. Was he putting me on?

Suspicious, I said, "You don't believe in Sarah's craft."

He groaned as he slid his legs to the floor. "I don't, but you guys do. I wouldn't mind a chance to figure out why."

I tilted my head. "In other words, you're bored and you want us to amuse you."

He shrugged. "Sure. Why not?"

Annoyed, I rose to stomp from the room.

Rebecca pulled me back. "Doesn't matter why he suggested it. Looking in Sarah Goode's book is a good idea."

Elvira, her eyes alert, nodded.

"See?" Roger said. "Even your cat agrees. So…"

Sighing, outnumbered, I went to my desk and took Sarah's *Book of Shadows* from the top drawer. As I brought the book and my magnifying glass to the sofa, I thought, *Maybe this is fate telling me something Sarah wrote will point to the monster.*

Roger leaned in the corner of my sofa nearest the French door. Rebecca slid to the sofa's corner next to my bookcases. I settled between them gently, so as not to jar Roger's wounded shoulder or leg. Even so, he winced when I sat.

Caring as I did for this man, I suffered when he hurt. "Let me get your pain meds," I told him.

His shoulders hunched, he bit the side of his lip and shook his head.

"Roger, it'll take the edge off your pain."

He gave me a sideways glare.

Just as he had learned to read Elvira's expressions, in the time we'd been a couple, I had learned to read his. The look he gave me said, *Pain meds? Do you think I'm a wuss?*

Men and their machismo!

After a minute, his face relaxed and he pointed to the book. "You gonna show me how you do it, or what?"

I looked at Rebecca.

She shrugged. "He's as stubborn as someone else I know," she said, and opened the calfskin cover.

On the first pages were entries Sarah had made in early 1691. In these she spoke of the wastefulness of her husband, William. Useless, she called him, spending hours in the tavern Bridget Bishop operated in her house. In March she wrote:

> *What more than shuffleboard* (she wrote this as shovel-board) *plays he with such a wench at unseasonable times of night when Master Howard, her husband, has travelled from this Salem Town?*

Several pages later she wrote of her growing affection for Minister George Burrows.

> *Kind is he, bringing in his smile and gentle touch compassion for one such as I, upon whom has been visited base poverty. A poverty, indeed, of the pittance left me by my father, then squandered by Daniel Poole whom I wed in haste on my mother's insistence and who bequeathed me naught but debt when he died. Now am I wed to William, who, complaining of this debt, increases my burden with his gaming. Yet more, now do I wear a poverty of spirit draped like a mean mantle across my shoulders, placed there by the pitying glances when, head low, I walk in this Salem Town. In dear George's eyes alone do I spy an image of what I might be.*

An entry I had read when my mother first gave this ancient book to me told how Sarah's love for George

Burrows came to nothing. At the height of the witch scare, accused by a few girls of stealing their affection, he fled from Salem.

"Nothing helpful here," I said as Rebecca and I continued to scan down the pages.

"I guess your book won't work if someone that doesn't believe is watching," Roger remarked.

I raised my elbow to jab him in the ribs. Fortunately, my brain sent a timely memo that reminded me of his wounds.

"Sometimes we've had to go through Sarah's book for an hour or two before we found an idea," Rebecca said. "This takes patience."

Clearly bored, Roger yawned. "Patience, huh? How does Emlyn do it, then?"

At that moment, I so wanted to let my elbow teach him what I knew about patience. I might have done it, if Rebecca hadn't knocked her shoulder against mine and said, "Read!"

Grumbling, I returned my attention to the book. Over the next hour or so, we turned page after page. Now and then we noticed an herbal remedy and stopped to discuss it. I didn't dare look at Roger while Rebecca explained the benefits and dangers of the mixtures my ancient relative described. Even a glance at him would have been an invitation for a remark. Knowing the nature of a remark he might make, I could have forgotten that, like a doctor, a Wiccan's cardinal rule is to do no harm.

As the autumn sun began to set, an entry made on February 20, 1692 caught my eye.

"Look at this!" I pushed the book onto Rebecca's lap, and handed her the magnifying glass.

Excited, I had forgotten my concern about the manner in which my guy might respond. I held my breath and glanced at him. His head was against the cushion. His eyes closed, he softly snored.

"What do you think?" I whispered to Rebecca.

Not at all worried about waking Roger, she read this aloud:

> *"Strange is now the spirit of this Salem Town. Whispers do I hear yet cannot determine the words. Fear has become a neighbor. Reverend Parris preaches of Satan hiding among the branches of the orchard where in autumn Bridget Bishops' apples will ripen. It is not Satan, I think, that covets this grove, but another, more evil, who would possess it. No friend to Goody Bishop am I, yet I must find the truth, for I fear this human devil desires more than her apple orchard.*
>
> *"That I might know of this, last night beneath the moon, into boiling water from the spring I mixed shredded bay leaves, mugwort and cinquefoil. As the steam rose, I breathed in the vapors. Then while I slept did I dream, yet the dream provided no answer. I saw only Bridget Bishop's home, her tavern, burnt, the ashes piled high on the ground. An old man, a stranger to this town, his back bent and clad in rags such as those I now wear, stopped and pointed at the ashes, then walked on.*
>
> *"I do not yet know the meaning of this omen. In one week when the moon is full, will I again brew my herbs. At that time I might see more clearly."*

Finished reading, Rebecca turned a page, then another. "Sarah didn't tell us anything. After this, she just talks about being arrested."

I took the book and scanned down a number of pages. Then I turned back to what my ancient relative wrote on February 20. Closing the cover, I said, "She didn't get a chance to do her divination spell. Betty Parris and Abigail Williams went crazy five days after she made this entry."

Nothing I had read in Sarah's book pointed me in the direction of who killed Daniel, Ray and Mrs. Scannado. Still, it struck me I might have gotten a glimpse of another crime—a series of murders that took place more than 325 years ago. Entries Sarah had written and research I'd done on the Salem witch trials—in which I now saw innuendos in the way the prosecution had been conducted and more innuendos in the identities of those people prosecuted—hinted that something lay beneath the accusations. The entry I'd just read gave me a clue as to the motive. I sat back and closed my eyes. In my mind, I built an imaginary murder board. Sarah and Bridget Bishop were on top. Below them I placed a man named Reverend Nicholas Noyes. Noyes had sat day and night in Sarah's cell, trying to force her to confess to practicing witchcraft. Did he have a hidden agenda in doing this? Next to Noyes I placed William Goode. Had Sarah told her husband she suspected somebody wanted to steal Bridget Bishop's orchard? Below them were Magistrates Corwin and Hathorne, who presided over Sarah's farce of a trial. In so quickly convicting her, had they acted in major part on a recommendation from Noyes? I also mentally placed Reverend Parris and his daughter, Betty on the chart. At the bottom I put the apple orchard, prime land that might have meant instant wealth to someone who grabbed it. Had an unknown person intended to take what Bridget Bishop refused to sell and arranged for the trials and hangings as a means of stealing her land? Like in Agatha Christie's *The ABC Murders*, had that person arranged for the killing of twenty or so people to mask the killing of the one person the killer intended to murder?

After a few minutes spent mentally examining the imaginary lines I drew between these people and Bishop's orchard, I opened my eyes and sat forward. "Is it possible?"

"Is what possible?" Roger said.

Startled by the baritone voice of the guy I thought to be soundly sleeping, I did a double-take.

Rebecca shrugged. "Your girlfriend was dreaming."

I glanced at the railroad clock on the wall near my bookcases. The clock showed it was a half-hour later than when I'd closed my eyes. Exhausted from the strain of the past few days, I had fallen asleep. Still, my mind must have been awake. The dream of a murder board actually pointed me in the right direction.

"Listen," I said. "I've got to tell you what I thought of."

"Uh-huh." Roger rolled his eyes. "You were thinking while you slept?"

Alert, Rebecca leaned over me to look at him. "She was, Roger. You have to listen to her. This is the way it works sometimes. We were reading about how Sarah Goode planned to find out what was going on in Salem."

He didn't look convinced. "That old woman used a spell to reach through time and tap Emlyn's shoulder?"

I smacked his wrist. "Without any wiseass remarks, will you just hear what I've realized?"

He raised his hand in mock surrender. "Okay, talk."

It took but a few minutes to describe the murder board in my dream.

"That's just great," Roger said when I finished. "You've solved a three hundred year-old murder that everyone knows *wasn't* a murder."

"No," I said, bending over to scoop Elvira from under the coffee table. "What I dreamed told me something about our case."

"*Our* case? *You* don't have a case. Me and Harry do, and you're staying out of it."

"Hey, didn't you tell me to find something in Sarah's book?" I looked at Rebecca. "You heard him say that, didn't you?"

She nodded. "Yep, I heard him."

"So there, wise guy." This time I did poke him in the ribs.

"Ouch!"

The cat twisted her neck, and stared at Roger. This might have been her way of saying, *You deserved that. Now ask Emlyn what the dream told her. Go ahead, ask her!*

I didn't wait for the question. "What I dreamed told me Harry's looking in the wrong direction. The answer's not in Kline's office. If he ever had a copy of that land grant, knowing people were killed because of it, he's destroyed it by now. Plus, that contract I saw? It might be for the development of condos at Crystal Beach, but the only names on it were corporations, and they're probably all shell companies."

A light seemed to flash in Roger's eyes. He had seen me do this enough times to recognize I might be onto something. "What should Harry be doing?" he asked.

"He's got to talk to the four people in my writers' group who are still alive. One of them will know who's at the bottom of this well."

While I spoke, I couldn't shake the feeling that my dream hid the final clue. I didn't flail wildly to grab for it. *One of Rebecca's brews should help me remember.*

Chapter Twenty-Two

What I Missed

For the next fifteen minutes, I explained to Roger the lines leading from Sarah's suspicion that Hathorne, Corwin, Noyes or Parris might have created the witch scare in order to steal Bridget Bishop's land to my conclusion that one of the four remaining writers in my group had to be the killer. Seeing in his eyes a blankness that told me he couldn't read my oral roadmap, I grabbed a yellow pad and some pens from my desk. Sitting again next to him, I drew the murder board I'd constructed in my dream. In blue ink, I drew lines connecting the events from Sarah's vision through her arrest and trial. In red, I wrote the questions she had asked. After inspecting what I'd drawn, I handed the pad to him.

"Do you see what I mean?"

Elvira nodded.

Roger shook his head.

I took back the pad. In black ink, I wrote the name of each one of my writer friends under those of Hathorne, Corwin, Noyes and Parris. "Now, do you see?"

"I *do*." Rebecca pointed to the pad. "I see the connection."

Roger stared at the pad with narrowed eyes. Again shaking his head, he muttered, "I don't get it."

Elvira squiggled from my arms. Wiggling her large derriere, she started for the kitchen. As she reached the hall she stopped, glanced back and snorted in a way that seemed to say, *Men are* so *dense!*

"All right." I sighed. "I'll show you again."

"No, don't bother," Roger said. "Just give me my phone."

The cellphone in his hand, he punched in seven numbers. A moment later, he said, "Yeah, Chief, it's me. Listen, Emlyn says forget Kline. You won't get anything from him." Roger glanced at me and smiled. "Yeah, that's what she said would happen."

"What did I say?"

"The chief told me Judge Aldernado wouldn't give him a subpoena for Kline's files." Again, into the phone, Roger said, "Emlyn says you've gotta question Smart, Wold, Maitland and Nash again. She's more sure than ever it's one of them calling the shots." He listened for a minute, then said, "I've got no idea what's making her so sure. She and Rebecca were reading in that old book of hers, and... Yeah, I'd do it if I could. We've seen her hunches be right more than not."

When Roger placed his phone on the coffee table, I said, "He's going to talk to them?"

"He is," he replied. "Gonna try to get 'em all into the station tonight."

"So what do we do now?" Rebecca asked.

Roger picked up the television remote. "We wait."

He clicked through the channels until he found Joel McRae as *The Virginian* riding into Medicine Bow. The bit of romance in the movie grabbed Rebecca's attention.

I'm far from an expert on waiting. One time in high school, Freddy Silbert and I were told to sit outside Principal Magrath's office. The principal said that when he returned from lunch, he'd decide on our punishment for substituting stag-film slides for the ones on the Civil War our history teacher planned to show. The principal didn't buy into our argument that the class had more interest in the subject of sex education. After ten minutes squirming on those hard wooden chairs, Freddy and I decided to perform a service for the school. As soon as the secretary went to the ladies room, we reorganized all of her files. Needless to say, my mother was less than thrilled when she received another phone call from Principal Magrath.

Since I found waiting no easier now than it had been in high school, I picked up Sarah's book, then dragged Rebecca away from *The Virginian* and into the kitchen. While I pulled the ingredients for shrimp fettuccine Alfredo—one of Roger's favorite meals—from the fridge, I told her, "There's something in what Sarah wrote that would drag whoever's doing this out of the shadows."

"What?" Rebecca asked.

She must have stared intently at my back, because I felt my skin tingle.

"That's the problem. I've replayed in my mind what we read, but I can't..." I groaned and turned from the stove. "Maybe if you read that February 20 entry again, you'll see what I'm missing."

It took her a few minutes to find the page and minutes more to read and reread what Sarah wrote about an apple orchard, a bent old man and bay leaves, mugwort, and cinquefoil producing a divination vapor. While she read, sometimes silently, sometimes aloud, I put water for the pasta up to boil and started working on the sauce. I mixed a roux of flour and bacon fat (Harriet Sovronsky had taught me this trick—bacon fat adds more flavor than butter), then whisked in half and half and parmesan cheese ("be careful not to overdo the cheese," Harriet had warned). Finally I stirred in the butter in which I'd sautéed the seasoned shrimp.

When I spooned the sauce over the pasta, a white head popped up from her food bowl. Tilting her head, the cat stared at me as if to say, *Hey! How about some of that for me? And don't forget to give me shrimp—lots of it!*

I stooped and spooned some into her bowl. When I stood, she looked up at me and ran her tongue across her lips. Now it was as if she said, *That's all you're gonna give me? I'm a growing cat.*

"You're a cat that's about to be put on a diet," I told her.

Just then, the two-legged creature in my house called from the living room, "Dinner ready? I'm coming." This was followed by the sound of the wheelchair rolling on the wood hall floor. I found it interesting that Roger could move without grunting and groaning when his belly sensed sustenance.

I pulled a seat away from the round white dinette table. Wheeling his chair with just his uninjured arm, it took Roger a few minutes to reach the kitchen door.

Rebecca saw him struggle to push down on one wheel then reach across his body to push the other. Stepping into the hall, she said, "Let me help you."

Through a clenched jaw, he responded, "Won't be an invalid. I've gotta do this myself."

Strong, independent, how could I even think of another man when I had this guy in my life? I gulped. This thought recalled Roger's desire that we marry. After my unfortunate marriage to a man who'd had trouble keeping his fly zipped, it frightened me that I considered marrying a second time. I mean, Roger was nothing like my ex. Still…

"Don't be silly," I said as I rushed to the kitchen door. "I'm here for you."

"Always?"

I bent and kissed his forehead.

At last pushed up to the table, he glanced at the calfskin-covered book Rebecca had moved next to my dish. With a grin, he asked, "What trouble are you two plotting to cause this time?"

I opened the book and turned the pages. When I found the right one, I placed my finger on the paragraph Rebecca and I had read. "There's something here I'm not seeing, and I can't shake the feeling it's important."

"I didn't see anything that'd help," Rebecca said.

I handed her the book. "Read it one more time. I know it's there—it's got to be."

Roger reached over and closed the book. "Do you two really think you can solve three murders with anything you find in this? Crimes are solved by police work—by cops out in the street, asking questions." Like a traffic cop, he raised his hand to stop me before I could interrupt. "Yes, your hunches have helped—you might have narrowed this down to four suspects. But nothing in that book is gonna tell us which one it is. And nothing in what you read is gonna get that one to confess."

I grumbled. Though I didn't like it, Roger was right. I knew what the killings were about—my flights to Crystal Beach in the past, what I'd seen on the page the roustabout showed his girl, the copy of a land grant Daniel had shown me at the writers' group meeting, and the contract in Howard Kline's file. All of this unvaryingly pointed to a threat to the company building the condos at Crystal Beach, a threat that could only be eliminated by destroying the original and every copy of the land grant. And, maybe, anyone who knew of its existence. I knew why it had to be one of the four others left in my group—only one of them could have seen what Daniel showed me, then panicked over it. I had no idea, though, how I might figure out which of the four it was.

While I chewed on my flights to the past, something crawled from behind the vines in my subconscious mind and slithered closer to awareness. I had just thrown out a grappling hook to try and reel it in when Elvira's head came up from her bowl. A whole shrimp dangling from her mouth, she stared in the direction of my front door. Five seconds later, I heard a knock. After another knock, Harry called from the stoop, "No need to grab your pistol, Detective. It's just me."

Rebecca jumped from her chair. "I'll get it!"

The front door opened; the front door closed. Two minutes passed. Roger looked at me.

"She's happy to see him," I said.

"Happy as you'd be if we were together all the time?"

I didn't intend to nod. I surely didn't. It… just happened.

"And maybe even get married?" he added.

"I-I-I…"

I got no more out, because just then Harry led Rebecca into the kitchen. Looking at Roger, he said, "What canary did you swallow, Detective?"

My cheeks burning, I looked away.

Elvira's head snapped around. Her eyes wide open, she licked her lips, then mewed as if to say, *Canary? I didn't know we have one of those.*

At the same time, Rebecca said, "Oh?"

"Oh what?" Harry looked confused.

She kissed his cheek. "I'll tell you later."

He looked from her to Roger, then at my stove. "Got any more of that food? I'm half-starved."

While I heated a portion of the Alfredo sauce and shrimp, I said, "Were you able to talk to the members of my group?"

He spread a napkin across his lap. "I got three of 'em in. The Smart woman wasn't home when my guys got to her house. He husband said he didn't know where she went. We'll look for her again tomorrow."

Dana couldn't be found? Interesting. I recalled that she had shown up at the hospital. I wondered now, as I had then, whether she'd gone to Roger's room to learn if the police had found any evidence linking her to Daniel's murder. Thinking of Mark, who had been with her, I asked Harry, "What about the others?"

"The three we talked to, their alibis held. At the time Daniel Bennet was murdered, Nash was with his sister. Wold and Maitland were out searching for our victim, and both were in crowded places where people they knew saw them."

"That just leaves Dana," I said, then shook my head. "It can't be her. Daniel wasn't very tall or muscular, but she's shorter than he was and too slight to have overpowered him so she could cut his throat." That would mean it had been Mark who wanted to learn if he'd been linked to the killing.

Rebecca pulled my mind back to Dana. Twirling pasta around her fork, she suggested, "Maybe it *could* be Dana Smart. She could've used a Taser. You know, stopped him with that, then killed him while he was on the floor."

"Can't be," Harry said. "New York State treats Tasers like guns. If she has one, she'd have to have a license for it, which she doesn't. The others don't, either. We thought of that, and checked."

Roger poked me. "That's what I said about police work. And that's why you have to leave all the legwork to us."

I looked at him. "Someone bent on killing doesn't bother about licensing laws. She could've gotten a Taser on the black market."

He shook his head and grunted.

"Forget about Tasers," Harry said. "The ME didn't find any marks on the bodies that would indicate one had been used. If you're right about it, the answers are with these four people. What about them—their backgrounds, families, friends? Things like that."

This wasn't the first time I had been asked about this, and it still bothered me not to have an answer. I sighed. "All these years working with my friends in Writer's Refuge, and I know so little of them. I only just found out that Ray..." I choked back a tear for another lost friend. "Ray Scannado was an Iroquois." I closed Sarah's book and pushed my chair back from the table. "Well, I'm going to fix that!"

Roger grabbed my wrist. "Nuh-uh. You're not. One of those four might be a killer, and I don't need you dead just when you agreed to marry me."

Rebecca, nearly choking on a bite of linguini, held her napkin to her mouth. "You did? And you didn't tell me?"

"I-I didn't. I mean, I did, but I-I—" I slumped in my chair, burying my face in my hands.

"You did," Roger said. "I asked and you nodded. I saw you."

In my mind, I saw the gold flakes in his hazel eyes glitter and his grin grow so broad that the cleft in his chin almost disappeared.

Harry reached across the table. "Congratulations, Detective. "It's about time someone threw a rope around this heifer."

Their case on hold until the next morning, these two cops could relax and feel free to tease. I was the *teasee*.

"I-I…" I groaned.

"Too late to change your mind, Emlyn," Harry said. "I think a lawyer would call this a verbal contract."

"That's right." Roger let out his resonant laugh. "Don't go through with it, I can sue you."

I glared at him.

My cat nodded. A bit too vigorously, I thought.

"Yeah," Rebecca said with a giggle. "Roger, you might wanna talk to Howard Kline about this verbal contract."

The mention of Kline brought the land grant back to my mind, which in turn brought back images of Daniel, Ray and Ray's mother. The mirth of the moment vanished behind a dark cloud. I sat up straight and ran my wrist across my eyes.

"Save this for later," I said. "I won't think of anything else until whoever killed my friends is caught."

Rebecca shot me a look of annoyance. "What's wrong with you? The day you get engaged should be exciting. Can't you let go for a minute?"

"I can't even think about... you know..." I glanced at Roger.

Bless my hero. He let me off the hook. Sort of. "Well, all right then," he said. "When I solve this case, you'll be my reward."

Ignoring my snort, Harry said, "If that's what we've gotta do to finally get you two married, let's do it. You've been lying around here all day, Detective. Got any ideas?"

His smile gone, Roger thought for a second, then said, "I do have one. Been wondering about this. How firm is Daniel Bennet's time of death?"

Harry pulled a notebook from his jacket pocket, and flipped a few pages. "The ME puts it at six o'clock or so, but says it could've been earlier by as much as—" He ran a finger down the page. "—three or four hours. Blood at the scene was dried, so there's no way Doctor Jack can get closer."

Doctor Jack Markowitz was the Niagara County Medical Examiner.

"That's what I thought." Roger nodded. "So—"

"That means no one has an alibi for the time Daniel was killed..." I stopped, and stared down at my plate.

"You still here?" Roger touched my hand. "Earth to Emlyn."

I blinked several times. "Something just occurred to me. If Daniel was dead three or four hours—"

"Yeah?"

"Who called me? Who called *any* of us in the group?" If Daniel hadn't called me—he'd been dead by the time I received that call—he hadn't died because I'd failed him. The guilt I felt for not getting to my friend in time began to release its grip. As it faded, I recalled something. At Dana's house, Daniel had told me he knew where the original land grant was hidden, but whoever called me said something about *thinking* he knew the hiding place. If I had remembered that at the time, I would've known it couldn't have been Daniel who called me. Exasperated, I smacked my forehead and said, "I knew I didn't recognize the voice on the phone!"

"But it was a male voice?" Roger asked.

"I thought so."

"Then it could've been Maitland or Nash." Harry took a deep breath and sat back. "Good. We're narrowing down the list of suspects."

Roger shook his head. "Or it could've been Partridge."

"Or Dana or Samantha disguising their voices." I closed my eyes and sighed.

Harry seemed to consider all of this for a minute, then the brief expression of hope left his face. "That means we're back at the beginning."

Rebecca stroked his cheek. "I'm sorry. All that work you've been doing is nothing but ashes."

Perhaps the harvest moon shining through my kitchen window caused another puzzle piece to slide into place. I have no other explanation for why, after all this time, I saw it. My eyes wide, my head snapped around. "What did you say?"

Rebecca stared hard at me. "I said Harry's work would be ashes. I don't… Hey, wait a minute. You thought of something?"

With the smallest of smiles, I nodded. "I know where Daniel hid the land grant… At least, I think I do. The answer's been there all along—in what old Sarah wrote about her vision of an old man looking at the ashes of Bridget Bishop's house. More important, it was in something Daniel said to me at the writers' group meeting."

With her brow knitted, Rebecca asked," What'd he tell you? You told me every little detail about that meeting, but I don't—"

"We were in Dana's yard, looking across the lake at Crystal Beach. Just before he spotted someone listening to us and hid the copy of the land grant, he said it would be in ashes."

The guys leaned toward me. "Where is it?" they said at the same time.

Entirely focused on the image in my mind, I hardly heard them. "I saw it when we entered the house. Why didn't it register?" I muttered. "If it had, Ray and his mother wouldn't have been killed."

From the hole into which I'd fallen, I heard Rebecca say, "You always do this—talking to yourself." She raised her fist. "Oh, I'm gonna beat you till you burst! Where is it?"

Harry grabbed her hand and eased her back onto her chair. Quietly he asked, "Where is it, Emlyn?"

I closed my eyes and pictured the living room of the Bennet House. Moth-eaten curtains half-fallen from the windows, yellow stained sheets on the chairs and tables, a chipped brick fireplace. In the center of the room I saw Daniel, transparent, streaks of red running down his neck. He pointed to the mantel...

I pointed my finger in the way, in my imagination, I saw Daniel point. "It's in there," I whispered.

"Somebody hit her!" Rebecca shouted. "Where is it?"

Her voice pricked like a needle in my mind and pulled me back to my kitchen. With a groan, I said, "It's in Carlton Bennet's urn."

Chapter Twenty-Three

A Plan is Born

Harry sat back and ran a hand across his gray military-cut hair. "You're sure that paper is stuck in with old man Bennet's ashes?

Roger took my hand. "After how her hunches have paid off for us in the past? I wouldn't doubt her."

My cat glared at him. Her *meow* could only have meant, *Whaddaya mean, hunch? What Emlyn does is science!*

Sighing, Harry said, "All our guys digging around in there… Never thought to check out that urn." He reached around and took his cellphone from the corduroy jacket he'd hung on the back of his chair. "Better call the precinct, get some officers over to the Bennet House."

As Rebecca carried our dishes to the sink, she asked, "Don't you need a warrant or something to do that?"

"Not in this case." He began to punch numbers into his phone. "The place is an open crime scene."

Before he hit the last number, a thought stuck me. I put my hand over his phone "Don't, Harry. Leave the grant where it is."

"What are you talking about? That paper's the key to these murders. It's evidence."

"It is, but—"

Perfectly in tune with me, Roger finished my sentence. "If our killer finds out we've got it, he'll dive into his rabbit hole and we'll never find out who he is."

Harry glanced down at his phone, then laid it on the table. "You got a better idea?"

As Roger started to speak, I said, "I think *I* might. I'm not sure you're going to like it, though."

Rebecca turned from the sink. Roger and Harry looked at me.

"The way you're smiling worries me," Roger said. "When you look like that, you're about to get in trouble."

"Not if I can help it."

He shook his head. "That's the problem. You can't help it. It's the way you're built."

Have I mentioned that Roger also knew me too well?

"Hold on, Detective. Let her talk," Harry said. "I'm curious about what she has in mind."

Rebecca gripped the sink. Her knuckles white, she said, "Somebody clamp a hand on her mouth. When she gets in trouble, she always drags me into it with her."

"Not this time. If my idea's going to work, I'll have to do it by myself."

"No! Nuh-uh. You're not putting yourself at risk!"

"Slow down, Detective."

"Chief, you can't let her."

His hand raised, Harry said, "I'm not saying we're gonna do anything. I just want to hear what Emlyn's thinking."

I took a deep breath. "We should leave the land grant where it is. Then, one at a time, I'll call the others in my writers' group, tell them I know where it is, and ask them to meet me at the Bennet House. I'll say I need help to dig it out so I can give it to the police. Then, like whoever imitated Daniel did, I'll tell each one he or she is the only one I can trust."

It must have hurt Roger when he jumped from his wheelchair. Balancing himself on one leg, with his left hand on the table, he shouted, "No! Not gonna happen!"

"Why not? I've thought this out," I said, though I'd been putting the idea together while I spoke. "The ones who aren't involved will be curious, and will encourage me to call the police as soon as I take the land grant from the urn."

"Yeah, and the one who's killing people will slit your throat, and walk off laughing with that paper in his hand." With lines of pain around his eyes, Roger eased himself back down in his chair. "Besides, even if that paper was in Carl Bennet's urn, how do you know that thing's still there? The killer could've found it already."

"Either way we'll have an answer."

"How so?" Harry asked.

"These people are writers. That means they're curious about everything—"

Rebecca laughed. "You mean they're nosey like you are."

I stuck out my tongue at her. "I mean, they'll want to see it and find out how I knew where to find it. If one of them already has it, he'll make some excuse for why he can't meet me."

"And if none of them have it?" Harry asked. From the look on his face, he must have been considering my plan. "What if it turns out to be Partridge?"

I hadn't thought of him. Still, as the expression goes, shooting from my hip, I said, "If it's him, he's sure to be lurking around the Bennet House. When I go in, he'll show himself. Then you can nab him."

"What if he kills you first?" Roger turned to his boss. "See? That's what I mean. This is a lousy idea."

His lips pursed and his eyes closed, Harry leaned back in the dinette chair with his hands folded across his stomach. In this position he reminded me of Rex Stout's detective, Nero Wolfe. After a moment, he said, "Actually, Emlyn's idea could work. We'd have to get the house set up with microphones, and have officers planted to rush into the living room the minute Emlyn's threatened… But yeah.

Her plan has some merit." He smiled at me. "I wish you'd been my strategist when I was in Iraq."

Elvira had been under the round dinette table, listening while my plan developed. Now she rubbed against my leg and purred as if to say, *That's my human. I knew I'm supposed to be with you for a reason.*

Rebecca glared at the cat. "Sure, *you* think this is a smart idea. You'll be napping on your chair while Emlyn's getting herself killed."

With a snort, Elvira threw back her head and sauntered to her food bowl.

"Not to worry," Harry said. "We won't let her get hurt." He rose from the table and moved behind Roger's wheelchair. "Me and you, Detective, are going to the living room to work out the surveillance. You ladies stay in here and work out what to tell our suspects."

As the Niagara Falls detective chief rolled the chair though the door, Roger twisted to look up at him. "I don't like this. Too much can go wrong. There's gotta be another way."

"I've got it covered," Harry said. "Listen…" His voice dropped to a whisper.

"You're crazy. You know that, don't you?" Rebecca said as she rubbed the wash cloth so hard on a dinner dish, I though any minute it could cry for mercy. "You're a big coward, have you forgotten that?"

I couldn't disagree with her. I *was* a coward. But once again words had gotten out of my mouth without first passing through my brain. Now that the words were out, I was afraid to take them back. In short, I was afraid to be a target—even though the police would be watching and listening—and I was afraid not to do it. If that isn't crazy, I don't know what is. I could think of only one reason I'd gotten myself into this fix. It had to be the damn spell that kept taking me out of my body.

While I gazed around my cozy—and safe—kitchen, my over-active imagination constructed a scene in which I stood alone in the dark in the Bennet House living room, waiting for the person who had committed the crimes.

I know who it is, who it has to be, but to prove it I have to draw the killer out of the shadows. Shivering in my heavy coat, though the night is far from cold, I furtively glance in the direction of Carlton Bennet's urn. Now I hear whispers from the corners of the room. Could these be voices of ghosts in this cursed haunted house? Minutes pass and the whispers grow more pronounced. Someone touches my ear. Startled, I twist to see who it is. No one's there. When I turn back, a shadow steps from the corner. As it comes toward me, it passes through a ray of moonlight. Dressed in deerskin leggings and moccasins, the figure's hair is cut in a Mohawk. Without knowing why I know, I know this is the Tuscarora brave who cursed this place. Something in his hand glints. A knife. He raises his arm to slash my throat…

I gasped.

Rebecca turned from the sink. "Now what's wrong?"

"I, uh… was thinking…" I again felt my cheeks grow warm.

"Don't do that!" She threw the dish towel at me. "You thinking is what gets *us* into trouble."

"No, listen." I pulled the old book in front of me. "I think I need protection. Help me see whether Sarah wrote about a combination of herbs that'll do that."

My cat looked up from her bowl, shook her head and *meowed*.

"I agree, Elvira," Rebecca said. "If Sarah had figured out a protection spell that worked, she wouldn't have gotten hanged."

Another thing I hadn't thought of. With a sigh, I said, "Then what can I do?"

"Walk into your living room and tell the guys you changed your mind."

Recalling the scene I'd just imagined, I decided I would take my friend's sage advice. But when I tried to get up from the table, it felt as though my pants had been glued to the seat.

Rebecca must have seen my struggle and guessed the cause. Pulling a dinette chair next to mine, she stroked my hand. "I was afraid this would happen."

I looked a question at her.

"Remember what I told you about using that clairvoyance spell, how it could drag you back to the past when someone's gonna die? There's another thing about it."

"What?" From the heaviness of her voice, I wasn't sure I wanted to know.

"Since that spell warned *you* of the death, you're the one that has to make it right."

I gulped.

"Okay, I read something in a book in my shop that might help. Here's what you have to do. After Roger goes to sleep tonight, go outside and burn incense made of frankincense, sandalwood and rosemary. While it burns, concentrate on the place where you'll need to be protected and ask the God and Goddess to watch over you."

I looked at her. "Aren't you going to do the ceremony with me?"

She groaned. "You're kidding, right? Much as I don't want anything to do with this, I have to work the spell with you. If I don't watch what you're doing, you might blow up the neighborhood." She turned away and groaned again.

***

A crisp, clear autumn night. Cloudless. Perfect for reaching out to the Goddess and God. Elvira at our heels,

Rebecca and I carried the low steel-meshed white table from my patio to the far end of my back yard and placed it at edge of the line of trees bordering the Niagara River. Crowded though it was, we set up an altar on this small table. On a purple felt cloth, we placed candles to the left and to the right—yellow to represent the God, white for the Goddess. To the left, in front of the Goddess's candle, we placed a bowl of water, a cup, a crystal and a bell. To the left we placed a bowl of salt, my athame and the incense we would burn in the censer. On a piece of construction paper in the center, I drew a pentacle with the point facing up. If the point faced down it would invite evil—the last thing I would need when I returned to the Bennet House.

The altar now organized, we took a long strand of cord and laid it in a nine-foot diameter around the altar. Nine, the number of the Goddess, whose protection I hoped to invoke. This done, I raised my left hand in the shape of a crescent moon. I held up my right hand with my middle two fingers bent and held down by my thumb and my pointer and pinky straight out. Then, Rebecca, the cat and I in the circle, with my eyes closed I imagined a sphere of safety encasing us.

"Gracious Goddess, queen of the Gods, lamp of the night, mother of woman and man, descend, I pray, and bring your protective power here to our circle." We intoned this in unison. Well, Rebecca and I did. Elvira let out a long *meeeow*—I hoped the Goddess spoke cat.

My friend lit the incense and slowly moved her hands to draw the smoke to us. Leaning close to me, she whispered, "Okay, now's when you tell the Goddess the stupid thing you did—volunteering to get yourself killed."

I grumbled.

"Hey, don't growl at me," Rebecca said. "I'm not the one that got you into this mess."

It looked as if my cat rolled her pink eyes.

Jabbing me with her elbow, Rebecca pointed upward. "Go on. Tell the Goddess what you need."

Elvira yawned, then poked me with her paw and mewed, as if to say, *Tell the Goddess already, will ya? It's late. I need my beauty sleep!*

I sighed, and took a deep breath. "Mighty Goddess, I think I need your help—"

"There's no thinking about it Goddess," Rebecca said. "Emlyn's in trouble again."

"Someone killed my friends, and Harry and Roger—you remember them?—they don't know who did it, so I, uh…"

Rebecca looked up to the starlit sky. "This idiot thinks she's invincible, Goddess, and she's about to get into trouble. Again." Now she turned her eyes to me. "Go ahead. Tell the goddess what you need. Concentrate. Think about where the killer will come after you."

Again closing my eyes, I pictured the living room of the Bennet House, focusing in turn on each detail of the room. Then I fervently prayed, "Please, Goddess, spread your protective arms over that place and keep me safe."

My prayer completed, Rebecca sprinkled salt in the water bowl and poured it around our circle. "Thank you for hearing us, great Goddess," she intoned. "Our ceremony is over."

Feeling protected—more or less—I worked with Rebecca to clear away all remnants of our ritual. I didn't need a nosey neighbor noticing what we'd been doing and telling Gossip-Grace Linden about it.

As I walked back to my house, a dark cloud passed over the moon. From the way my cat twisted to look up at the cloud, I wondered whether this might be an evil omen.

Chapter Twenty-Four

In Need of Protection

I slept fitfully that night, unable to shake the sight of a dark cloud passing in front of the moon. Because the moon is the Goddess's domain, I feared this was an omen that didn't bode well for what lay ahead of me. After turning in bed for what felt like three nights, I rolled onto my side and opened my eyes. The digital display on my clock radio said 5:53. I patted the bed next to me, feeling for Roger. How quickly I had grown accustomed to having him next to me while I slept. How safe I felt in his embrace. Injured now and not able to climb the stairs, he slept on my sofa. I laid awake upstairs in my bed with my fear curled up against my back.

Weary, I climbed from my bed, went to the window and raised the blind. Scratching my arm, I peered out at the black line of trees that stood like soldiers guarding the bank of the Niagara River. Would those soldiers protect me? I threw on my flannel housecoat as if it were a suit of armor. Quietly, I went downstairs.

In my living room, I saw the green and red floral cushions from the back of the sofa piled on the floor, and Elvira cuddled next to Roger where I should have been. Pulling back my hair, I bent, and kissed his forehead.

His lips turned up in a wisp of a smile. "I love you, too," he murmured.

What would I do without this guy? I stroked his cheek, then took Sarah Goode's *Book of Shadows* from my desk draw.

In the kitchen, I put up a pot of coffee and settled at the dinette table. I hoped Sarah's book would provide a clue as to who had killed people in my small city. If it did, I could tell Harry the name, he would nail the perpetrator and I would not have to stand alone in the Bennet House, waiting for the murderer to strike. Of all the dumb ideas I'd had in recent years, this one topped the list!

After about twenty minutes, an entry Sarah made on July 14, 1692 caught my attention.

> *Four months are now passed since two false-swearing children said in the Salem Town Meeting House I had bewitched them. Each day since does Reverend Noyes come to this dark windowless cell in which, like a mad woman, am I confined. Still does he demand that which he did when he sat in judgement of me. Soon to Gallows Hill will I be taken, he tells me. Do I dare to face God's wrath having not confessed my mortal sin? I say to this false saver of souls that which said I to him during my trial at the Meeting House. "How can I confess what I have not done? I am no more a witch than you are a wizard," said I. "Take my life and God will give you blood to drink!"*
>
> *Now near my final day, lacking herbs with which I might escape from this Salem Town that has naught but pointed at me with fingers of fear and hate, I can but ask of God if there be one with a key to this cell that I might fly free.*

Sipping from my white mug, I read the entry three times. At last, like a gear, what Sarah wrote began to mesh with something I had seen or heard.

Holding my mug, I moved from the table to the sink and gazed out the window. "What am I not seeing?" I muttered as I stared across at the almost naked trees on the other side of River Road. From memory, I repeated each word Sarah had written. "Judgement. False-swearing. Confined."

A squirrel scampered across my lawn. A panel truck sputtered down the street, the beginning of the weekday morning traffic. I watched the truck pass my neighbor's driveway. That neighbor, Professor Harvey Nelson, came from his house, leaving for work at Buffalo State University where he taught American History. A friend, Harvey had often helped when I needed historical facts for a story. As he approached his car with his briefcase, he fumbled with his key. He dropped it, bent, and picked it up.

"Oh!" I said. Once again Professor Nelson had helped me find a missing fact.

"What are you shouting about?" Roger called from the living room.

"I've got it!" I said, loud enough to be heard two planets away from Earth. I rushed to the living room, knocking my shin on a stool as I passed the kitchen counter. "I know who did it. Who it has to be." I dropped into my overstuffed wingback chair and rubbed my shin.

Elvira's head came up from between Roger and the back of the sofa. Blinking, she looked at me with an expression that seemed to say, *Keep it down, will ya! Some of us are trying to sleep.*

I threw the *TV Guide* at her but missed.

Can a cat giggle?

Roger sat up, rubbing his eyes. "Who did what?"

"I know who the killer is. It's the only way it could have been done, and he's the only one that could have done it."

"Whoa. Slow down, Tonto," Roger raised his hand. "You're galloping too fast. I just woke up, and you're way ahead of me." He yawned, then stretched. "Okay, now, quietly. Who do you think it is?"

"Eli Nash, of course."

Again he yawned. "Uh-huh. Of course. Just how do you figure that?"

"It's the key. He's the one that had it."

"Um-hmm. The key. What key?"

"To the Bennet House!" I hissed, growing impatient with my guy's cross-examination. "Call Harry and tell him."

He closed his eyes and took a deep breath. "And what would Nash's motive be?"

"Motive?"

"Yeah, you know. The reason he decided to start killing people?"

I didn't need sarcasm at that moment—not when I had just solved a triple murder. Maybe a quadruple murder, if Eli had also been responsible for Richard Bennet's death at Attica. I threw a pillow at Roger.

He easily batted it aside with his left hand. "A snit won't make me forget my question. Tell me what you think is the reason he killed three people."

"Well... It has to have something to do with the Crystal Beach land grant, but I haven't figured how he's involved. Still, I'll bet anything I'm right."

Roger's grin told me I should not have made so ambitious a wager. "I'll take that bet," he said with the deep laugh that sent tingles through me. "And this is my ante: if you lose, you'll marry me."

"And if *you* lose?"

His smile grew so wide it wrinkled his forehead. "In that case, I'll marry you."

The man was playing with me, of course. He wouldn't propose marriage as a bet. Would he? No, I decided, he wouldn't. Well, I could play this game, too. My arms crossed on my chest, I said, "Okay, wise guy, you're on. Now call Harry. Tell him to haul Eli in, and we'll see who's right."

Roger shook his head. "Have you forgotten Partridge in all of this? He also could've opened the house."

I had no need to think about that. "Partridge couldn't have gotten into the Bennet House. No key. And remember, he had his guys watching the house from outside."

Still smiling, Roger said, "*You* need to remember something, Sherlock. The kitchen window was broken. Partridge could've gotten in that way."

What I keep saying about a writer's need to be observant? "*You* need to remember that the glass on the lawn out back means the window got broken from the inside," I said. "If Partridge had broken the window to get in, the glass would have been on the kitchen floor."

His smile fled. He opened his mouth, then closed it.

"And another thing," I said. "What you and Harry were talking about—the killer's *modus operandi*?"

"Yeah, yeah. Partridge wouldn't've used a knife on Bennet and the Scannados."

"Which brings us back to Eli. So, call Harry, get Eli in. Question him until he confesses!"

"The chief's questioned the guy twice now. Call him in again, he'll wanna talk to his lawyer. Harry won't budge him without evidence, and there's none. Can't see any way at this point but to go with your idea of you being bait. Problem is I hate that idea and don't want you anywhere near the guy." He reached out to me.

I left my chair, sat on the carpet next to the sofa and rested my head against him.

Stroking my hair, he said, "If it is Nash, he's not fooling around. Three people are already dead…" I heard a choke in his voice. "Emlyn, I couldn't stand it if he hurt you." He lifted my chin and looked into my eyes. "The chief swore to me he'll have you completely covered or I wouldn't let you…" He let out a deep sigh. "Just promise you'll be careful. Listen to everything you're told to do. Every detail. Please."

I couldn't answer. My mouth was busy kissing him.

***

As I got ready to meet Eli Nash at the Bennet House, I couldn't help but wonder whether learning the craft for which my ancient ancestor had been hanged was the reason things I only thought about had begun to actually happen. Last year, while I struggled to prove my mother hadn't murdered a high school classmate, Rebecca warned me that a witch's stray thoughts could be cast out as spells. Did the same hold true for my writer's imagination? If this were so, one day I might get dropped into a boiling cauldron or maybe shoved in the middle of two warring zombie armies. Or Jack the Ripper might jump out from behind the beech tree in my backyard and, knife blade flashing in the moonlight, cut out my insides and skin me. What brought this to my mind? While breaking into Howard Kline's office a few days earlier, I had imagined myself to be Jamie Bond Super Spy, staring danger in the eyes. As a tech specialist from the Niagara Falls Police Department strung wires from what seemed to be my breastbone to my navel, I felt like a spy being readied for a suicide mission.

This, though, came later in the day. Hours before I got strung like a Christmas tree, Harry and Rebecca knocked on my front door.

"Just a minute," I sang.

"Do I smell coffee?" Harry said when I opened the door.

"You do," I said. "And I can put up some eggs and toast if you're hungry."

Rebecca peered at me. "You sound chipper this morning."

I glanced over my shoulder to where Roger lay, his blanket and sheet pushed against the back of the sofa. Clearly, I had been curled up next to him.

"Oh? He's feeling better this morning?" Rebecca said.

I answered with a smile.

"I'd feel a whole lot better if we came up with another way to snag the killer," Roger called. This was followed by a grunt, an *uff* and the sound of wheels rolling on the wood hall floor.

"We talked about this, Detective." Harry took a sip from the mug of coffee I poured him. "No one's come up with another way to lure the perp out."

I took a carton of eggs from the refrigerator. Holding it against my chest, my voice filled with hope, I said, "Maybe we don't have to lure him out."

When I turned, I saw Harry staring at me.

"I know who the killer is."

"You figured it out?" Rebecca sounded incredulous.

"Well…" My cheeks growing warm, I glanced at Harry. "Actually, Sarah told me."

He rolled his eyes, and said to Roger, "Now we've got a ghost solving crimes?"

Rebecca smacked his arm. "You've been around Emlyn enough to know what she means. Something she read in Sarah Goode's book gave her the idea. Right?"

I nodded. Leaving the eggs on the counter, I picked up the old book, and read them Sarah's July 14, 1692 entry. When I finished, I closed the book, and said, "See? She wrote about a *key*."

"Uh-huh. A key." Harry shook his head.

Frustrated, I snarled at him. "You're not listening! Only one person could have killed Daniel Bennet."

Roger cleared his throat. "You'll wanna hear her out, Chief. What she told me about this—I think she may be right."

Harry gave a sharp nod. "If you think so, Detective. Okay, Emlyn, talk to me."

In five minutes or so I laid it out: the shift in the time of death meant that Eli could have gotten the key, then met Daniel at the house a few hours before we arrived. He could then have gone to his sister's house to wait—had anyone asked Eli's sister what *time* she'd given him the house key? To discount Agent Partridge as Daniels' killer, I explained that I'd seen the shattered window glass on the lawn outside the Bennet House kitchen. This meant no one had broken in. That, in turn, meant whoever got into the house used a key. Since only Eli had a key to the house, it had to have been he who let Daniel in. In fact—though I was guessing about this—it seemed probable that, knowing Eli's sister was the real estate agent for the house, Daniel had phoned Eli and asked him to get the key to let him in so he could take the land grant from his grandfather's urn. That would be when Eli killed Daniel—before Daniel took the grant from the urn. That would be the only explanation for why Ray and Mrs. Scannado were killed.

"Daniel wanted the grant so he could give it to Ray," I said. "Remember, Roger? That's what Ray told us. It's why he took us to Bennet House for the ghost hunt. He planned to meet Daniel there and get the grant."

When I finished my explanation, Harry rubbed his chin. "I see. Uh-huh. Yes, I..." He slipped into silence.

"So, now that we know Eli's killing people, you can arrest him and I won't have to trick him into meeting me at the Bennet House." I grinned with relief.

Harry didn't answer.

"Right?" I said. "You can arrest him?"

"I'm afraid it can't work that way." Harry shook his head. "No. Having the key isn't enough to hold him. Not even enough to call him in for more questioning. See, even though Nash had the house key, there's no evidence he *killed* anyone."

I looked to Roger for help.

He closed his eyes, and sighed. "Isn't there another way, Chief? Maybe get a woman from the squad out there dressed like Emlyn?"

Rebecca pointed at him. "Good idea. You can use a policewoman who's trained to handle a man with a knife."

Again, Harry shook his head. "Somebody clever as Nash seems to have been, he's gotta know we're getting close. He'll be cautious. If he even senses it's not Emlyn in the house, he won't go near the place."

"But he might," I said.

"Yeah, it's possible. But if he does, when he sees it's not you in there, he'll act surprised, and not make his move on the land grant."

I groaned. As I said, this idea was far from the brightest I'd ever had. Now I was stuck with it.

"Not to worry, Emlyn." Harry reached out, and patted my hand. "We're already getting the Bennet House wired, and we'll have officers hidden in the kitchen and on the second floor, ready to move as soon as Nash comes for you. We'll have you covered every which way from Sunday."

This might have made me feel better about being fish bait if I hadn't seen lines of worry ringing Harry's eyes.

So, snared in a trap of my own design, with my cell phone on speaker, I made the call to Eli. Forcing excitement into my voice, I told him, "I know where that land grant is hidden."

"What..." He hesitated. "...land grant? What are you, uh...? What land grant are you talking about?"

I caught my breath. Eli's voice... *He* had called me, pretending to be Daniel. Hearing the slight rasp in his voice—the remnant of his cold—I was certain of it.

Gathering myself, I said, "I don't know what it's for. I just know Daniel thought it was important. Do you know why?"

It took a moment before he responded—it struck me he might have covered his phone with his hand. At last, he said, "I have no idea what you're talking about."

Harry tapped my shoulder, then rotated his finger, cuing me to press Eli.

I started to scratch my arm. I've mentioned that I was a very poor liar. When I tried to tell even a small fib, I would develop a rash. Roger and Rebecca knew this about me and now they looked at each other, trying hard not to giggle.

"How's she gonna pull this off without scarring her whole body with those long nails of hers?" Rebecca whispered.

Harry waved his hand, signaling her to be quiet.

"Gee." I scratched my armpit. "I was sure you'd know. Because you were a school principal, Daniel thought you were the smartest in our group and you'd know what to do about that piece of paper."

"Dan… told you that?" Eli sounded flattered.

"He did. And he made me promise if anything happened to him, I'd get it to you right away."

Again he hesitated. "Your, uh… friend… Roger. He's a detective. If that land grant got Daniel and Ray killed, why don't you give it to him? You don't want to also be killed because you *have* it."

Eli had just made his first mistake. A big one. How could he know that Ray had been killed? The police hadn't released that. Also, the way he suggested possessing the grant would put me in danger sounded like a veiled threat.

A wisp of a smile played on Harry's lips. Clearly, he had also caught Eli's slips.

My churning stomach and the itch that now spread to my chest told me to finish this conversation. "I promised

Daniel I wouldn't get the police involved. Look, he asked me to call and get you the grant, so that's what I'm doing. If you don't want to take it…" I let the suggestion hang.

"Okay. I'll come by your house and you can give it to me."

I took a deep breath, ready to snap the bear trap on his leg. "I don't have it—and, frankly, I don't even want to touch it. Meet me at the Bennet House tonight. I'll show you where it is."

"Just tell me where to find it, and I'll get it."

"It's, uh… kind of hard to describe. Meet me there. Please."

It took a moment, but he at last agreed.

"Nicely done," Harry said when I clicked off the phone.

Instead of answering him, I ran from the kitchen, and tore up the stairs to my bathroom.

"What got onto her?" Harry asked.

Rebecca laughed. "I made her a salve from spurge laurel that'll stop the itching she got from telling all those lies. It's in her medicine cabinet."

Chapter Twenty-Five

One Fact Forgotten

The evening arrived. Time to meet Eli at the Bennet House. Wired (in more than one way), I drove down Pine Avenue muttering, "Stay calm. You can do this. It'll be over soon. Harry has your back."

Past eight o'clock on an early November weekday night, the streets were silent, deserted, dark, except for lights in Michael's Restaurant, Como's and the Cataract Grill, where late diners finished their meals. A man and a woman slipped out of Club Joey's. Hand-in-hand, laughing, they strolled to a gray Honda. Watching the couple, I thought of Roger and the times he and I had wandered this way after an evening out. Tears in the corners of my eyes, I longed for those quiet times with the guy I loved. If anything went wrong tonight I would never again know such times. Never again know… anything.

Gripping my steering wheel tighter, I swore, "No more. If I don't get killed tonight, I'll never again get involved in a murder. Even if it's a friend that's killed, even if someone begs me, I'll let the police do their job."

At just over 30 miles-per-hour, I passed the Holy Family Church. I passed Portage Road, where just up the street I had searched for Daniel at the Tops Market. I passed Memorial Hospital from where last year my mother had disappeared, and to where, just few days earlier, Roger had been taken after getting shot in the house I intended to enter.

My right foot eased up on the gas pedal, and my Malibu slowed to 15 miles-per-hour. Did I really want to do this? I could make a left, then another left on Ferry Street and head back home where I could snuggle next to Roger on the sofa. Even watch sports analysts banter about the next week's games. At the moment, marrying the man and spending the rest of my life at his side seemed a far better idea than the one that had dropped me into a car headed for the Bennet House.

"I've changed my mind, Harry," I said aloud. "Find another way to nab Eli."

I didn't know whether he heard me through the wires stung over my body. He had no way to answer.

The light on Main Street turned green. I didn't move until the car behind me honked. Taking a deep breath, I told myself, *Harry has the Bennet House filled with cops. Eli can't hurt me there.* I gulped, trying hard to believe that.

Plucking up a bit of the courage with which I endowed the fictional heroines I had created, I toed the gas pedal, crossed Main and turned onto Park Place.

As I drove slowly up the block, a figure in a brown hooded jacket stepped from between two parked cars. His hand raised, he motioned me to stop.

I clicked on my bright headlights, and leaned over the steering wheel to get a good look at the person.

The figure waived to me, then pushed back his hood. Medium height, a round face with an easy smile, and a hairline well past his forehead.

I pulled up next to him, and lowered my window. "Eli, why are you here? The house is up the block—"

I got no further. Another hooded figure rushed from between the parked cars, reached out and slammed my head against my car door. Dizzy from the blow, the world around me dimmed. I felt my head lifted. I felt a gauze placed over my nose and mouth. It had a hospital smell. Just before the world went totally black, I heard a woman say, "Shove her over and follow me."

***

I had no notion as to where I'd been taken. My next recollection was of being pushed and poked. Groggy, I blinked. I tried to glance around, but my eyes refused to cooperate. Someone shook me.

"Wake up!" a distant voice demanded.

I groaned.

"Come on. Open your eyes!" Hands grasped my face, and rocked my head. The fingers seemed to be thin. Long nails scratched my cheeks.

A woman whispered, "I told you not to use so much ether."

A man replied, "How was I supposed to know? No one uses that stuff anymore."

As my mind cleared, the voices moved closer. I recognized one of the voices as Eli's. The other... Still groggy I couldn't tell anything but that it was female.

"Didn't you ask?" the female said.

"Black market, you don't ask questions," Eli responded.

I shook my head to free it from the hands that held me.

"She's coming around." The female whispered, I supposed, because she hoped to disguise her voice.

Eli sneezed. "Let's get this over with."

The female again grabbed my head and forced me to look at her. "Where is it?"

I swallowed hard and opened my eyes. At last aware, I realized I was laying on a bed of sodden leaves among tall brown reeds. I tried to shift. If I could roll, I might be able get to my feet and run. Not knowing where I'd been taken, I had no idea where I would run to, but anyplace had to be better than wherever *here* was.

Hands shoved me back. When I tried to kick out at the hands, I realized my legs were bound and my arms were tied behind me.

The female had a hood over her head and a black scarf wound around the lower part of her face. Kneeling next to me, she leaned down until her head nearly touched mine.

"Where is it?" she hissed.

I turned my eyes to the right. Eli, his hands at his sides, stood among reeds near a leafless tree, about five yards away from the female.

My throat dry from the anesthetic I'd been given, I rasped, "You don't want to do this."

Eli turned away.

"Tell me!" the female said.

"Why should I? You're gonna kill me anyway."

She reached into her pocket. When her hand emerged, it held something long and black. She pushed a button, and a blade flicked open. She raised the knife. The blade flashed in the moonlight. In a swift motion, the blade slashed through the shoulder of my coat and cut into me. I cried out.

As she again raised the knife, strands of hair slipped from her hood. Wheat colored hair. The color of the woman's hair I'd seen in Howard Kline's office. Though I had worked with her for a number of years, I hadn't recognized her then because she had her face turned down to the page she read, and her hair fell loose in front her. If Kline hadn't closed the door, and if I'd gotten a better look at her, I would not have misread the heading of the contract in the lawyer's file. Had I read it correctly, the pieces of this puzzle would have fallen into place days ago. Ray and his mother would not have been killed, Roger would not have been shot, and I would not now be lying here as if I were on a platter, about to get carved up like a Thanksgiving turkey.

Holding the point of the knife to my throat, the woman whispered, "We can do this the easy way or the hard way."

My stomach in knots, I should have thought of last words that would live on in literature. Once again, though, my brain failed in its proofreading duty. My voice quivering, I said, "Samantha, you really have to stop using clichés."

She sat up straight. With a growl, she yanked the scarf from her face. Hatred in her eyes, she snarled, "Just because you've had some books published it doesn't mean you know everything!" She raised the knife, ready to strike. "Your cop boyfriend isn't going to save you this time."

"Samantha, stop!" Eli shouted. "The land grant. She hasn't told us where it is."

She hesitated a moment, considering, I supposed, whether hatred trumped her need for an old sheet of paper. Thank God—and all the Wicca Gods and Goddesses—that moment of hesitation proved to be enough. I heard a dog bark nearby, then all at once bright lights clicked on and night became day. An amplified voice filled the air: "Drop the knife and lie face down on the ground!"

Brandishing the switchblade, Samantha Wold looked over her shoulder. "Stay away or I'll kill her!"

"Don't do it, Samantha," I said, sounding far braver than I felt. "The police have guns. Are *you* ready to die?"

"Put down the knife. I won't tell you again." This time the voice didn't come through an electronic megaphone. Again a dog barked. Now Harry Woodward stomped through the reeds, his pistol drawn and aimed at Samantha. Never had I been so happy to see this giant of a man.

Sneezing, Eli dropped to his knees with his hands locked behind his head. Two uniformed officers grabbed him.

Samantha looked at Harry, then to her left and right, where other cops moved toward her. Among the cops I saw a woman in a red quilted jacket. A brown and black German Shepherd stood next to her. The dog snarled and leaned forward as if ready to race to me. Bless this dog. Clearly it had found me within this mire of reeds.

"Stay, Kash." The woman raised her hand, and the dog sat. I recognized the dog handler. Kathy Boone, a trainer of search and rescue dogs. I had been introduced to her a few years ago while researching a story about a child lost in the woods south of Ellicottville.

"I'll slit her throat. I swear I will!" Samantha shouted.

Her knife again flashed. As it came down, I whimpered, seeing my entire life pass before my eyes. Instead of cutting me, she slashed the cord that bound my legs. Holding the knife against my throat, she told me to stand up.

My hands still tied behind me, I struggled to get to my feet.

Again the dog snarled.

"Kash, quiet," Kathy Boone said.

Samantha pulled me in front of her, like a shield. "You want Emlyn alive, you'll let me walk away from here." Pulling me with her, she backed up two steps.

Flanked by officers, Harry came closer. "You're not going anywhere."

Like an advancing army, the officers to Harry's left and right moved to encircle us.

"L-let me leave." Samantha's voice shook. "I-I'll let Emlyn go as soon as I get to the border."

I knew she wouldn't. Hoarse from fear, I said, "I don't want to die, Samantha, and neither do you."

The officers continued to move toward us. One of them raised a rifle. A red laser beam scanned down

Samantha's body from her forehead to her knees. "She's in my sights, Chief," he called.

"It's over," Harry said. "Drop your knife. Step away from Emlyn."

Samantha's hand shaking, the point of the blade stuck my throat.

I closed my eyes. My legs like rubber, I dropped to my knees.

A single shot rang out. I heard Samantha cry, felt her twist away.

Trembling, I opened my eyes, and saw Harry, his pistol at his side, standing in front of me. "You sure took your time getting here," I rasped. Yes, my statement had the same element of cliché as that which I'd accused Samantha of using. I didn't care.

Harry nodded.

I glanced behind me. "Is she dead?"

On the ground, Samantha answered with a moan.

"Collins, get the EMTs over here," Harry commanded. He knelt beside Samantha, picked her knife from the ground, and slit the leg of her running suit to expose her wound. The police marksman had apparently shot out her kneecap. "You're gonna live," Harry told her. "Then you're going away for the rest your life."

While one of my writer friends—or I should say, *former* writer friends—was restrained and marched to a patrol car and the other wheeled off on a gurney, the Niagara Falls detective chief crouched at my side and cut the binding from my hands.

"I thought I was dead," I told him. "How did you know they took me here? You said you'd set the trap at the Bennet House."

He gave me his signature smile—not much more than the twitching of his lips. I've mentioned that as a writer I'd learned to pick up on the slightest verbal and physical nuances. So when I saw Harry's eyes flick, I knew he didn't want to tell me something. Instead explaining how the police had followed my car, he said, "Your shoulder seems to be bleeding a bit. So's your neck." He touched my throat, then pulled my jacket aside. As he looked at my wounded shoulder, he called, "I need a paramedic!"

Just then a breeze rippled the reeds around us. The search and rescue dog raised its head and sniffed the air. Its head turned. After another sniff, it jumped to its feet and ran off.

"Kash!" Kathy Boone called. She chased after her dog.

I lost sight of them when an EMT came toward me. It took him just a few minutes to clean and bandage my shoulder and neck. "Not much more than scratches," he said when he finished. "Check with your primary in the morning." To Harry, he added, "Didn't cut any major arteries, not much bleeding. No need to take her to the hospital."

When the EMT walked back to his van, I turned to Harry. "You didn't tell me. How did you know to look for me here?"

"Collins," he called. "Are those two on their way to lockup?"

"Harry?" I said.

He sighed. "Roger and I knew there had to be two people involved in these murders, and we figured they might pull something like this. So while I had you wired, I had another tech put a homing device in one of the wheel wells of your car. Then I got hold of Kathy Boone and asked her to join us."

"Why didn't you tell me? They had me so scared I might have died from a heart attack."

He glanced off to where a couple of officers toed the underbrush. The German Shepherd sat near them.

"Roger figured if you knew, you might give it away. Then these two would switch cars and we'd never catch 'em."

"Oh, Roger thought that, did he?" I snapped and loosened my jacket. I suddenly felt so hot, steam might have shot from my ears. "You'd better hide that man in a cell, because if I get my hands on him you'll have to lock *me* up!"

I might have said more, maybe tossed out a stray thought that would turn into a spell and smack into Roger like a tsunami. I didn't get the chance. An officer standing near the search and rescue dog shouted, "Chief! Over here!"

Harry stood. At a slow pace, he made his way through the reeds. I looked around, now certain I was in the strip of land between Sewage Plant Road and the Niagara River—the same place I'd been told Eli and Samantha had dumped Ray's body. I got to my feet, and followed Harry. When I caught up with him, he and a group of officers were staring down at a pit hidden among the reeds. I pushed up next to one of the officers.

Leaves covered most of what lay in the pit. I could, though, make out a polished shoe and the cuff of one pants leg. A bit further up, I saw what appeared to be the edge of a black jacket.

Harry nodded to his left then his right, and two officers climbed into the pit. With gloved hands they shoved aside the leaves. First they exposed a face as gray in death as was the body's straight hair. Next they uncovered the torso, and I saw a black jacket and a black vest that had BORDER PATROL written across it. Where had I seen this person?

Harry provided the answer. "So this is where Border Agent Partridge disappeared to." He pulled out his cellphone. After punching in some numbers, he said, "Sergeant Cummings, we're gonna need crime scene and a bus down by Sewage Plant Road." In a few words, he told the precinct's desk sergeant precisely where we were. Then he took my arm and led me to my car, where he again punched numbers into his phone.

"Roger," he said. "Yeah. We got her…" He listened for a second or two, then said, "A small cut on her shoulder and one on her neck, but not much the worse for wear. I've got a crime scene to supervise, so I've gotta stay… Yeah, I'll tell you about it later… Emlyn? No need for the hospital. I'm sending her home and having Collins follow her. When she gets there, keep her in the house—cuff her to a chair if you've gotta." He laughed. "Yeah. She might be a bit hard to handle—she got out of me that not telling her we had her car bugged was your idea." Again he laughed. "She doesn't have a gun, so I don't think you'll need protection." He glanced down at me, then added, "From anything but her mouth."

I glared at Harry. Even with the phone nowhere near my ear, I could have sworn I heard Roger gasp.

When I climbed into my car, I sat for a long time completely still, clutching the keys in my hand. Now that the killing spree had ended and Eli and Samantha would soon be locked away where they could do no more harm, it dawned on me how lucky I had been. I, who take such pride in my ability to be observant, had failed to recall three facts. Missing them nearly cost me my life. The first: two people had to have been involved in this mayhem. Harry and his crime scene team had mentioned this when they investigated Mrs. Scannado's body hung like a Halloween decoration in my backyard. They had said they found two sets of tracks leading to and from my beech tree. I have no excuse for missing this. With all that had happened, I just forgot. Thank goodness Roger and Harry hadn't.

The second fact I can't be blamed for missing. If Howard Kline had not walked into his office when he did, I would have had more time to examine the contract I found in his file. With an extra ten minutes or so, I know I would have noticed I had misread the name of a party to the contract. Had I not, in my haste, misread it, I would have realized the contractor constructing the condos at Crystal Beach was not World Development Corporation, but *Wold* Development. Had this registered in my mind, this case might have ended before it began. One more thing I'd forgotten, though at the time I had no reason to think about it. The way Samantha Wold ran after our last writers' group meeting ended should have told me it was she who had seen the land grant Daniel showed me. So many things I should have recalled… Hercule Poirot wouldn't have forgotten them. Neither would Jane Marple nor Nero Wolfe.

Sitting in my car, staring through the windshield, I considered that, with mistakes such as these, not even the most powerful protection spell could have saved me. *So*, I thought, *thank goodness Roger and Harry were more alert than I'd been...* But then I thought, *Hmm. Maybe they were so alert* because *of my protection spell. I'll have to talk to Rebecca about this.*

Epilogue

I've always considered February the *Dead Month*. The glow of the holiday season will have faded and March, with its promise of spring, will still be weeks away.

That year, when February crept onto my calendar, inches of snow from the most recent winter storm were piled up on both sides of the road and along my driveway. I saw this when we pulled off River Road. The penalty phase of the trial had just ended and Eli Nash had been found guilty of four counts of murder in the second degree. Daniel Bennet, Ray Scannado and his mother and Partridge, the border patrol agent. He hadn't been charged with murder in the first, because, according to the testimony he gave at Samantha Wold's trial, it had been she who wielded the throat-cutting switchblade. Eli had said, "I was merely her unwilling accomplice." The jury hadn't believed the *unwilling* part of his statement.

Samantha Wold had been found guilty of murder in the first degree.

Roger, dressed in gray slacks and a navy blue top-coat over his equally blue jacket, climbed from behind the wheel of his Trailblazer. Fully recovered from his wounds, he opened the passenger door and said, "It's over now."

"It is," I said. "Now I can get back to writing." For the past month the ADA, Dan Petit, had me on-call as a witness in the two trials.

Roger smiled at me. "You had no doubt they'd be convicted, did you?"

I stared past him, peering at the blood red maple. Its branches bare, the tree stood forlorn on my lawn. I felt as forlorn as that tree. "I had no doubt at all. Still, in a way I'm sorry about it."

"How can you say that?" He looked shocked. "Those two are monsters." As if to prove he still had the strength of the man he'd been prior to being shot, he lifted me from the passenger seat of his SUV and set me gently on the blacktop.

Holding his arm, I stood on tiptoe and kissed his cheek. "I know that, but…" I sighed. "In the years we worked together in our writers' group, they were so open and so… nice. Plus they both wrote so well, saying things in a way I wish I could. I've learned so much from each of them."

Roger responded with the question I had been asked just after I found Daniel Bennet's body. "Just goes to show. What did you really know about them?" In a rare moment of philosophizing, he added, "What do we know about anyone?"

"I know all I need to about *you*." I again kissed him, this time full on his lips.

Harry Woodward's Buick pulled into my driveway behind Roger's SUV. As he and Rebecca climbed from the car and approached us, Harry said, "That's over with. Can't wait to get back to real police work." The lead detective on the case, Harry had undergone heavy questioning by both the prosecutor and the lawyers for the defendants.

"Maybe tomorrow," Roger said. "Wanna relax some first." He took my arm and walked with me to my front door.

"I know what you mean," Harry said as he followed us inside. He pulled off his gloves and glanced at Rebecca. "I could use something warm to drink."

Smiling, she scooped up Elvira. As always, my cat seemed to know I would be home minutes before I actually arrived. She handed the cat to me and removed her coat. Instead of her usual maroon floral slacks and wool top and vest, she wore a gray wool sweater set. While she went into the kitchen to brew tea from something she carried in her shoulder bag, Roger, Harry and I got comfortable in the living room.

Sitting on the side of the sofa nearest my bookcases, Harry said, "Notice Kline's face each time they had him in the witness box? Hadda be eating his insides out that he wasn't defending those two."

Though Howard Kline had argued that he represented both Eli and Samantha and attorney-client privilege prevented him from testifying for the prosecution, based on evidence Dan Petit presented, Judge Aldernado had ruled Kline appeared to be a participant in the crimes— at least an unintended one—and therefore the privilege didn't apply. The Judge then said that because he would be a witness, Kline could not serve as their defense counsel.

Rebecca set a tray of mugs on my coffee table. "Drink this. It'll relax you."

"What's in it?" Roger asked.

Harry laughed. "You don't wanna know, Detective."

After sipping our tea in silence for a few minutes, Harry said, "You could've knocked me over with a feather when the judge told Kline he was lucky he wasn't being charged with complicity."

"That sleazy SOB should be in jail." Roger rubbed the shoulder in which he'd been shot. "He's the one who started all this."

"True, that." Rebecca said. "What did Samantha Wold say when she testified?"

I pulled my writer's journal from my purse and turned a few pages. "Ah, here it is. She said Kline brought a copy of the land grant to her father, and used it to worm his way into representing Wold Construction in the Crystal Beach condo project."

Roger put his mug on the lamp table. "Yeah. And Kline said he'd gotten that copy of the grant from Richard Bennet as part payment for defending him when he murdered his wife. He probably figured he was safe to bring it out after Bennet got shanked in Attica." He learned toward Harry. "You know, Chief, we ought to investigate whether Kline had something to do with Richard Bennet getting killed. He sure profited from it."

"I thought about that." Harry shook his head. "There just isn't any evidence of his involvement in Bennet's murder."

"Still—"

"I know you'd like to get him, Roger." Harry's voice softened as he spoke to his friend rather than his second-in-command. With a glance at me, he continued, "We all would, but we've got other fish to fry. The mayor says we've gotta find who's responsible for those break-and-enters along Independence Avenue. He's getting pressure from the community."

"I understand you have to focus on that," I said. "But the defense Kline used for Richard Bennet— remember, I was on the jury—was just so…" I rolled my eyes. "The Tuscarora's Curse made him kill his wife? Thinking about it now, it was as if he wanted Bennet to be found guilty."

Bennet sent to a penitentiary, how hard would it have been for Kline to have him killed? He might have had that whole scenario planned—the shoddy Tuscarora's Curse defense, then getting rid of Bennet—once he realized the value of the land grant. I made a mental note to look into this.

"What I don't understand," Rebecca said, "is why they used a gun on Roger. They didn't shoot any of the others."

Her question brought me back from wandering in a dark scenario—one which Ray Scannado might have constructed—in which Howard Kline was the archenemy behind all that had happened. "They denied shooting Roger and—"

Rebecca broke in. "Yeah, but they both swore they didn't kill anyone."

Roger loosened his tie and stretched his legs out on the coffee table. "You're both forgetting something. Remember the conversation we had about the different MOs? The ballistic tests on the bullets that hit me and the ones crime scene pulled from your kitchen wall, Emlyn, all came from a border patrol weapon assigned to Agent Partridge." He smiled. "Seems you forgot a number of things in this case."

"She certainly did," Harry said. "And any one of 'em could've gotten her killed." He shot his Marine colonel stare first at me, then at Rebecca. "That's why you have to leave chasing criminals to the police."

I felt tempted to say, *Yeah, like you guys never forget anything.* For once, though, the proofreader in my brain did its job. Instead of speaking, I rose to take the empty mugs to the kitchen.

As I left the room, Rebecca said, "I don't get why Agent Partridge shot at us and Roger."

Leaning across the kitchen counter, I said, "*I* know—at least, I'm pretty certain I'm right. Partridge was after the same thing Samantha and Eli wanted. That's why he concocted that story about illegal aliens using the Bennet House."

"Probably," Harry said. "That would also explain why Wold and Nash killed him. But how Partridge found out about the land grant and what he planned to do once he got his hands on it is another thing we'll never know."

I'm glad the others didn't see a grin light my face. If they had, they would have known I intended to investigate this. Yes, I knew I had sworn twice that I would never again get into the middle of a murder investigation. But at the time I vowed this, I had been certain I was about to die, so my oath didn't count. Besides, the murders I planned to look into weren't going to be investigated by the police.

When I returned from the kitchen, I saw Roger at my étagère, pouring merlot into four wine glasses.

"Are we celebrating the end of the case?" I said.

"That plus my winning our bet."

"Bet? What bet?" I asked, though I knew very well the bet he spoke of.

Roger handed me a glass of wine. "This case was never as complicated as you made it, Emlyn. The killers' motives were simple. Classic, really. Greed. Wold's father owned the construction company that bought the Crystal Beach property. If that land grant got out, they would've lost the land and the small fortune they'd invested in the project. That happened, his daughter would've been out of her cushy job."

"And Eli Nash?" Rebecca asked.

"Almost the same motive." Roger handed her a glass of wine. "He worked for his sister's real estate agency. They're the ones that brokered the land purchase for Wold Development. That grant surfaced, they would've had to return the hefty commission they got." He turned to me. "So, you see, it was plain old police work that got those two convicted—beating the pavement, talking to people—not sitting in that chair of yours, hoping something your old relative wrote in her book would give you the answer."

"Nice try," I said. "But not quite accurate. Without what Sarah Goode wrote, you never would have unraveled this case."

"Still, it took police work to figure out two people were involved." Holding his glass, Roger sat next to me on the sofa. "So, a toast. I won the bet, and Emlyn's gotta marry me."

"Whoa, hold on a minute!" I said. "You didn't win any bet. I bet Eli killed everyone."

"Yup," he said. "But he just got the victims close enough for Wold to do the job. So I won."

"No, no. I was right. Eli was the key."

His grin grew so large, his jaw seemed to square his entire face. "Okay, I surrender. You won the bet."

"Good," I said. "So that's that."

"Yup. You won, and that means *I've* gotta marry *you.*"

"What?" My eyes shot open wide.

"Hey, that's what we bet. Rebecca, you heard it."

I gave my friend a glare that threatened murder and mayhem if she agreed with Roger.

She poked her finger at her cheek. "I heard it, all right." She raised her glass and drank down the wine.

About Susan Lynn Solomon

Formerly a Manhattan entertainment attorney and a contributing editor to the quarterly art magazine SunStorm Fine Art, Susan Lynn Solomon now lives in Niagara Falls, New York, the setting of many of her stories. She is the facilitator of the Just Buffalo Literary Center Writer's Critique Group.

Since 2007 her short stories have appeared in numerous literary journals. These include, Abigail Bender (awarded an Honorable Mention in a short romance competition), Ginger Man, Elvira, The Memory Tree, Going Home, Yesterday's Wings, Smoker's Lament, Kaddish, and Sabbath (nominated for 2013 Best of the Net, and winner of second place in the 2017 Word Weaver Writing Competition). A collection of her short stories, Voices In My Head, has been published by Solstice Publishing.

Susan Solomon is the author of the Emlyn Goode Mysteries. A finalist in M&M's Chanticleer's Mystery & Mayhem Novel Contest, and a finalist for the 2016 Book Excellence Award, her first Emlyn Goode Mystery novel, The Magic of Murder, has received rave reviews, as have the novelettes, Bella Vita, and The Day the Music Died, and the novel, Dead Again, which was a finalist for the 2017 McGrath House Indie Book of the Year. In each of these Emlyn Goode Mysteries she demonstrates that murder has a sense of humor.

Social Media

Website: http://www.susanlynnsolomon.com

Facebook: http://www.facebook.com/susanlynnsolomon

LinkedIn: https://www.linkedin.com/in/susan-solomon-8183b129

Acknowledgements

I wish to thank the members of Writers Refuge, to whom this book is dedicated. Wonderful writers, they painstakingly reviewed and commented on chapters, pointing out things I'd missed, and offering suggestions that made both my writing and this story tighter. I also wish to thank Kathy Boone, a noted trainer of search and rescue dogs for her detailed information. Plus, I must thank Tony Kohler for a marvelous job in editing Writing is Murder, and Kathi Sprayberry, Kate Collins, and the rest of the Solstice Publishing team for their constant encouragement.

If you enjoyed this story, check out these other Solstice Publishing books by Susan Lynn Solomon:

Emlyn Goode Mysteries

The Magic of Murder

When his partner is discovered in a frozen alley with eight bullets in his chest, Niagara Falls Police Detective Roger Frey swears vengeance. But Detective Chief Woodward has forbidden him or anyone else on the detective squad to work the case. Emlyn Goode knows Roger will disobey his boss, which will cost him his job and his freedom. Because she cares for him more than she'll admit, she needs to stop him. Desperate, she can think of but one way.

Emlyn recently learned she's a direct descendant of a woman hanged as a witch in 1692. She has a book filled with arcane recipes and chants passed down through her family. Possessed of, or perhaps by a vivid imagination, she intends to use these to solve Jimmy's murder before Roger takes revenge on the killer. But she's new to this "witch thing," and needs help from her friend Rebecca Nurse, whose ancestor also took a short drop from a Salem tree. Rebecca's not much better at deciphering the ancient directions, and while the women stumble over spell after spell, the number possible killers grows. When Chief Woodward's wife is shot and a bottle bomb bursts through Emlyn's window, it becomes clear she's next on the killer's list.

https://bookgoodies.com/a/B015OQO5LO

Dead Again

When Emlyn Goode's mother returns to Niagara Falls for a high school reunion, so does murder. During the reunion, a woman's body is found in the ladies room. Is this killing connected to one that occurred 40 years before in the woods below the town of Lewiston? Harry Woodward, a young police officer working his first murder case suspected Emlyn's mother of the crime, although there wasn't enough evidence to arrest her.

Home from a year-long leave, Harry—now the Niagara Falls Chief of Detectives—together with Emlyn's friend, Detective Roger Frey, investigates the latest killing. Distraught over indications her mother might have been involved in both murders, Emlyn, with her cohort, Rebecca Nurse, sets out to prove otherwise. But, danger lurks in the shadows when amateurs—even ones with witchy skills—get involved with murder.

https://bookgoodies.com/a/B01N0OA1IV

Bella Vita

A car burns in the parking lot behind Bella Vita Hair Salon. The corpse in the front seat has a short sword pushed into his ribs. Beneath the car is a cast-iron cauldron filled with flowers. This seems to be a sacrificial rite Rebecca Nurse had been teaching Emlyn Goode. But is it? The corpse has been identified as George Malone, and earlier on this summer solstice day, he and his wife had severe argument. Could it be that Angela Malone has murdered her husband? Prodded by Elvira, an overly-large albino cat that wants the case solved so she can get some sleep, to Rebecca's dismay

Emlyn again dips into her ancient relatives Book of Shadows to find the answer before her friend and neighbor, Detective Roger Fry, can.

https://bookgoodies.com/a/B01I01WEWW

The Day the Music Died

A rock star's murder leaves Emlyn Goode questioning everything she knows about herself.

Amanda Stone, a rock and roll icon who vanished at the peak of her career in 1986, has returned to her hometown of Niagara Falls. She brings with her a message that causes Emlyn Goode to question everything she knows about herself. When Stone is murdered, Emlyn must use the craft her ancient relative wrote of in a Book of Shadows to solve the crime. If she fails, she'll never know if what Stone told her is true.

https://bookgoodies.com/a/B0747V1DPT

'Twas the Season

Food, friends… and murder—how Emlyn Good celebrates Christmas!

"How do I get involved in these things?" Emlyn Goode asks.

It's Christmas Eve. Instead of singing carols around a fire, Emlyn and Roger Frey are at the historic Echo Club for the Niagara Falls police precinct's annual holiday celebration. Tonight there will be good food, dancing, and time with friends. A joyous night—that is, until the body of a man Emlyn knows too well is found in the Club's stairwell. Now she refuses to rest until she figures out who killed him,   and   why.

But, each time Emlyn's gotten involved in a murder, the killer has come after her. Can she find a clue in her ancient relative's Book of Shadows before that happens again?

https://bookgoodies.com/a/B07884XTJV

www.ingramcontent.com/pod-product-compliance
Lightning Source LLC
Chambersburg PA
CBHW070909180626
46817CB00003B/986